Praise for
The Cranberry Cove Mysteries

"Peg Cochran has a truly entertaining writing style that is filled with humor, mystery, fun, and intrigue. You cannot ask for a lot more in a super cozy!"

—Open Book Society

"A fun whodunnit with quirky characters and a satisfying mystery. This new series is as sweet and sharp as the heroine's cranberry salsa."

—Sofie Kelly, *New York Times* bestselling
author of the Magical Cats Mysteries

"Cozy fans and foodies rejoice—there's a place just for you and it's called Cranberry Cove."

—Ellery Adams, *New York Times* bestselling
author of the Supper Club Mysteries

"I can't wait for Monica's next tasty adventure—and I'm not just saying that because I covet her cranberry relish recipe."

—Victoria Abbott, national bestselling author
of the Book Collector Mysteries

Books by Peg Cochran

The Cranberry Cove Mysteries

Berried Secrets
Berry the Hatchet
Dead and Berried
Berried at Sea
Berried in the Past
Berried Motives
Berry the Evidence

The Lucille Mysteries

Confession Is Murder
Unholy Matrimony
Hit and Nun
A Room with a Pew
Cannoli to Die For

Farmer's Daughter Mysteries

No Farm, No Foul
Sowed to Death
Bought the Farm

More Books by Peg Cochran

The Gourmet De-Lite Mysteries

Allergic to Death
Steamed to Death
Iced to Death

Murder, She Reported Mysteries

Murder, She Reported
Murder, She Uncovered
Murder, She Encountered

Young Adult Books

Oh, Brother!
Truth or Dare

Writing as Meg London

Murder Unmentionable
Laced with Poison
A Fatal Slip

Berry the Evidence

A
CRANBERRY COVE
Mystery

Peg Cochran

Berry the Evidence
Peg Cochran
Beyond the Page Books
are published by
Beyond the Page Publishing
www.beyondthepagepub.com

ISBN: 978-1-958384-25-1

Chapter 1

Hercule wove in and out between Monica Albertson's legs, barking excitedly and wagging his tail as she tipped food into his dog dish.

Hercule had appeared out of the blue one day at Book 'Em, Monica's husband Greg's new and used bookstore. They had tried to find his owner but had failed. And Hercule had adopted them as much as they had adopted him.

Monica glanced out the kitchen window. The forecast for Cranberry Cove had been typical for late November—temperatures dropping, wind and some rain. The weatherman was proving to be right, with the skies heavy with dark clouds and wind whipping the fallen leaves into a mini tornado.

She was adding some water to her cat Mittens's bowl when there was a knock on her back door. Mittens brushed against her leg and meowed in protest as she headed to answer it. Before she could open the door, the visitor knocked again, harder this time. *Patience,* Monica thought as she reached for the knob and pulled open the door.

Gina, her stepmother, was standing on the doorstep. She was so pale that her artfully applied rouge stood out on her cheeks like a clown's makeup and her hair was coming down from its updo, making it look as if she'd walked through a gale.

"He's dead," she cried as she stumbled into the kitchen, the heel of her black suede bootie catching on the saddle. She was shaking as violently as the branches of the tree outside.

"Who's dead?" Monica could have sworn that her heart stopped beating, but she could clearly hear it hammering in her ears.

"I must have fallen asleep, and when I woke up, he was dead." Gina moaned and put her head in her hands.

"Not Mickey?" Monica said. Gina had finally fallen in love and settled down with Mickey Welch after Monica's father left her, and to have that snatched away from her so soon would be a tragedy.

Gina shook her head impatiently and her twist wobbled precariously. "No, not him," she said somewhat testily.

She walked over to the kitchen table, her high-heeled boots tapping against the floor, sank into a chair and put her hands over her face.

Monica's panic was increasing by the minute. Who was dead? Please, don't let it be Greg or Jeff or anyone else she knew. The doctor had told her to try to avoid stress. She was doing a fine job of that, wasn't she?

"You have to tell me what's happened." She sat down opposite Gina. Her legs were feeling decidedly wobbly. "Who's dead? What happened? Start at the beginning."

Gina took a deep, shuddering breath. "My realtor. Richard Taylor. Everyone calls him Rip."

"As in Rip-off?" Monica said. "Did you know him well?" She had never heard Gina mention him before.

Gina didn't answer. Her hands were still trembling and she clasped them tightly in her lap. "Rip had just shown me a house—Mickey already saw it last night and we agreed it was just what we wanted. It's a seller's market these days so we didn't want to waste any time. We put in an offer on the spot."

"And?" Monica said when Gina paused for several long seconds.

"We sat in Rip's car—you should see it, a brand-new Jaguar in my favorite color, red."

Business must be good, Monica thought.

"We sat in his car waiting to hear if the owner would accept our offer. We wanted to sign the papers immediately. Rip said last week he'd negotiated a deal but before the documents could be signed, someone slipped in with a better offer. In cash."

"But you said he was dead—Rip, your realtor."

Gina held up a hand. "I'm getting to that. Like I said, we were waiting in Rip's car for an answer to our bid. He had the heater going, it was warm and . . . well, I fell asleep." She began to shake again. She looked at Monica. "I could use a little something to . . ."

Monica jumped up from her chair. She opened one of the cupboards and pulled out a dusty bottle of Jack Daniel's she'd bought the time her father came to visit. She poured a finger's worth into a glass and handed it to Gina, who downed it in one gulp.

Gina coughed and patted her chest with her hand. She held the glass out to Monica. "I'll take another one of those, please."

Monica refilled the glass with another finger's worth of whiskey and Gina downed the second shot as quickly as she had the first.

"So, you fell asleep," Monica prompted.

"Yes. I don't know what came over me. One minute I was complaining about this dog that was across the street yapping and yapping—it was really getting on my nerves—and the next minute I was asleep."

"Maybe you were tired? Maybe you didn't sleep well last night?"

"I think I slept okay. I did dream that someone was staring at me and I woke up briefly, but then I went back to sleep. Or maybe that was the dream I had while I was in Rip's car." Gina rubbed her forehead. "I just can't remember. It was stuffy in the Jaguar and suddenly I couldn't keep my eyes open and believe me, I tried. It was like I'd been drugged or something."

"Maybe you had been," Monica said. "Did you have anything to eat or drink?"

She'd heard of men spiking women's drinks but that usually happened in bars or at parties. Gina liked to think of herself as a cougar, so maybe Rip was trying to seduce her?

Gina shook her head. "No. Nothing. I was going to stop by the Pepper Pot and have lunch with Mickey afterward." She smacked her hands down on the table. "I almost forgot. I did have some coffee. Rip always kept a thermos of it in his car. He said he couldn't get through the day without some caffeine and he couldn't see paying a ridiculous amount of money for a cup at one of those fancy coffee places."

"Did Rip drink some of the coffee, too?"

"Yes. He gave me the thermos cup and poured his into a foam cup left over from the last time he got take-out for lunch and ate in his car."

Monica's head was spinning. She was trying to process what Gina was telling her, but it wasn't making any sense.

"And when you woke up . . ."

"When I woke up, Rip was dead."

"You're sure he wasn't sleeping?"

Gina shook her head vigorously. "That's what I thought at first. I was a little embarrassed—you know how your mouth sometimes falls open when you sleep and you make those little snoring noises? I must have been a sight."

"Did you check Rip for a pulse?" Monica couldn't sit still any longer. She jumped up and took Gina's empty glass to the sink, where she rinsed it and put it in the dishwasher.

Icy rain had started and was pattering against the window with a brisk *rat-a-tat-tat*.

"I didn't have to." Gina swiveled in her chair to face Monica.

"Someone had shot him in the head. There was blood all over." She shuddered. "It was quite a sight."

Monica gasped. No wonder Gina was shaken up. "How dreadful. Do the police have any idea who did it?" Monica was beginning to feel as if she could use a shot of Jack Daniel's herself but it was off-limits in her condition.

Gina looked at the floor, the wall, anywhere but at Monica.

"You must have called the police?" Monica said. "Didn't you?" Her voice rose and Hercule looked up from where he was napping next to Mittens.

"I panicked." Gina laid her hands out on the table, palms up. "I didn't know what had happened. It was like I was having a terrible nightmare only I was no longer asleep. All I knew was that Rip was dead, and for all I knew, the killer was still around. My first instinct was to get out of there."

"But what if some kids find him like that?" Monica glanced at the clock. "They'll be on their way home from school in an hour. They shouldn't have to see something like that." Monica could easily imagine the nightmares they would have.

"Don't worry. I called in an anonymous tip from my car," Gina said.

Monica couldn't believe what Gina was saying. "You left the scene of a crime!" she cried. "And not just any crime . . . murder!"

"Don't look at me like that." Gina put her hands over her eyes. "I panicked, okay? Now what do I do?"

"You have to go to the police." Monica collapsed into a chair.

Gina groaned. "I'm so embarrassed."

"Frankly, that's the least of your problems at the moment."

• • •

Monica took a few minutes to collect her thoughts after Gina left. Gina was in a sticky situation but they both knew Detective Tammy Stevens, and Monica thought she would understand why Gina had panicked and fled the scene. Surely, she wouldn't consider Gina a suspect. It was preposterous.

Hercule and Mittens were both napping at either end of the living room sofa. Monica smiled at them fondly as she got her coat from the closet. She needed to get to the farm kitchen—a recent addition to

Sassamanash Farm, her half brother Jeff's cranberry farm — and get to work on some baking.

Her mother, Nancy, had recently arrived from her home in Chicago to help Monica in the kitchen since her current employee, Kit Tanner, was going to be running the café in Book 'Em as soon as it opened. Nancy had found a darling cottage to rent and Monica wouldn't be surprised if she opted to stay permanently. It would certainly be a relief to have some help after the baby was born.

Monica closed and locked the back door of her cottage and headed out. The wind had stripped any remaining dead flowers still clinging to the trellis bordering her small garden and their curling brown petals littered the slate walkway.

She glanced at the cranberry bogs as she walked past them. The tangled vines were bare, the last of the berries having been harvested in October. When winter arrived, Jeff would flood the bogs and ice would form, protecting them until warm weather came again.

Judging by the feel of the wind on the back of her neck, Monica wouldn't be surprised if they had a frost that night. Fortunately, Jeff had installed a warning system. If the temperature dropped below freezing it would set off an alarm and allow him to start the pumps that would send water to the bogs to cover the cranberry vines.

By now Monica had nearly reached the farm kitchen. She'd outgrown the kitchen in her cottage when her baked goods and cranberry salsa had taken off and Jeff had thought it wise to invest in a larger, commercial kitchen. It certainly made things easier, Monica thought as she approached the extension to the processing shed that housed the kitchen.

Kit was at the counter measuring flour into the mixer when Monica opened the door. He had jet-black hair that he cut and then grew out again on a regular basis. Earlier in the fall he'd had a long ponytail, and before that it had been shaved up the sides. This time he'd opted for buzzed sides with the longer hair on top of his head gelled into spikes. It was the same routine with his facial hair — Monica never knew whether he'd be clean-shaven, have a bit of scruff or a full-on beard. She knew people tended to look askance at him because of his rather unusual appearance — unusual for Cranberry Cove, at least — but he was kind, funny and hardworking.

He smiled when he saw Monica and sketched a mock salute.

"Good afternoon, boss. How are you feeling?"

"Right as rain. How about you? How was your dance class last night?" she said as she slipped off her jacket and hung it on a hook by the door.

Kit and his partner, Sean, were taking dance lessons in preparation for their wedding in the spring.

Kit made a face. "I don't think I did too much damage to Sean's feet."

Monica laughed. "Good for you. I'm sure you're going to put Fred Astaire to shame by the time the reception rolls around."

Monica's mother was seated at the small table they used for their lunch. She had a spool of cranberry-colored ribbon by her elbow and was snipping off lengths, which she then tied around the jars of salsa Monica had made.

Her hair was perfectly coiffed, as usual, and she was elegantly dressed in slim black pants and a royal blue blouse with an apron tied around her waist.

"Mom," Monica said, as she walked toward her. "You don't have to do that."

Nancy looked at Monica over the tops of her reading glasses.

"I thought it gave your product a bit of pizzazz. It's called branding, dear. I read all about it in an article in that paper your father used to subscribe to. Someone left a copy of it at the hairdressers."

"I wouldn't have thought that that would have been your first choice of reading material."

Nancy sighed. "There wasn't much of a selection. It was either that or one of those magazines that write about actors and pop stars I've never heard of." She sniffed. "I have handbags older than some of those kids." She picked up the scissors and snipped another length of ribbon. "It said if you want your product to succeed, you need to create a consistent brand image."

Did her mother even know what that meant? Monica wondered. She shrugged. There was no point in arguing with her. She knew she didn't stand a chance of winning.

"How did your appointment go?" Nancy looked up from the bow she was tying.

"Fine." Monica sat down in the chair opposite. "The doctor said everything looked good."

"Are you taking your vitamins? Drinking plenty of milk?"

Monica nodded silently and then yawned. The urge to lie down and take a nap had suddenly hit her like a sledgehammer.

"You can't be too careful, you know." Nancy reached for another jar of salsa and fastened the piece of ribbon around it. She put the finished jar to the side and raised an eyebrow at Monica. She waved a hand toward the long butcher block counter. "I've been thinking. It would be more efficient if you moved the mixer down toward this end. That would give you more room for rolling out the dough."

Monica barely refrained from rolling her eyes. The next couple of months were going to be very long, she feared. Very long indeed.

• • •

By four o'clock, Monica could no longer ignore her need for a nap.

"I feel guilty leaving it all to you," she said to Kit as she put on her jacket.

Kit stopped, put down his rolling pin and stood with his hands on his hips.

"Don't give it another thought, dear. We've got it covered." He turned to Monica's mother. "Right, Mrs. A?"

"Yes. You go on home now and get some rest. You've got precious cargo aboard." Nancy made a shooing motion with her hand.

Monica smiled. "I can tell when I'm not wanted." She laughed as she opened the door and stepped outside.

The wind immediately blew her hair across her face and she brushed it away impatiently. She was walking past one of the bogs when she noticed Jeff headed toward her.

"Hey, sis," he said as he came abreast of her. "How's my niece or nephew doing?" He was wearing a heavy sweatshirt with *Sassamanash Farm* written on it and a knit cap pulled down over his dark hair.

"To be honest with you, making me very tired. I'm headed home for a nap." Monica cocked her head. "What are you up to today?"

Jeff ran a hand around the back of his neck. "We're pretty busy. Everyone wants cranberries for Thanksgiving." He grinned. "We're packing and shipping them as quickly as we can."

"I wonder if the Pilgrims had cranberry sauce at the first Thanksgiving?"

Jeff shrugged. "The Wampanoag tribe celebrated with the Pilgrims and they used cranberries in a lot of different ways—as dye and in medicine as well as for food. They probably made pemmican, a dish of crushed cranberries and dried meat."

"You've done your homework. I'm impressed."

Jeff ducked his head. "I wanted to know everything I could about the product I'm growing."

There was a shout in the distance and Monica turned to see one of the workers beckoning Jeff.

"Gotta run. See you later." Jeff took off at a trot.

Monica let herself into the cottage as quietly as possible but Hercule was already waiting at the door, his pink tongue lolling out of his mouth and his tail wagging a mile a minute.

As Monica bent down to pet his shaggy head, Mittens strolled over and rubbed against her leg. She scratched the cat's chin with her other hand.

"Okay, you two," she said. "I'm going to lie down for a bit."

She contemplated going upstairs to get in bed but decided instead to stretch out on the sofa. The cushions were soft and comforting and she snuggled under the mohair throw they kept tossed over the arm of the sofa.

Monica closed her eyes but sleep was illusive. She sighed, reached for the remote and flipped on the television. The logo for the local news flashed on the screen just as her eyelids were drifting closed but they shot open again when she heard the name Richard "Rip" Taylor.

A news reporter in a sleeveless sheath despite the cold weather and with long blond hair that had the perfect amount of curl was standing in a driveway in front of a white colonial with black shutters. She breathlessly informed the audience that this was where the murder had occurred. She pointed to a spot where Rip's Jaguar still stood roped off now by yellow crime scene tape.

A small crowd had gathered in the background, blowing on their hands and stamping their feet against the cold.

Another woman entered the screen and Monica recognized her as Detective Tammy Stevens. The two of them had become quite well acquainted over the course of several murder cases. Stevens was wearing a trench coat falling open to reveal navy trousers and a plain white blouse. She scowled at the camera.

The reporter, whose name was apparently Isabella, shoved the microphone in front of Stevens's face. Stevens looked momentarily confused but then began to speak.

Monica's stomach dropped lower with each word Stevens said.

"We believe someone was in the car with Mr. Taylor either when he was murdered or shortly before. We found a cup with red lipstick on the rim," Stevens said, her face grim.

Monica pictured Gina sitting at her kitchen table earlier that day, her lips painted a glossy crimson.

"We are hoping this individual will come forward," Stevens continued, "since she might be able to shed some light on this tragedy. If anyone has any information, please call . . ." And she rattled off a telephone number. The number was also flashed across the bottom of the screen in large white type.

So, Gina hadn't gone to the police after all, Monica thought. The delay was only going to make things worse. Gina had no reason to want Rip Taylor dead, at least not that Monica was aware of, but now it looked as if she was hiding something. Gina was soon going to find herself out of the frying pan and into the fire.

Chapter 2

Monica felt a touch on her shoulder and slowly opened her eyes. She sat up and rubbed her hands over her face.

"I must have dozed off," she said.

Greg smiled at her. "That's good. You need the rest."

The events of the afternoon came flooding back and Monica grimaced.

"What's wrong?" Greg sat down beside Monica and put a hand over hers.

Monica took a deep breath. "Gina woke up next to a dead man earlier today."

Greg's eyebrows shot up and his expression was so comical that Monica actually laughed. But then the gravity of the situation hit her anew and she turned serious.

She told Greg everything that Gina had told her.

"The police don't suspect her . . . do they?"

Monica played with a loose thread on the throw. "Gina didn't wait around for the police. She panicked and left the scene. She came here instead."

Greg pinched the bridge of his nose. "I assume you told her to go to the police."

Monica sat up straighter. "I certainly did. But you know Gina. She has a mind of her own. They announced on the news tonight that they are looking for the woman who had been in the car with the victim."

Greg shook his head. "So, she obviously didn't take your advice. Can you talk to her again?"

"I'm going to have to," Monica said. She picked up the throw and began to fold it.

"What's that noise?" Greg said, putting a hand to his ear. "Sounds like someone is knocking on the back door."

Monica followed Greg as he strode out to the kitchen. They could see Jeff standing outside through a gap in the curtains. He nearly burst over the threshold when Greg opened the door.

"Have you heard about my mother," he said, throwing himself into one of the kitchen chairs. Cold was coming off of him in waves.

She wondered if she needed to get the bottle of Jack Daniel's out again. She was shocked to see her half brother like this. He was normally so cool in a crisis. After all, he'd survived a tour of duty in Afghanistan, although he had come home injured and with a partially paralyzed arm. Monica had closed up her small café in Chicago to come to Cranberry Cove to help him.

"We've got to do something." Jeff put his head in his hands and moaned.

Greg put an arm around Monica's shoulders. "Monica urged her to go to the police immediately."

Jeff was sitting with his elbows on his knees and his head in his hands. He looked up, his expression troubled.

"I told her the same thing," he said. "But no luck. She wouldn't listen. She's convinced they're going to think she's guilty."

"But she barely knew the victim," Monica said. "He was helping her look for a house. Why would the police even suspect her?"

Jeff shrugged. "She seems to think that they'll seize on her as the easiest solution to the crime."

Monica shook her head. "I don't believe Detective Stevens would do that. I've seen how she works and she's methodical and fair."

Jeff let out an enormous sigh. "I hope you're right." His expression brightened. "Maybe you could help out. You know — look into it a bit? You've done it before."

Greg was already shaking his head but Monica responded before he could speak.

"I don't think so, Jeff. Not this time." She patted her still-flat stomach. "I've got someone else to think of now."

Jeff hung his head. "Will you at least talk to my mother again? Please? Get her to see reason."

"Of course," Monica said.

Later, as she was cleaning up the dinner dishes, she thought about Jeff and how distressed he'd been. She hoped Stevens found the real murderer soon and put all of their minds at rest.

Monica glanced at her laptop sitting out on the kitchen table. It wouldn't hurt to do a little research on Rip Taylor though, would it? She'd hardly be in any danger sitting in her own house. There were a lot of ways to investigate that wouldn't put her in harm's way. Besides, she was bored and it would help fill the time until the baby came. The months ahead felt as if they were stretching out endlessly.

• • •

Monica's alarm went off early Saturday morning and her first instinct was to throw it at the wall. Instead, she hit the snooze button a couple of times and luxuriated in the few extra minutes in bed. But she couldn't linger forever, as much as she wanted to. She had a new employee starting that morning and she had to be there to meet her.

With Kit taking over the Book 'Em café soon, Monica needed an extra pair of hands to help with the baking, especially after the baby arrived. She'd put an ad in the classified section of the local paper and had had no responses. Fortunately, the VanVelsen sisters, who ran Gumdrops in town, knew of someone looking for a job. Janice Bakker was an older woman—Monica judged her to be around sixty—and she'd worked at the Roskam Baking Company in Grand Rapids. Monica counted herself lucky to have found someone who was both mature and had experience and she was relieved when Janice accepted the job.

Greg had already left for work by the time Monica got up. He was checking out an estate sale over an hour away and wanted to get an early start. Monica pulled the comforter up over the now empty bed and headed to the bathroom.

She showered quickly and then pulled a pair of jeans from her closet. She slipped them on and was surprised to see she had to struggle a bit to get them buttoned. It seemed as if she'd gained weight overnight.

Hercule stirred in his bed and finally lifted his head, his ears cocked.

Monica motioned to him. "Come on, Hercule. It's time for breakfast."

Hercule leapt gracefully over the side of his dog bed and followed Monica down the stairs to the kitchen, where Mittens was already waiting by her bowl.

Monica filled Hercule's and Mittens's bowls and then scrambled some eggs for herself. She'd been lucky to have dodged the plague of morning sickness. As a matter of fact, she was ravenous all the time and was surprised she hadn't yet put on any significant amount of weight.

She finished her breakfast, put the dirty dishes in the dishwasher, and with five minutes to spare headed out the door and toward the farm kitchen.

By the time Monica reached the kitchen, Janice had already arrived and was seated at the table with Nancy. Steam coiled from the cup of tea in front of her and a half-eaten scone was on a napkin by her elbow.

She was wearing worn corduroy trousers, a sweatshirt with appliquéd teddy bears on it and a pair of clogs. There were lines under her pale blue eyes and her frizzy gray hair resembled a tumbleweed.

"Here you are," Nancy said as if Monica was half an hour late instead of right on time.

Monica felt a burst of irritation, which she quickly quelled. She gave a pained smile and sank into a chair at the table.

Janice beamed at her. "Your mother has been telling me that you have a bun in the oven."

Monica groaned inwardly. Did everyone have to know so soon? She knew she couldn't hide her pregnancy forever, but she and Greg had wanted to keep it to themselves a bit longer.

Janice looked Monica over carefully. "How is your morning sickness?"

Monica was taken aback by the question. "I haven't really had any," she stammered.

Janice shook a finger at her. "You're having a girl then. I had the worst morning sickness with my two boys—Jed and Bobby—but none with my daughter, Jodie." She shook her finger at Monica again. "You wait and you'll see I'm right. It's a little girl you're carrying."

Monica barely managed another pained smile and was relieved when she heard whistling and the door opened.

Kit bounded in with his usual energy, the tip of his nose and ears red from the brisk wind. He unwound his scarf, took off his jacket and hung them both on the hooks by the door.

Monica got to her feet. "Kit, this is Janice Bakker. She'll be taking over for you when the café opens."

Kit smiled and held out his hand. "Pleased to meet you, Janice Bakker the baker." He grinned.

Janice giggled. "I certainly lived up to my name, didn't I? Everyone said I would someday. I baked my first cake when I was eight years old. Of course, my mama had to turn the oven on for me, but I did all the rest myself." She gave a self-satisfied smile.

Monica's mother had originally insisted that the two of them could handle the baking alone, but so far Nancy had done little more than tie ribbons on jars and rearrange the storage room. Monica was glad she would have Janice's help.

"Shall we get started?" Kit said, rubbing his hands together.

Janice got up from her chair with a groan and walked to the counter. She had a bit of a limp and her hips rocked up and down as she walked.

She must have noticed Monica looking at her.

"I've got a bit of a hitch in my giddy-up," she said, smacking a hand against her hip. "The doctor wants to do one of those hip replacements but I'm not too keen to go under the knife, if you know what I mean."

"Why don't I show you where everything is?" Kit interjected, leading Janice to the storage room.

Nancy sidled up to Monica and raised her eyebrow. "I don't know about this," she said.

Monica groaned. "I know. But she had great references and apparently knows her stuff. If I'm going to be out with the baby, I need someone I can count on."

Nancy pursed her lips. "Let's hope her hip doesn't give out then." She glanced at the door to the storage room then patted Monica on the arm. "Don't worry. I'll stay as long as you need me. I'm renting that darling cottage by the lake and it's such a nice change from the suburbs of Chicago."

"Are you sure?"

Nancy nodded briskly. "I'm sure we'll manage just fine."

• • •

Monica was pleased to see that Janice worked efficiently and caught on quickly as she and Kit showed her how to make the various cranberry products sold in the farm store—scones, cookies, bread and Monica's popular salsa.

By lunchtime they had baked enough to restock the store for the afternoon customers and Monica felt comfortable leaving things in Kit and Janice's hands while she ran into town. She needed to pick up something for dinner and she wanted to stop by Gina's aromatherapy shop. She was going to take another crack at urging her to go to the police. She wasn't looking forward to it, but she'd promised Jeff.

She slipped into her jacket and headed back to her cottage, where she checked Mittens's bowls and took Hercule for a brief walk before grabbing her car keys.

The drive into town didn't take long. Monica paused at the crest of the hill where she could see Cranberry Cove spread out below with the waters of Lake Michigan just beyond. The lake was gray and forbidding today with white foam capping the waves rolling briskly toward shore.

Monica turned onto Beach Hollow Road, which bordered the lake, and found a parking space in front of the Cranberry Cove Diner. A man in overalls and a Carhartt jacket opened the door and the smell of bacon frying drifted out. Monica's stomach rumbled even though she'd had a turkey sandwich for lunch.

She passed Book 'Em, Greg's shop, and peeked in the window. Greg looked up from the counter and waved to her. The last time Monica had been past the shop, there had been the sound of hammering and sawing coming from the second floor, but now the café was nearly done and it was only a matter of the finishing touches — paint, wallpaper and furniture.

Bart's Butcher was right next door. The refrigerated case in front of the display window was filled with plump pork chops, rounds of beef tenderloin and succulent lamb chops all neatly arranged.

A bell rang when Monica pushed open the door. Bart looked up from the steak he was trimming and smiled at her.

"You're looking well," he said as he wiped his hands on his apron. "What can I get for you?"

"My mother is coming to dinner so I'll take three of those pork chops, please." Monica pointed behind her toward the display case in the window.

"Excellent choice." Bart grinned at her as he came out from behind the counter to retrieve the chops. "Have to keep your strength up," he said as he laid the chops on a piece of butcher paper. He gestured toward them. "Protein is what you'll need. Plenty of protein. It puts iron in the blood, as my oma used to say."

Monica inhaled sharply. Did Bart know she was expecting? Did everyone? So far, she'd only told Greg, Jeff, Nancy, Gina, and Kit.

Bart pulled a length of string from a dispenser on the counter and quickly tied up the package. "Here you go," he said, handing it to Monica.

He rang up the purchase with a flourish. Monica glanced at the total, took some money from her purse and handed it to Bart.

"You make sure that fellow of yours takes good care of you now," Bart said with a twinkle in his eye as Monica left the shop.

Gina's store, Scentsational, was a few doors down at the end of the block. The large display window was filled with bottles of essential oils and diffusers made of all sorts of materials, from polished wood to handmade glass in the shape of a teardrop. Most of Gina's customers were summer visitors or tourists on autumn color tours, although a number of Cranberry Cove residents had been converted to the benefits of aromatherapy.

The shop was empty of customers when Monica pushed open the door, and Gina was wielding a feather duster on the glass shelves behind the front counter. She jumped when she heard Monica come in.

"You scared me," she said, tucking the feather duster under her arm. She frowned. "Nothing's wrong, is it? You look so serious."

Monica fiddled with a loose string on her jacket. "Not wrong exactly, but I'm worried about what the police are going to think if you don't turn yourself in and tell them you were in the car with Rip when he was murdered."

Gina scowled, her expression mulish. "I don't particularly care for that phrase *turn yourself in*. It makes me sound like a criminal, and you know as well as I do I'm perfectly innocent."

Monica held out a hand. "I didn't mean it to sound like that. Honest."

Gina leaned her elbows on the counter and the thick gold necklace she was wearing that looked like a heavy-duty bicycle chain swung forward and hit the glass with a clunk.

"You have to go to the police and admit you were there," Monica said, her voice pleading. "It's going to look suspicious otherwise."

"But what if it gets out that I was in the car with Rip? You know how reporters are. They'll worm the information out of the police somehow. They always seem to, anyway." She drummed her fingers on the glass counter. "The killer might come after me." She pointed at her chest with her index finger.

"Why would the killer—"

Gina began to pace up and down in the space behind the counter. "Because they might think I saw something. They might want to shut me up." She drew a finger across her neck.

"But you were asleep. You couldn't have seen anything."

"But they don't know that, do they? I might have been faking it."

Monica shook her head. "But you weren't."

Gina shook her head. "I don't know. The killer killed once. What's to stop them from doing away with me as well?"

Monica gave an exasperated sigh. "But they've already seen you. They know what you look like."

"Maybe not," Gina said. "I was slumped down in the front seat."

Her hands shook as she picked up a bottle, pulled out the stopper and sniffed the contents. She held the bottle toward Monica. "Lavender. It's calming and reduces anxiety."

"I could use some of that," Monica said. She took a sniff and waited for a sense of calm to come over her.

Gina suddenly slammed the bottle down on the counter and put a hand to her mouth, a horrified expression on her face. "Oh! What if the killer had missed? They could have shot me instead."

"I think we need another sniff of that lavender essential oil," Monica said. "It's worn off."

Gina grunted. "I think what we need is a drink."

Chapter 3

Monica was washing lettuce for a salad when there was a tap on her back door.

"Come in," she yelled.

"What's that delicious smell?" Nancy said as she walked into the kitchen.

"Pork chops." Monica spun the salad spinner and watched as it went round and round, rattling against the kitchen sink. "Smothered pork chops baked on top of onions and potatoes with a cream sauce and a cheese topping."

"Sounds wonderful." Nancy unwound her scarf and slipped off her coat. "And if that aroma is anything to go by, they will be as delicious as they smell."

"You can hang your jacket on the hook by the door," Monica said. She transferred the lettuce leaves to a large wooden bowl. "By the way, how did you and Janice make out after I left?"

Nancy rolled her eyes. "We did fine. But I had to be quite firm with her about how to do things. She kept insisting on doing them her own way."

"She is a trained baker . . ." Monica opened the refrigerator, took out a cucumber and began to peel it.

She fervently hoped there wasn't going to be trouble between Nancy and Janice. It had been difficult enough to find someone to take the job. On the other hand, she was grateful for her mother's help and didn't want to offend her or get into an argument about Janice's qualifications. It was that old proverbial saying she thought, caught between a rock and a hard place.

Nancy sank into one of the kitchen chairs with an audible groan.

Monica turned around and eyed her mother. "You're not doing too much, are you?" she said in alarm. Maybe she could convince her mother to let Janice do the lion's share of the work. Janice was used to hard work and the most taxing thing her mother had ever done had been long ago when secretaries were still using typewriters.

Nancy waved a hand. "Don't worry about me. I'm perfectly fine. Just normal aches and pains. That's what happens when you get old."

"You're not old," Monica said. She turned away, but then something about her mother's appearance registered and she glanced back at her again. "You look different."

"It must be the light." Nancy pointed to the overhead fixture.

"No, I don't think so. It's your face. I didn't notice it before but it looks . . . tighter. Or something," she added somewhat lamely. She put her hands on either side of her face and pulled the skin taut. "Like this."

A flush colored Nancy's cheeks. "Okay, I'm busted. I have a confession to make. I had a teeny tiny bit of Botox done yesterday morning while you were at the doctor." She frowned. "What do you think? Does it look okay?"

Monica knew her mother liked to look her best—her hair was always done and her outfit chosen with care—but she'd never thought she would go so far as to get Botox.

"It looks great, but I thought you looked fine before."

"That's what everyone always says." Nancy snorted. "When they've been secretly sneering at your wrinkles all along."

"But . . . why? Why now?"

"You mean now that I'm so old?" Nancy said. There was an edge to her voice.

"That's not what I meant," Monica said, flustered. She went to the oven, opened the door and peered inside to check on the pork chops. The cheese on top was bubbling nicely.

"You don't know what it's like." Nancy rummaged in her handbag for a tissue. She dabbed at her eyes. "I'm lonely. I'd like to meet someone—a companion." She spun around toward Monica. "And please don't tell me to get a dog or a cat."

"I wasn't going to," Monica said in a small voice, knowing she had been about to do exactly that.

"You have your Greg and you're so happy. Gina has Mickey now and she seems to be very happy. I'd like to be happy, too." She dabbed at her eyes again. "But men my age all seem to want younger women. And if I found someone old enough to think I'm young . . ." She shuddered. "I thought if I looked a little less . . . ancient . . . I might meet someone."

Monica felt a twinge of guilt. Her mother would be much more likely to meet someone back in Chicago and not in a tiny town like Cranberry Cove, spending her time helping Monica out.

The back door opened and cold air rushed in as Greg stepped into the kitchen, a newspaper tucked under his arm. He greeted Monica with a kiss on the cheek.

"Brrr." Monica shivered. "Your face is cold."

"The temperature is dropping," he said as he hung up his jacket.

"I hope there isn't a freeze." Monica opened the oven and pulled out the casserole dish. The steam billowing from the top bathed her face. "That would mean a long night for Jeff." She set the casserole on a trivet on the table.

Greg pulled out a chair and took a seat. "By the way, I heard on the radio on the way home that the coffee Gina said she and Rip drank had been laced with benzodiazepines. That's what knocked them out."

"Sedatives?" Nancy said, unfurling her napkin and placing it in her lap. "So the killer put the drugs in his coffee?"

"Apparently he or she did." Greg helped himself to a pork chop. "I wonder how the killer got hold of benzodiazepines?"

"Maybe they had a prescription." Nancy shrugged. "Back in the fifties they used to hand them out like candy. Fortunately, doctors have wised up since then and they're harder to come by now."

"But wouldn't that point a finger at the killer? Find someone who has a prescription for tranquilizers and a motive and bingo, you've got your killer." Greg picked up his knife and fork.

"Maybe they didn't have a prescription but had access to the drug somehow," Monica said.

"A doctor?" Nancy said.

"Or a nurse." Monica cut off a piece of her pork chop.

"Or a pharmacist," Greg added. "They have access to all sorts of drugs. Easy enough for a few pills to go missing."

"So, we're looking for a medical professional," Monica said.

Greg's and Nancy's heads both swung in her direction.

"*We*"—Nancy put emphasis on the word—"aren't looking for anyone. The police are doing the looking."

"Right. Absolutely," Monica said.

• • •

Monica gave her mother a brief hug and stood at the open door while Nancy walked to her car. She shivered and wrapped her arms around herself. The air was sharply colder than it had been earlier and she feared that Jeff would have to flood the cranberry vines for the first time that season.

Greg had helped her with the dishes and was now watching television in the living room. Monica wiped down the counters and then picked up the newspaper Greg had brought home with him. She wasn't in the mood for television and she wasn't quite ready for bed yet, although she'd had to stifle several yawns during dinner.

Greg obviously hadn't gotten around to reading the paper—it was still crisp and in its usual precise folds. Monica spread it out on the kitchen table and began to thumb through it. An article on the second page caught her eye. It was about Rip Taylor's murder—no surprise, since it was the most exciting thing that had happened in Cranberry Cove since that truck had overturned on Beach Hollow Road, sending cartons of buttermilk bursting all over the street. The reporter had interviewed Detective Stevens. Monica skimmed the article. There wasn't much she didn't already know.

She folded the paper, turned out the lights and joined Greg in the living room. She was surprised to see that the ten o'clock news had already started. She hadn't realized it had gotten that late. No wonder she couldn't stop yawning.

She was about to say good night to Greg and head upstairs to bed, when she heard the reporter say Rip Taylor's name. She perched on the end of the sofa, one hand on Greg's shoulder.

The reporter was standing in front of a small white house with dark green shutters and an empty planter in the shape of a windmill by the front door. The wind blew his hair over his forehead and he brushed it away impatiently and stared at the camera with a serious expression.

"Right now, we are standing here with Mrs. Mary Vandenberg of Twenty-two Sandstone Lane in Cranberry Cove." He smiled at the woman. She had short gray hair and slightly yellow teeth that overlapped in the front and was wearing ill-fitting jeans and a buffalo plaid jacket.

"Mrs. Vandenberg has something to tell us," the reporter said, shoving the microphone in her face.

Mrs. Vandenberg stared at the camera for a moment, blinking rapidly, then wet her lips and cleared her throat.

"It was the day that fellow was killed. Mr. Richard Taylor. My friend Maureen and I went to the Pepper Pot for breakfast. Maureen likes their eggs Benedict but it's a bit too rich for me." She patted her stomach.

The reporter looked pained. "And what did you see at the Pepper Pot, Mrs. Vandenberg?" He barely stifled a sigh.

"I saw that fellow Richard Taylor."

The reporter pulled the microphone back. "How do you know it was Mr. Taylor?" he said, his eyes trained on the camera.

"He sold me my house." She gestured toward the bungalow behind her. "He was very nice and helpful."

The reporter's eyes were beginning to glaze over. "And what else did you see, Mrs. Vandenberg?"

"A woman." She nodded at the camera. "He was having breakfast with a woman." A sly expression came over her face. "They looked quite . . . *cozy*, if you know what I mean."

Monica half expected Mrs. Vandenberg to wink at the camera.

"And this was right before the murder was reported to have taken place, is that correct?"

Mrs. Vandenberg nodded. "Yes. I saw it on the news later that night."

"Can you describe the woman to us?"

"She had her hair in one of those fancy updos." She twirled a hand over the top of her head. "And was wearing one of those necklaces like the ones they sell at that shop in town—Twilight." She frowned in obvious disapproval.

The reporter jerked the microphone back and the camera moved, taking Mrs. Vandenberg out of the shot.

"Could that woman have been the killer?" the reporter said in somber tones. "Stay tuned to WZZZ as we bring you the latest on this fascinating case."

Greg stood up, stretched and turned off the television. "I'm for bed. How about you?" he asked Monica as he followed her up the stairs. Hercule was right behind him, occasionally bumping Greg's leg with his nose, as if to hurry him along.

"That reporter looked a bit frustrated with Mrs. Vandenberg," Greg said when they reached the landing. "That wasn't much of a description she gave."

"No, it wasn't."

Hercule ran ahead of them, jumped into his bed and began to walk in a tight circle before plunking down with a loud sigh. Mittens was already curled up and asleep on her cushion positioned near the heating vent, where she liked it.

Something about the description bothered Monica as she changed into her pajamas, but she was too tired to think about it now. She wondered if prompting Mrs. Vandenberg might help her remember more about the mysterious woman. The woman might have been a totally innocent breakfast companion, but it looked as if this was the first lead they had had on the case, unless Stevens was holding back information.

Monica tried to put it out of her mind as she settled down to sleep, but as she dozed off, she'd already decided to talk to Mrs. Vandenberg herself.

Chapter 4

The farm store didn't open until noon on Sunday and closed earlier than usual in the afternoon. It was just enough time for people to stop by and pick up some of the store's baked goods to enjoy after church.

Monica had planned to sleep in, but as luck would have it, she woke up a little after seven o'clock and, try as she might, she couldn't get back to sleep. Finally, she gave up—there was no point in wasting time lying in bed. Besides, the delicious smells coming from the kitchen were enticing her to get up.

She glanced at Hercule's bed. It was empty. Apparently, the heady aromas had lured him as well.

Greg was at the stove with an apron tied around his waist flipping cranberry pancakes when Monica got downstairs. A plate with crisp bacon was already on the table. Hercule was standing by Greg's side licking his lips and Mittens was curled up in the pale sunbeam coming in the window.

"Hercule wants you to make some for him, too," Monica said, patting the dog on the head.

"He's already had some," Greg said. "I gave him a tiny bite of bacon." Greg flipped the last pancake and added it to the platter on the counter.

Monica carried the platter to the table and slipped into a chair. Steam was rising from the pile of pancakes as she grabbed two with her fork and added them to her plate. She added a pat of butter and a swirl of maple syrup.

"How are they?" Greg asked as Monica forked up her first bite.

"Delicious," she mumbled around the food in her mouth.

Satisfied, Greg reached for the pancakes himself. "I hope you can rest today. I have to go to an estate sale near Lansing. The executor contacted me about some early Ngaio Marsh first editions that are for sale. He's giving me a first look, otherwise I would put it off until tomorrow."

"I plan to curl up on the sofa with the newspaper and relax for a bit before going down to the kitchen," Monica said.

After they did the dishes and Greg left, Monica did curl up on the sofa. She glanced through several sections of the Sunday paper but she couldn't focus on any of the stories. She kept thinking about Mrs. Vandenberg. Surely, she must remember more about the woman she saw having breakfast with Rip Taylor. Even the smallest detail might help to identify her.

After paging through the final section of the paper without really seeing it, Monica made a decision. She would go to see Mrs. Vandenberg herself. She was sure she could coax more information out of her than that wooden excuse of a television reporter. He'd seemed more interested in making sure his face was on the screen than getting at the truth.

Within five minutes Monica was in her car and on the road driving toward Sandstone Lane. Mrs. Vandenberg's house was easy enough to find — Monica recognized the windmill planter outside her front door from the news report.

A dusty Ford Escape with a *Pure Michigan* bumper sticker sat in the driveway. Monica hoped that meant Mrs. Vandenberg was at home.

She parked her car at the curb, made her way up the slate path to the front door and rang the bell. It sounded inside the house with a melodic tinkle.

Monica was beginning to wonder if she was doing the right thing and was about to turn around and leave when the door suddenly opened. She smiled quickly.

"Mrs. Vandenberg?"

"Yes?" The woman tilted her head to one side. She was dressed in neatly pressed black slacks and a pale blue sweater.

Monica wet her lips. "I saw your interview on WZZZ yesterday."

Mrs. Vandenberg broke into a smile. "All my friends are calling me to say, Mary, you're a celebrity. We saw you on television." She put her hands on either side of her face. "I never expected it." She motioned toward the interior of the house. "Won't you come in?"

Monica gratefully accepted the invitation and followed Mrs. Vandenberg into a small parlor filled with plants overflowing their containers, numerous mementos, knickknacks scattered on every surface and comfortable, old-fashioned furniture.

"Please. Sit." Mrs. Vandenberg gestured toward the sofa.

Monica perched on the edge uneasily. She felt like an intruder. She *was* an intruder.

"I was wondering about that woman you saw in the restaurant

having breakfast with Rip Taylor, the man who was killed," Monica said softly.

"Oh, are you from the newspaper? Are you going to write about it?"

"Not exactly—"

But Mrs. Vandenberg wasn't listening. "I never expected so much attention just because I was eating breakfast at the Pepper Pot at the same time as a murder victim." She shook her head. "Poor man, blissfully eating his scrambled eggs, not knowing that was his last meal." She shivered.

"He was eating scrambled eggs?" Monica said, leaning forward slightly.

"Yes. I noticed he put ketchup on them just like my father used to do." She laughed and shook her head. "Mother used to tease him about it, saying only truck drivers did that." She leaned closer to Monica. "My father was a bookkeeper at Steelcase and never drove a truck in his life."

"If you noticed that little detail," Monica said, "you must be very observant."

Mrs. Vandenberg preened like a peacock.

"Since that's the case, perhaps you noticed a bit more about the woman who was with Mr. Taylor."

"I most certainly did," Mrs. Vandenberg said, "but that young man from the television station barely gave me a chance to say a thing." She crossed her arms over her chest. "Young people can be so impatient these days. It's all that—what do they call it—social media. They have the attention span of a gnat."

Monica smiled. "What do you remember then? What are the details you didn't get to reveal?"

Mrs. Vandenberg put a finger on her chin. "She ordered eggs Benedict just like my friend Maureen. I mentioned the necklace to the reporter, didn't I? It had a silver symbol on a leather cord—it looked a bit like a cross but the top was different. They sell jewelry like that at that shop Twilight. I don't know what Cranberry Cove is coming to, allowing a store like that to open here. I've heard the owner is a Wiccan?"

Monica mumbled something indistinct.

Mrs. Vandenberg shook her head slowly. "I do remember the woman was dressed rather . . . oddly." She ran a hand up her pants leg.

"She was in these leopard-print leggings and a sweater with a very deep V in front." She sniffed. "Not the sort of thing you usually see around Cranberry Cove." She plucked at a piece of lint on her sweater. "We go for more practical clothes here."

Monica felt her stomach knot. That description sounded a lot like Gina. Too much like Gina. Who else in Cranberry Cove would go out for breakfast wearing leopard-print leggings?

Monica was suddenly glad that Mrs. Vandenberg hadn't had a chance to tell the reporter more about what she'd seen. But had she told the police?

"Have you told the police this?" Monica said.

Mrs. Vandenberg shook her head. "They haven't asked me."

And hopefully they wouldn't, Monica thought as she said goodbye to Mrs. Vandenberg and returned to her car.

Monica left Mrs. Vandenberg's, passing through downtown Cranberry Cove on her way home. Most of the shops were closed, although the door to the diner was propped open in anticipation of the after-church crowd looking for a hearty breakfast. As she passed Twilight, she noticed the lights were on. She quickly put on her blinker and pulled into a space out front.

She peered through the window and could see Tempest Storm, the owner, moving around inside. She knocked on the door.

Tempest looked up from the box she was unpacking and frowned. When she realized it was Monica, her expression changed and she hurried toward the door.

Monica heard the locks clicking and then the door was flung open.

"Monica. How lovely to see you," Tempest said. She was wearing a blood red velvet tunic over black pants and dangly crystal earrings. "Please come in." She gestured toward the interior of the shop.

"I was feeling restless—these overcast November days are so dreary—so I decided to come in and unpack some stock. It always cheers me up to look at the pretty things I've ordered."

"What's in the box?" Monica asked as Tempest slipped behind the counter.

"Crystals." Tempest's face lit up. She pulled out a small plastic pouch with a stone inside and held it up. The light overhead glinted off the pale pink surface. "This is rose quartz. It encourages love, trust and harmony." Her expression changed. "I've been summoned for jury duty. Some case where a fellow seriously injured someone in a bar fight. Obviously, we could use a little more love and harmony these days."

Tempest slipped the crystal out of the plastic pouch, opened the counter and set it on a black velvet display cloth.

Monica glanced at the objects arranged in the display. A necklace caught her eye—it was a silver emblem that looked vaguely like a cross and was hung on a black leather cord. She pointed at it.

"That's an interesting piece," she said to Tempest.

Tempest slid the necklace out of the case and placed it on the counter.

"It's an ankh. It's the ancient Egyptian symbol of life. It was created by the Africans and thought to be the original cross. Would you like to try it on?"

Monica shook her head. "I'm looking for a gift for Gina . . ."

"How funny," Tempest said. "She bought herself one just like it a couple of weeks ago."

Monica laughed, but inside her stomach did a nosedive. "I guess I'll have to think of something else then."

Tempest waved a hand over the counter. "What else can I show you?"

"I don't want to be a bother," Monica said. "I saw your light was on and I thought I'd stop in and say hello. I don't want to keep you. I'll come back next week when you're open."

"How are you feeling?" Tempest closed the counter and locked it with a key that was on a bracelet around her wrist.

Goodness, had the news of her pregnancy spread all throughout town? Monica wondered. Bart already knew about it and now Tempest as well. Pretty soon Gus, who fried eggs and flipped burgers at the Cranberry Cove Diner, would be in on it too.

"I hope you're not letting yourself get too tired," Tempest said, raising an eyebrow.

"I'm fine." Monica gave a strained smile.

She thanked Tempest, said goodbye and left the shop. She was quite sure the necklace Mrs. Vandenberg had been describing was the one Gina had recently bought, and the description of the woman's outfit fit Gina to a tee.

How long before Detective Stevens learned about it and came to the same conclusion? It wasn't a giant leap from Gina having breakfast with Rip Taylor to Gina being the woman in the car with him when he was shot.

It was in Gina's best interests to go to the police before she found them on her doorstep one morning. Monica just had to convince her of that.

Chapter 5

Monday morning, Monica and Greg had an appointment with Deirdre Swanson, a local architect. Monica was excited. They were finally drawing up plans for the house they were going to build on some land Greg had bought ages ago. Their dream was coming true.

Deirdre's office was located in a small white clapboard building on Beach Hollow Road at the point where it curved away from the shoreline. She was waiting at her desk when Monica and Greg arrived.

Her office was very sleek, with a glass-topped desk, a tufted black leather sofa and a drafting table set in front of a large window where pale sunlight poured in. A bright yellow hard hat sat atop a pile of papers on the desk.

"Please, have a seat on the sofa," Deirdre said after greeting them.

Monica noticed there were some papers on the coffee table in front of the sofa. They were rolled up and held together with an elastic band. She supposed those were the plans for their new house and she felt butterflies in her stomach.

Deirdre sat in a black leather chair opposite them, one leg crossed over the other. She was as streamlined as her office in a well-cut black pantsuit, a plain beige shell underneath the fitted jacket, and a pair of large pearl earrings.

She reached for the papers and then stopped. "I'm sorry. Can I get you anything? Coffee? Tea? Water?"

Both Monica and Greg shook their heads.

"Well then, let's get to the exciting part, shall we?" She smiled at them as she pulled the elastic band off the roll of papers and spread them out in front of Monica and Greg.

"These are the tentative plans I drew up based on what we discussed. Your wish list," she said with a smile. She pointed to the drawing. "Here you have your kitchen. There's plenty of counter space and a lot of cupboards."

Monica and Greg exchanged a glance. "That will be an improvement," Monica said.

She loved her little cottage, but the kitchen was small and when the baby came, they were undoubtedly going to feel cramped.

"The kitchen opens to the family room here." Deirdre tapped the rendering with her pencil.

Monica leaned forward, trying to picture how the sketches would look when they came to life. She and Greg had agreed they wanted an open-concept floor plan. The house wasn't going to be particularly large or grand but it would have all the space they needed, and Monica couldn't wait until they started building.

Deirdre pointed at the drawing again. "This is the staircase to the second floor and the three bedrooms. I added this little detail—a window seat. Perfect for a child if you ever have a family."

Monica felt heat rise to her face. Did Deirdre suspect . . . ?

But Deirdre had moved on to the closets and storage space. Monica's mind drifted, imagining a little boy or girl curled up on the window seat with a book. She jumped when Greg touched her arm.

"Deirdre wants to know what we think?"

"It's lovely. Perfect." Monica couldn't find the words to describe what she felt.

"Good." Deirdre rolled up the papers and slipped on the elastic band again. "We can finalize things then."

Monica noticed a newspaper sitting at the edge of the coffee table atop a pile of books. It was folded open to an inner page and the headline of an article on Rip Taylor's murder was visible.

"Did you know him?" Monica pointed toward the paper.

"Rip Taylor?" Deirdre snorted. "I did and I wish I hadn't."

"Oh?" Monica said.

Deirdre leaned back in her chair and folded her arms across her chest.

"He took advantage of my niece, Emily Meyer." She raised an eyebrow. "Granted, she is a bit naïve despite having earned her bachelor of science degree at Michigan State." She shook her head. "What do they teach them in college these days?" She sighed.

"What happened to Emily?" Monica shifted in her seat. Her back was beginning to ache.

Deirdre pursed her lips. "He pulled a fast one on her. She was living in the house she inherited from my older brother. He passed away a number of years ago."

Monica and Greg made sympathetic noises.

"Emily was perfectly happy and had no intention of selling the property until Rip came along. He knocked on her door one day and invited himself in. He told her the house was in terrible repair and the only thing with any value was the land. Emily was horrified. He reassured her"—Deirdre made air quotes with her fingers—"and told her he had a client who would be interested in buying it. Or taking it off her hands, as he put it."

She leaned forward, her elbows on her knees. "Emily didn't know anything about real estate or what houses or land are worth. She was scared and she jumped at the chance to get out from under what Rip had managed to convince her was an enormous burden."

"She sold it to his client?" Greg said.

Deirdre nodded. "For a ridiculously low price. If only Emily had consulted someone first. She's always been somewhat impetuous. Of course, Rip's client just happened to be a developer who planned to build two huge brand-new houses on what had been Emily's land. And no doubt Rip would have been the agent brokering the deal when it was ready for sale. It would have earned him a nice commission. A very nice commission indeed.

"That's not going to do him any good now that he's dead, of course, but that's not much of a consolation for what he did to Emily."

Deirdre cleared her throat. "Well," she said briskly, clapping her hands. "Enough of that. This is all very exciting for you, I'm sure. I'll be in touch as soon as I have a construction schedule to share with you."

Monica and Greg said goodbye and Deirdre stood at the door and waved to them as they walked toward Greg's car, which was parked in front of the building.

"It doesn't sound as if that Rip Taylor is going to be missed all that much," Greg said as he beeped open the car doors.

"At least not by Deirdre Swanson or her niece." Monica slid into the passenger seat and fastened her seat belt.

Greg pulled out of the parking space and began to drive toward downtown Cranberry Cove. Monica barely noticed the scenery passing by. She was thinking about Rip Taylor. According to Deirdre, he was something of a con artist, or what her great-grandmother Albertson would have called a snake oil salesman.

And it sounded as if he had made some enemies along the way, Emily included. Was one of them the killer?

• • •

The farm kitchen was bustling with activity when Monica arrived. Kit was whistling while rolling out dough, Janice was folding cranberries into some batter for muffins and Nancy was filling a basket with cranberry scones.

"How did the meeting with the architect go?" Nancy said as Monica was unbuttoning her jacket.

"Very well." Monica could tell her face was flushed with excitement. "I'm beginning to think it's really going to happen." She hung up her jacket. "What do you need me to do?" she asked as she walked toward the counter.

Kit put down his rolling pin. "Nora called to say the store is completely out of cranberry walnut chocolate chunk cookies and could we bake some for the afternoon rush. And the Cranberry Cove Inn called and asked if there's any more cranberry salsa."

Monica felt a slight sense of panic. She was already tired from their morning at the architect's and was fighting the urge to put her head down and nap. Instead, she went into the storeroom to get the ingredients she needed to begin working on a batch of cookies. She'd tackle the salsa after lunch.

She went to the shelf where she kept the walnuts and froze. They were gone. She knew she'd received a shipment of them just last week. They couldn't possibly have used them all up. Now she was in a full-blown panic. Her hands were shaking as she walked back into the kitchen.

"I can't find the walnuts," she said, her voice trembling. "They're not on the shelf where I always keep them."

She wouldn't normally panic like this. She supposed it was the pregnancy hormones putting her on edge.

"My goodness," Nancy said. "You've gotten so pale. Maybe you should sit down."

Monica waved a hand. "I'm fine. But I need to know what happened to the walnuts." Even she could hear the querulous note in her voice.

Janice, who had been taking a batch of scones from the oven, turned around.

"I moved them," she said. "I felt the storeroom could have been organized more efficiently." She pulled off her oven mitts. "I'll get them for you."

Kit rolled his eyes and Nancy gave Monica an *I told you so* look. Monica gritted her teeth so hard she felt the muscle in her jaw clenching.

"Please clear things with me first, okay?" Monica said to Janice when Janice handed her the bag of walnuts.

If Janice was offended, she didn't show it. Monica tried to put the episode out of her mind as she measured out butter and sugar for the cookies. No doubt Janice had meant well. She should be pleased she'd found an employee willing to take the initiative.

It was approaching noon when Monica's energy began to flag, and she'd noticed her mother looking at her from time to time, her brow wrinkled in concern.

Finally, Nancy took the rolling pin out of Monica's hands. "Sit," she said, leading Monica over to the table.

Monica was more than happy to comply. She dropped into the chair with a sigh. A newspaper was sitting on the table and she pulled it toward her and began to thumb through it.

Rip Taylor's obituary was in the second section. The photograph that accompanied it looked as if it had been taken for Rip's business cards. He was wearing a dark suit, tie, and a broad smile. Monica supposed the smile was meant to make him look warm and welcoming but she thought it made him look more like a shark. Or was her perception colored by what she'd learned about Emily Meyer and how he'd swindled her?

Monica scanned the obituary. Richard "Rip" Taylor had been thirty-four years old. He had been married to the former Lacey Van der Zee but the marriage ended in divorce. He had been employed by Cranberry Cove Realty for ten years. He'd been a running back for the Cranberry Cove Cougars in high school and held the record for the most touchdowns scored in one game. He went on to play for the Michigan State Spartans.

That must have come in handy in his real estate career, Monica thought. Any number of people in Cranberry Cove probably knew who Rip was and immediately thought of their own homegrown star football player when they wanted to buy or sell a house.

Which was going to make it easier for her to get some information on Rip—what his wife was like, did he have any money problems or any addictions. Any one of those things could reveal what he might have become entangled with that would have given someone a motive for murder.

• • •

Monica finished up her baking by late afternoon. She'd been dragging nearly all day, but then she had a sudden burst of energy she suspected was brought on by her insatiable curiosity. She was anxious to know more about Rip Taylor. How could she dig up some useful information? She thought about it as she walked back to her cottage. Suddenly she had an idea. What if she pretended to be interested in buying a house? Maybe she could glean some office gossip from Rip's coworkers at Cranberry Cove Realty.

Hercule and Mittens were both waiting patiently when Monica pushed open the door. She clipped on Hercule's leash and took him for a quick walk. He bounded out the door and nearly yanked the leash from Monica's hand. He wanted to chase some squirrels that were foraging for food in her garden but he finally got down to business, and Monica managed to convince him to go back inside.

She checked Hercule's and Mittens's water bowls, added a bit of food to Mittens's bowl and went upstairs to change. She hardly looked like she was in the market for a house in the flour-covered jeans and sweater she'd worn all day.

Hercule was stretched out dozing in a sunbeam and Mittens was curled up on the sofa, her tail tucked under her, when Monica finally shut the back door and went to her car.

Cranberry Cove Realty was on Beach Hollow Road just beyond the Bread and Cheese Gourmet Shop. Monica pulled up out front and parked. Pictures of houses were tucked in the large display window and she paused for a moment to look at them. They ranged from a modestly priced Cape Cod–style home to a mansion sitting on a rise above the town with a spectacular view of the blue waters of Lake Michigan in the distance.

A bell tinkled when Monica pushed open the door. The desk at the front of the office was vacant, although the papers strewn across it indicated that its owner wouldn't be gone for long. Behind it were two more rows of desks. A woman sitting at one of them got up as Monica walked in.

"I'm Vera Roth. Can I help you?" She gave a practiced smile and held out her hand.

She was a tall, blowsy-looking blond wearing a navy blue suit. She had a white blouse under her jacket and her skirt was pulled across her hips as if it was too tight.

"Umm, I'm looking for a house," Monica said as they shook hands.

Vera tilted her head to the side and appeared to be waiting for something, so Monica continued. "A small house." She named a price. "Three bedrooms and two bathrooms if possible."

"Let's see what we can do," Vera said, clapping her hands together. She slipped on a pair of reading glasses, went to her computer and began clicking through files. The charm bracelet on her wrist jangled as she tapped the keys. "I think I've found the perfect property for you. Let me see if it's convenient for the owner if we go look at it now." She reached for the telephone.

Monica bit the side of her thumb. She hadn't intended to take the charade this far. She'd thought she would be able to get Vera talking about Rip and that would be that.

Vera spoke on the phone briefly. She hung up and smiled at Monica. "We're in luck. The owner's about to go out. Why don't we go in my car since I know the way. It's right outside."

Monica nodded as Vera dug in her capacious handbag for her car keys and then followed her meekly out the door to a sleek BMW parked at the curb.

The inside of the car still smelled like new and Monica surreptitiously ran her hand over the smooth black leather upholstery.

Vera got behind the wheel, started the car and pulled away from the curb.

It was now or never, Monica thought. "I was sorry to hear that one of your colleagues was murdered—Richard Taylor. That must have been a terrible shock."

Vera's head briefly swiveled toward Monica. "Rip? Yes, quite a shock. You don't expect someone you know to be murdered, do you? It's something you read about in the papers or see on television."

"I can't imagine shooting someone." Monica shivered. "Did Rip have enemies that you know of? I suppose it could have been a random killing. The police haven't revealed much about the case."

Monica noticed they had now entered a small neighborhood—one of the original developments in Cranberry Cove. The houses were smaller and older but were well-maintained.

"I think Rip was skating on thin ice financially," Vera said as they pulled into the driveway of a modest ranch house with a bicycle leaning against the garage door. "Bill collectors were calling him all the time at the office. He was always dodging calls — letting his phone ring until it went to voicemail. You don't do that in this business. You might miss a client or offend one. After all, they can always take their business elsewhere. Another real estate agent can show them the same house."

Vera led Monica up the slate path to the front door.

"He was living with his girlfriend, Kayla Moore. She's a defense attorney. You should see her house — she inherited it from her parents, who made a fortune in supplying uniforms to factories. The cynical part of me wonders if that's part of the reason Rip was attracted to her. I don't know what happened to all his money — he was quite a successful agent and should have been making good commissions. Maybe his first wife cleaned him out in the divorce."

Vera fiddled with the lockbox on the door. "I remember when Jane Williams went on maternity leave. We all chipped in to buy her a stroller. Everyone except Rip. No matter how many times we bugged him, he never seemed to have the money to pay his share. You could see he was walking a tightrope trying to keep all the balls in the air at one time."

"Did he have any enemies?" Monica said.

Vera shrugged. "I don't know. But it's possible he borrowed money from some people who took it personally when he couldn't pay it back." The lock clicked and Vera pushed open the front door.

Monica shivered as they stepped into the foyer of the house. She didn't know very much about loan sharks, but she knew they often extracted a high price if a loan wasn't repaid. Had they resorted to murder? Was that why Rip had been shot? To make an example of him, perhaps?

Monica paid almost no attention as Vera led her on a tour of the house. At one point, Vera asked her what she thought of the layout and Monica stared at her blankly for a moment before finally coming up with an answer.

As Vera drove her back to the real estate agency, something occurred to Monica. How did Rip, who was by all accounts flat broke, afford the fancy car he drove? Gina had said he'd picked her up in a Jaguar. Monica didn't know all that much about cars but one thing she did know—Jaguars didn't come cheap.

Chapter 6

Monica was in her car, heading home, as unanswered questions continued to swirl in her head. Who put the sedatives in Rip's thermos of coffee? He lived with his girlfriend, Kayla Moore—had she prepared the coffee that morning and had she added something a little extra?

There was one way to find out—ask her. There was no guarantee she'd answer. She might even throw Monica out, but Monica thought it was worth a try. She pulled into a parking lot and dug her phone out of her purse. She typed Kayla's name into a search engine and scanned the results. One of the entries that popped up was the Michigan resident database. She crossed her fingers as she clicked on the link.

Bingo, Monica thought. Kayla lived on Southwicke Street in a development on the fringes of Cranberry Cove. She plugged the information into the GPS on her phone and glanced at the map that came up on the screen. Interestingly enough, it looked like Kayla's house was a block away from the house Gina had been looking at when Rip was killed.

It didn't take long to get there. Monica followed the directions on her phone and soon pulled up in front of an impressive brick Georgian home with elaborate topiary trees in ceramic pots on either side of the front door. The landscaping was impeccable and not a single fallen leaf marred the front lawn.

Monica felt her mouth go dry. What was she going to say if Kayla was home? She could hardly come out and ask her if she'd murdered her boyfriend. Kayla wouldn't let her past the threshold. She had to think of something. She was with the Welcome Wagon? No, Kayla had been living here for quite some time. She was selling something? Taking a survey? Finally, Monica hit upon a solution. She would claim to be a reporter writing an article on Rip's murder.

She poked around in her glove compartment and found a small notebook with a few blank pages left in it and a pen with *Douglas Construction* written on the barrel. She tucked them into her purse.

A wide slate walkway led to the glossy front door. Monica lifted the heavy brass knocker and let it drop.

The door was opened a few moments later by a woman in a pale blue uniform with a white apron tied around her waist. She was middle-aged with tired lines around her eyes and mouth.

"Miss Moore isn't in," she said before Monica could introduce herself.

"Perhaps I can speak to you then."

The woman hesitated but then opened the door wider, as if she was afraid of appearing rude. She led Monica down the hall and into an expansive kitchen that gleamed with stainless-steel appliances, white cabinets and white marble countertops.

She took a seat at the kitchen table and motioned for Monica to follow suit. She introduced herself as Joan.

Monica took a deep breath and introduced herself. "I'm writing an article on Mr. Taylor's murder from the . . . the human-interest perspective."

She didn't mention the name of the publication and was relieved when Joan didn't ask.

"I'm sure Mr. Taylor's murder has been a shock to you," Monica began. "I imagine you've known him for a long time."

Joan shook her head. "Only since he and Miss Moore starting going together. Miss Moore is the one I've known a long time. I worked for her parents before they died." She folded her hands and put them in her lap.

"Still, it must have been a shock. Someone you actually knew being killed like that."

Joan bobbed her head. "You don't expect it, do you? It's one thing to read about it in the papers or see it on television, and then suddenly it's real. It's hard to take in."

"What did you think of Mr. Taylor?" Monica had removed the pen and notepad from her purse and was pretending to take notes.

Joan shrugged. "He was okay, I guess." She frowned. "Except for him leaving his stuff all over the place. I was constantly picking up after him. His shoes kicked off by the sofa, empty glasses on the coffee table, candy wrappers stuffed between the seat cushions." She shook her head. "I'm not going to miss that."

Monica was still pretending to take notes. She looked up from her pad. "Did he and Miss Moore get along?"

She shrugged again. "Like any other couple, I suppose."

"They didn't fight?"

Joan hesitated. "All couples fight, don't they? It's only natural." She played with the edge of her apron. "Besides, none of the boyfriends stay very long."

Monica cocked her head. "Oh?"

Joan sighed. "The last one was here for six months. He was nice. Always said please and thank you. He treated me with respect. I liked him and I was disappointed when he left."

"And Mr. Taylor?" Monica cocked her head to the side.

Joan shrugged.

"I gather that Mr. Taylor always took a thermos of coffee with him when he left in the morning. Are you the one who made the coffee for him?"

"The police already asked me that." Joan's lips clamped together. "Miss Moore did it. She was the one." She pointed to a gleaming coffee machine on the counter. "I don't know how to work one of those things and I'm not about to learn. My mother used to make coffee on the stove. What's wrong with that?"

Nothing, Monica thought. She remembered the percolator sitting out on her mother's kitchen counter.

"Did you put the coffee in Mr. Taylor's thermos after Miss Moore made it?"

Monica hoped that Joan wouldn't realize where Monica's questions were going. She looked slightly suspicious and Monica was relieved when she answered.

"The police asked me that, too. No, Miss Moore did all that. I had enough to do with cleaning up the breakfast dishes. Miss Moore drank one of those smoothies, I think you call it." She shuddered. "Nasty-looking green stuff. Mr. Taylor liked a full breakfast—eggs, bacon, toast and hash browns, or sometimes pancakes and sausage. It was Miss Moore who took care of the coffee." Joan set her jaw firmly.

"Of course," Monica said in a soothing voice. She quickly changed the subject. "This is a lovely home."

Joan looked as proud as if she'd been the owner.

"The late Mr. Moore designed the house himself."

"I imagine Mr. Taylor enjoyed living here. What luck landing a girlfriend like Miss Moore."

Joan's eyelids flickered. "You can say that again." She crossed her arms over her chest.

"You said that Miss Moore and Mr. Taylor argued occasionally. Nothing serious, I assume? I'm sure Mr. Taylor wouldn't want to give up everything Miss Moore had to offer."

Joan sat up straighter and set her shoulders. A strange look passed over her face.

She didn't answer.

Monica wondered why as she packed up her things and left.

• • •

Monica opened the door to her cottage, glad to be home. Hercule greeted her exuberantly, wagging his tail and banging it against the leg of the kitchen table. Mittens was nowhere to be seen. The sound of the television was coming from the living room. Obviously, Greg was home early for once.

Monica gave her husband a peck on the cheek and collapsed on the sofa, where Mittens had curled up on one of the throw pillows. She gave Monica an indignant look. Monica pulled the ottoman closer and put her feet up.

"Tired?" Greg smiled at her.

"Just a bit. It feels good to sit down."

The local news channel was playing on the television. The news anchor, a young man with slicked-back hair and a bright blue tie, stumbled over a word.

"That poor guy," Greg said, pointing to the television screen, "he can't read the teleprompter to save his life. That ought to be a plum job. You'd think they could find someone better."

The camera switched to a news reporter standing outside a house. It was a low-slung ranch-style home with a large picture window and an autumn wreath on the front door.

A woman was standing with the reporter as he introduced the story. The lines on her face suggested she was well past middle age. She was wearing leggings, a bright fuchsia sweater with bat wing sleeves and an enormous gold cocktail ring with a red stone in the center. Her ash blond hair was teased into a French twist.

"This is Mrs. Lombardi." The reporter could barely contain his laughter as he turned to the woman. "Tell us how you came home and found the tank to your guest room toilet missing." He angled the microphone toward her.

Mrs. Lombardi was clearly enraged. "I come from New York," she said in a strong accent, "and even in New York City I never heard of someone stealing a toilet tank." Her head quivered. "And what a mess! Water everywhere. The carpet was soaked. The water even seeped into the bedroom, where it ruined my favorite pair of mules—leopard-print pony hair. Fortunately, we never use that bathroom."

The reporter turned toward the camera. "The thief was immediately apprehended—caught on the Lombardis' home security camera. A Mr. Jax Johnson," he said in grave tones. "Do you have anything you would like to say to Jax Johnson?" He pointed the microphone at Mrs. Lombardi.

"Yeah. What do you want with a toilet tank?" Indignant circles of red bloomed on her cheeks. "You can buy one at Home Depot. What do you mean stealing mine?"

"I imagine you're happy the thief has been caught and justice will be done?"

Mrs. Lombardi gave the reporter a look that said *Are you kidding?* "Of course. What do you think?"

"It must be a slow news night," Greg said, getting up to turn off the television. "I wonder why anyone would steal a toilet tank?"

"It is bizarre. Unless something was hidden in it. Some people keep cash in the house and hide it in strange places like the freezer."

"I'll bet you're right," Greg said. "Now, how about I make us some dinner while you rest?"

Monica smiled and curled up on the couch. "I think I like that idea."

• • •

Monica was at the farm kitchen bright and early on Tuesday morning. Janice was already there unpacking a delivery of fifty-pound bags of sugar. She wasn't putting them where Monica normally did and Monica had to bite her tongue to keep from saying something. She reminded herself of the old adage, *Good help is hard to find.* Besides, she was grateful she didn't have to lift them herself.

She heard Janice grunt as she hefted a bag out of the crate.

"Why don't you wait for Kit and let him do that," Monica said.

Janice looked up and brushed a strand of frizzy gray hair off her forehead.

"I can manage, thank you." She bent and lifted another bag out of the crate.

Monica watched her, her brow furrowed. She hoped Janice didn't hurt herself. The last thing she needed was to be shorthanded now that the bookstore café was nearly ready.

The door opened, sending a gust of wind through the kitchen and sweeping several dried leaves across the threshold.

"Looks like a storm is brewing," Kit said as he slipped off his coat.

"Is it raining?" Janice said, breathing heavily and standing with her hands on her hips. She wiped her face with the edge of her apron.

"It's starting," Kit said. "I had to tiptoe through the raindrops. He twirled and did a few dance steps.

Monica pulled out her cell to call her mother to tell her to wait till the storm had passed, but just then the door opened. Nancy stood in the doorway, closed her umbrella and shook it out.

"It's beastly out there," she said, propping her umbrella in the corner. She handed a white shopping bag with *Posh Baby Boutique* written on it in pink and blue letters to Monica. "I brought you something, dear." She gestured toward the package. "I know it's early, but I couldn't resist. They have the most darling things in that shop. You should see them."

Janice made a noise like a pig squealing. Monica looked at her in alarm.

"It's bad luck," she gasped, pointing at the package.

"What on earth do you mean?" Nancy said, raising her eyebrows.

"Receiving or opening baby gifts before the baby comes is bad luck. It brings misfortune and attracts evil spirits."

"Nonsense," Nancy sputtered. "That's an old wives' tale. There's no truth in it. Open it, Monica."

Monica hesitated. She didn't believe in ridiculous superstitions and absurd myths. Did she?

"Very well," Nancy said, reaching for the shopping bag. She reached inside and pulled out a tissue-wrapped bundle. "I'll take the bad luck then." She shot Janice a venomous look. "Here." She handed it to Monica.

Monica took the gift and carefully unwrapped the paper. "Oooooh," she breathed, holding up a darling ruffled white bib. "I love it."

Monica felt a flush of pleasure. Suddenly the pregnancy seemed real. She surreptitiously put a hand on her stomach. She couldn't feel anything yet but maybe soon.

Nancy grabbed an apron from a hook on the wall, fastened it around her waist, and rubbed her hands together.

"What can I do?" she said briskly, and looked at Monica.

"Let's start on some scones," Kit said, guiding Nancy behind the counter. "If you'll do the mixing, I'll roll out the dough.

Monica rewrapped the bib in the tissue paper and put it back in the bag. She hesitated for a moment. What should she work on first? She rubbed her forehead. Was it pregnancy that was rendering her so indecisive? She squared her shoulders and walked purposefully toward the storage room. She would work on some cranberry muffins. They were a big hit with the crowd—mostly women—who stopped by with their friends for a cup of coffee and a bite to eat in the morning.

She was measuring out flour when she heard the door open and the sound of a familiar voice. She looked up to see that Lauren was standing by the door.

"The rain is finally letting up." She pulled off her hat and shook out her blond hair. She was carrying a large tote bag, which she put down on the table.

"What's up?" Monica said, dusting her hands off on her jeans, something she'd promised herself she'd stop doing. "Any exciting news about the wedding plans?"

Lauren and Jeff were planning to be married that spring when the cranberry flowers were in bloom. They'd hoped to have had the ceremony by now but some family issues on Lauren's side had cropped up and plans had had to be delayed.

"Not really. I've come to talk about the bookstore café opening." Lauren took a seat at the table. "It's time to ramp up our marketing and public relations." She pulled some papers out of her tote bag and tapped them with her index finger. "I've got a whole social media campaign mapped out and ready to go. We're going to blast Instagram, Facebook, Twitter and TikTok."

"TikTok?" Monica raised her eyebrows.

"It's big right now. I'll need to arrange to take some short videos of you and Greg." She turned around and pointed at Kit. "And you too, Kit."

Kit posed with his hands under his chin. "I'm ready for my close-up, Mr. DeMille."

Lauren had certainly done a good job, Monica thought, when they'd finished going over her plan. After she'd graduated college with a degree in public relations and marketing, Jeff had been afraid that she would call off their engagement and head to Chicago for a job, but she'd decided to stay in Cranberry Cove where, thanks to the Internet, she'd been able to get a fairly successful freelance practice going even though her clients were scattered around the country.

Lauren put the papers back in her tote bag and drew out her phone. She tapped the buttons and scrolled through her calendar. "Let's set a date to make the TikTok video," she said.

They discussed available times and days and Monica promised to get back to her after checking with Greg on his schedule.

"I heard about that fellow Rip Taylor, the real estate agent, being murdered," Lauren said as she zipped up her tote. "Small world. I knew his ex-wife, Lacey Van der Zee."

"Oh?" Monica raised an eyebrow.

"We were in high school together."

"Were you friends?"

Lauren shook her head. "Hardly. We barely knew each other. We ran in different crowds. She was a cheerleader and I was . . . well, a nerd. She didn't have time for someone like me. I wasn't popular with the guys like Lacey. Besides, she was already a senior and I was a lowly freshman."

Monica couldn't picture any guy not noticing Lauren with her blond hair, clear complexion and willowy figure.

"Lacey cheered for Michigan State and then went on to become a cheerleader with the Detroit Lions after graduation. I had heard that she had wanted to join the Dallas Cowboys squad but didn't make the cut. What a blow," Lauren said sarcastically, rolling her eyes. "Still, she did alright for herself. She ended up marrying Lawrence Green, the Lions' running back. They had a nice house, fancy cars and plenty of money to party. And she didn't seem all that broken up when Green was killed in a car accident. Drunk driving. He hit a tree going one hundred and ten miles an hour in his Ferrari. She hooked up with Rip Taylor less than six months after she buried her husband."

Now that was interesting, Monica thought after Lauren had left and she'd gone back to working on her cranberry muffins. Rip had married Lacey, who had plenty of money. Then they'd divorced and he'd met Kayla, who also seemed to have lots of cash.

She wondered who had ended the marriage, Rip or Lacey? Somehow, she doubted it had been Rip—why end a relationship that had you living in the lap of luxury? Had Rip been stupid enough to cheat?

It would be interesting to find out what had gone wrong.

• • •

By ten o'clock, they had enough baked goods ready to warrant taking them down to the farm store. Monica slumped into a chair at the table, took off her shoes and began to rub the soles of her feet. It was warm in the kitchen with the ovens going full blast and she fanned herself with her hand. A stray lock of hair had plastered itself to her forehead and she brushed it out of the way.

"You're tired," Nancy said.

Judging by Nancy's tone, Monica suspected her mother's brow would have been furrowed if it hadn't been for her recent Botox injections.

"I'll take all this down to the farm store," Monica said, slipping her shoes back on. "I could use some fresh air.

"Are you sure?" Nancy said, hovering nearby.

Monica managed to restrain herself from rolling her eyes. How was she going to endure nearly seven months of this?

"But isn't it still raining?"

Kit went over to the window and peered out. "It's stopped and the clouds are shifting. I wouldn't be surprised if the sun came out this afternoon."

"It will do me good," Monica told her mother. "Standing in one spot is hard on your back."

Before her mother could object any further, she carefully packed up the muffins, scones and bread and put them on the cart she used to ferry things back and forth to the store.

"I'll be back." She put on her jacket and went out the door, pushing the trolley in front of her, its wheels squeaking in protest.

The fresh air felt fabulous on her face, which was still hot from the heat of the oven.

She pushed the trolley down the cement path they had laid between the kitchen and the store. The route took her past one of the bogs, which

Jeff had flooded the first night they had had a frost. The bare vines were now covered with a thin coating of ice. In a few more months, Jeff would be putting down a layer of sand on top of the ice. In the spring, the ice would melt and the sand would sift onto the vines and choke out the weeds.

Monica reached the farm store and pulled open the door. She bumped the trolley over the threshold and froze.

The counter looked like something out of a horror film with blood puddling on the surface and spatters on the floor. Nora was standing behind the counter with her hand swathed in paper towels. Her face had lost all its color and she was trembling.

"What happened?" Monica cried. She took a step toward Nora.

Nora grimaced. "I sliced my finger on the box cutter when I was opening up some cartons. I can't seem to get it to stop bleeding."

There was a first aid kit under the counter, but Monica didn't think a couple of bandages were going to do the job. Blood was already soaking through the paper towels and running down Nora's arm.

"We need to get you to the hospital," Monica said, pulling her cell phone from her pocket.

"But the store . . ." Nora protested.

"I'm calling my mother. She can mind the shop while I take you."

Nancy arrived minutes later, her hair ruffled by the wind and her coat hanging open.

"I came as fast as I could," she said breathlessly. She stopped short when she saw Nora.

"Do you think you can handle the store while we're gone?"

"Of course. Now go." She made a shooing motion with her hand. She pointed at Nora's hand. "You'd better hurry."

Monica grabbed Nora's coat and draped it over her shoulders for her. Jeff's jeep was in the parking lot and Monica prayed he was in the storage shed. This was the time of year when he usually took advantage of some downtime to do repairs and maintenance work on the equipment.

She left Nora leaning against the building while she went inside. Jeff was looking under the hood of a tractor, his good hand covered in grease and smears of it on his forehead.

"I need to borrow your Jeep," Monica said. She put a hand to her chest. She was having trouble catching her breath. "It's an emergency."

Jeff looked startled. "Sure." He reached into his pocket, pulled out a set of keys and tossed them to Monica.

Jeff's eyes darkened. "It's not the—"

"No," Monica said somewhat tersely.

She ran back to Nora, the keys jingling in her hand. She hastened to get her situated in the car, climbed in herself and started the engine.

Fortunately, the hospital was relatively close. Monica stole a glance at Nora as they pulled into the parking lot. Her face was even whiter and her eyes were closed.

"Here we are," Monica said, hoping to rouse Nora enough to get her inside.

She turned off the engine and helped Nora out of the car and toward the doors to the emergency room. The doors swung open automatically and the smell of antiseptic drifted out. The waiting room was fairly full but the triage nurse took one look at the bloodied paper towels around Nora's hand and rushed her and Monica into a vacant room.

A nurse immediately appeared to take Nora's blood pressure and clip an oximeter to her index finger. As soon as she left, a doctor pushed the curtain aside and stepped in.

She gently unwrapped the paper towels around Nora's finger and tossed them in the trash.

"Let's see what we have here." She examined Nora's finger carefully. "You've done quite a number on yourself," she said with a brief smile. "You're going to need some stitches."

She poked her head out of the curtain and yelled some instructions. A moment later, a nurse bustled in with a suture kit and placed it on a tray.

She hovered nearby as the doctor reached for a gauze pad to cleanse the wound. Her movements were brisk and efficient, and in no time she had Nora's finger sewn up and properly bandaged.

"I'll be in shortly with the discharge papers," the nurse said as she followed the doctor out of the room.

Moments later she reappeared holding a sheaf of papers. She smiled as she handed them to Nora.

She appeared to be in her early thirties with blond hair brushing her shoulders and a slight, almost fragile build.

"These are your discharge instructions," she said, pointing at the papers. "Be sure to keep the cut dry for forty-eight hours." She smiled. "Do you have any questions?"

Nora shook her head and Monica was glad to see that some color had come back into her face.

The nurse leaned closer and Monica glanced at the name on her ID badge. It read *Emily Meyer*.

The name sounded familiar and Monica tried to remember where she'd heard it before. They were in Jeff's Jeep headed back to the farm when it came to her. Emily Meyer was the niece of their architect, Deirdre Swanson. And according to Deirdre, Rip had conned Emily into selling her house for a price way below its real value.

Monica could imagine how furious that must have made Emily when she found out that she'd been conned. Monica didn't think she looked like the murderous type though. Did nurses take an oath like doctors—to do no harm?

Something else was teasing Monica—an idea that was tantalizingly out of reach. She thought about it as she drove Nora back to the farm store. It had something to do with Emily Meyer and nurses and hospitals. But what was it?

The harder Monica thought, the more elusive the connection became.

They finally reached the farm store and Monica pulled Jeff's Jeep back into its parking spot. A few cars were in the parking lot, and when they went inside, Monica was relieved to see that her mother had managed just fine in their absence.

"I've rearranged the case a little bit," Nancy said when she saw them. "I think it's more pleasing to the eye this way."

Monica and Nora exchanged a glance and Nora shrugged. This time Monica could tell that it was Nora who was trying to refrain from rolling her eyes.

Nancy grabbed her coat but then hesitated with one arm already in the sleeve. "Will you be able to manage with your finger all bandaged up like that? I can stay if you want." She looked from Nora to Monica and back again.

"It's fine," Nora said, looking panicked at the thought. "If I need anything, I'll call you."

Nancy looked slightly disappointed but she followed Monica out the door.

Monica was quiet as they walked along the path to the kitchen. The idea she'd been trying to get hold of since they left the hospital continued to scamper out of reach just as she thought she was finally going to pin it down. It was torture—like having an itch you couldn't scratch.

They had nearly reached the kitchen when Monica finally figured out what had been teasing her.

"Oh!" she said.

Nancy looked at her. "Is everything okay? Do you have a pain? Do we need to call the doctor?"

"No, nothing like that. I'm fine. Really," Monica reassured her. Were people going to make a fuss every time she made a sound? she wondered.

She'd finally made the connection she had been searching for. Emily was a nurse. As a nurse she had access to any number of drugs. And those drugs probably included benzodiazepines like the ones the killer had put in Rip's coffee.

Emily was no doubt furious with Rip. But the question was, had she been furious enough to resort to murder?

Chapter 7

With Nora safely returned to the Sassamanash Farm store, Monica and Nancy headed back to the kitchen to finish up the day. They were nearly there when Monica's cell phone buzzed. She pulled it from her pocket and looked at the caller ID. It was Greg.

He was excited about the progress on the bookstore café.

"You have to see it," he said, "can you take a break and come by?"

Monica promised him that she would check in with Kit and if things were going smoothly, she'd take the rest of the afternoon off and run into town.

Nancy had gone on ahead while Monica took the call and already had her apron on when Monica reached the kitchen.

Monica stood in the doorway with her hand on the knob. "Can you manage without me this afternoon? Greg wants me to see the progress on the bookstore café."

Monica had barely finished speaking before Nancy, Kit and Janice all answered with a resounding *yes*.

Monica hated to admit it, but she was glad to quit for the day. She was more tired than she'd realized. The shock of finding Nora bleeding and the rush to the hospital had worn her out.

She said goodbye and began the walk home to get her car and to check on the animals. When she got to her cottage, Hercule was waiting by the door, his tail thumping a brisk beat against the doorframe. Mittens was sunning herself in a sunbeam that was casting a ray of light across the kitchen floor and slowly wandered over when she heard Monica come in.

Monica clipped on Hercule's leash. "Just a short one this time, buddy. I promise you a longer walk later."

Hercule scampered among the fallen leaves then flipped on his back and began to roll in them.

Monica stifled a giggle. No point in encouraging him. Hercule was a bit of a clown and she was convinced that he enjoyed making her laugh.

"Okay, buddy, that's enough. Time to get down to business."

As soon as Hercule was finished, Monica took him back inside despite his attempt to stall and drag his feet. She filled Mittens's food and water bowls, and went upstairs to change. Her jeans were covered in flour and she was wearing an old sweater that had pilled from years of wear.

She pulled on the sweater her mother had given her for Christmas and slipped into a fresh pair of clean jeans. That was better, she thought. She went into the bathroom, combed her hair, powdered her nose and declared herself ready.

There was little traffic on the way into town. The rain had stopped, although heavy clouds still blanketed the sky and the water in the lake was a forbidding-looking gray with a bit of white froth capping the waves. It made Monica glad that the car's heater was putting out plenty of warm air.

Greg was standing in the doorway when Monica pulled into a parking space in front of Book 'Em. He was so excited he could barely wait for her to get out of the car.

"Wait till you see it," he said. "It's really coming together and it looks great."

He put a hand on Monica's back and shepherded her into the store. Several people were browsing on the first floor amid the jumble of volumes on the shelves and displayed on tables. Two customers were relaxing in the sagging armchairs, piles of books on their laps.

A spiral staircase led to the second floor, which overlooked the main level of the bookstore. Monica's excitement mounted with each step she took. She finally reached the top and looked around in awe.

The wallpaper was printed with bookcases full of books and the bistro tables and chairs that had been delivered were arranged around the space. Two men in white coveralls were busy maneuvering a glass display case into place. Monica could already imagine it filled with baskets of cranberry goodies — scones, muffins, cookies and more.

"What do you think?" Greg asked anxiously. He stood with his hands on his hips and a broad grin on his face.

"It's fantastic," Monica said, looking around the room again and taking in all the details. Greg seemed to have thought of everything.

"And right on schedule, too." Greg headed toward the back wall. "There's one more thing. This still needs to be hung, of course,"

He picked up a long sign that was leaning against the wall and turned it around. It read *Monica's Café*.

Monica felt tears spring into her eyes. "I don't believe it," she said. "I didn't know . . . how did you . . ."

Greg smiled. "I remembered your telling me about your little café in Chicago."

Monica nodded. "I closed it to come here to help Jeff with the farm." She gave Greg an enormous hug. "I hated having to leave it, although to be honest, it began losing money as soon as that chain coffee shop opened down the street."

"This calls for a celebration, don't you think?" Greg's eyes were twinkling. "How about lunch at the diner? I'm starved. Have you eaten?"

Monica shook her head. "Not yet."

"I admit, the diner isn't particularly festive," Greg said as they headed back downstairs. "It's not the Cranberry Cove Inn, but the fellow is coming to hang the sign in the café in an hour and I don't want to miss him."

"The diner is fine," Monica said. "A bowl of hot chili sounds wonderful. It's become quite bitter out."

The Cranberry Cove Diner was noted for its chili. It wasn't on the menu but it was a well-guarded secret known to most of the residents of Cranberry Cove. Gus Amentas, who was a fixture behind the counter effortlessly flipping burgers and frying eggs, was contemptuous of the tourists who came to town in the summer and early autumn. Visitors got no acknowledgment at all from him. Residents new to Cranberry Cove might be rewarded with a slight nod of his head—so subtle that they weren't always sure they'd actually seen it. Longtime residents got a smile that looked as if it was going to crack Gus's weather-beaten face.

Monica had finally achieved the status of a longtime resident and Gus welcomed her to the diner with a smile and occasionally even a gruff greeting.

As soon as Monica and Greg stepped onto the sidewalk, they were enveloped in the delicious aromas emanating from the diner. Monica's mouth began to water and she could almost taste the chili. Her appetite had been finicky at first but now it certainly seemed to be growing every day.

When they walked through the door, she was astonished to see that Gus was not in his usual spot behind the counter, a spatula in each hand, flipping, turning and cooking with all the precision of a maestro conducting an orchestra.

She couldn't believe it. To her knowledge, Gus had never taken a day off. He was as reliable as the sun rising in the morning and setting at night.

They found a vacant booth and had barely sat down before the waitress cruised by their table, plunking down silverware and glasses of water wet with condensation. She returned moments later with menus, but Greg waved them away.

"We're both having the chili," he said.

"By the way . . ." Monica touched the waitress's arm before she could run off again. "Where's Gus? I don't think I've ever been here when he wasn't behind the counter. Is everything okay?"

The waitress leaned in closer, clutching her order pad to her chest.

"There was an accident," she said in a low voice. "Something to do with hot oil. He burned his arms and chest. He's in the Cranberry Cove Hospital. They say he's going to be there for a bit and then I heard he would be transferred to a rehab facility." She shook her head. "I never thought I'd miss him with all his grumbling and complaining, but I do." She touched a finger to her eye.

"Oh, no," Monica said, glancing at Greg. "Will he be okay?"

"You know Gus. Nothing keeps him down." She chuckled. "But the medical bills." She whistled and rolled her eyes. "I heard he might have to sell the diner."

The cook behind the counter yelled for the waitress and she scuttled off like a crab trying to scramble away from a wave.

"Poor Gus," Monica said. She picked up her napkin and without even realizing what she was doing, began to shred it. "I wish there was something we could do."

Greg frowned and wiped a bit of condensation off his water glass. "I know. The Cranberry Cove Diner wouldn't be the same without Gus behind the counter slinging burgers and frying potatoes."

Monica drew in a breath and looked up suddenly. "Maybe there is something we can do." Her voice became animated. "We can take up a collection for his medical bills. Everyone in town knows Gus. They'll certainly want to contribute a little something. They won't want some stranger coming in here and taking over the diner any more than we do."

"True." Greg took a sip of his water. "We could end up with some city slicker who'll put things like eggs Benedict and spinach quiche on the menu." He laughed. "I can't begin to imagine what the regulars would think of that."

"I could go door to door and speak to all the merchants. I'm sure they'd want to pitch in."

Greg's eyes brightened. "We can make some posters and ask all the shops to put them out with a can for donations."

"That's a great idea." Greg reached out and touched Monica's cheek. "Don't wear yourself out though, okay?"

"I won't. I promise."

Monica felt slightly guilty. She truly did want to help Gus, but she had an ulterior motive as well. Collecting money would give her an excuse for chatting with people, and since Rip's murder was on everyone's mind, it would seem natural if the talk turned in that direction.

And hopefully no one would suspect she wasn't making idle conversation but was actually investigating.

• • •

Monica got to the farm kitchen early the next morning. It was nice to be alone for a few minutes before everyone else arrived. She made herself a cup of tea — decaf, of course — and made a list of the things that needed to be done that day.

The Cranberry Cove Inn had put in an order for some more of her cranberry salsa. The jars were all ready to go, neatly packed into a carton. As soon as Kit, Janice and Nancy arrived, she would head into town to deliver them.

Monica was taking an inventory of supplies when there was a knock on the door.

She opened the door. "Lauren. Is everything okay?"

"Yes, totally. I thought I'd stop by and fill you in on some of the plans for the bookstore café opening." She breezed into the kitchen, bringing a whiff of fresh air with her. Her cheeks were pink from the cold. She yanked off her hat, sat down at the table and pulled out her phone.

"I've already begun putting pictures up on Instagram," she said, handing the phone to Monica. "I stopped by Book 'Em to take some photos. The café looks absolutely darling." She took her phone back and switched to another app. "I've also scheduled some entries on Facebook."

"You've thought of everything," Monica said with a smile.

"We still have to deal with TikTok," Lauren said, sliding her phone into her pocket.

Monica sighed. She wasn't looking forward to making videos for TikTok. She didn't even like having her picture taken.

"There's something else," Monica said. "I'm hoping you can do me a favor." She told Lauren about Gus.

"How awful! We can't let him sell the diner. It's such a fixture in Cranberry Cove."

"I know. I'm afraid someone will buy it and turn it into a gourmet diner serving things like ahi tuna and cold brew coffee."

Lauren laughed. "I think the natives would revolt if that happened."

"But the tourists would love it—the atmosphere of a diner but the menu of a gourmet restaurant."

Lauren nodded. "Totally bougie."

Monica raised her eyebrows. "Bougie?"

"Yes." Lauren gestured with her hands. "Bourgeois. Pretentious."

"We certainly don't want that. Where would we get our famous diner chili or perfectly done eggs over easy with hash browns?" Monica laid her hands on the table. "That's why I'm hoping you can help me."

Lauren raised her eyebrows. "Sure. Anything."

"I'm planning on taking up a collection to help pay Gus's medical bills. I'm thinking posters in all the shops along Beach Hollow Road with a canister for donations."

"That's a great idea." Lauren's face brightened. "I can get some posters made for you. I know a great graphic designer and a printer that's very reasonable."

"Would you? That would be wonderful."

The door opened and they both jumped. Kit breezed in with Janice right behind him.

"I'd better be going," Lauren said, pushing back her chair. "I have a virtual meeting with a client in Chicago."

The door closed behind Lauren and the kitchen settled into its usual routine—Kit rolling out dough for scones, Janice making batter for cranberry nut bread and Nancy, who had arrived, measuring out chocolate chips.

"I'm going to deliver the carton of cranberry salsa to the Inn," Monica announced as she reached for her coat.

Kit rushed over and grabbed the carton. "Let me carry this to your car for you."

Kit gushed over his and Sean's plans for their upcoming wedding as they walked along the path that led to Monica's cottage.

"We're trying to decide about the cake. Sean wants lemon but I want red velvet." He giggled. "Can you imagine the reaction when we cut into that?"

By now they had reached Monica's driveway. She popped open the trunk of her car and he placed the carton inside.

"Don't you dare try to pick this up yourself," he admonished as he slammed the lid shut.

Monica got into the driver's seat. "Don't worry. I've called the Inn and someone will be waiting by the service entrance."

She put the car in gear and waved goodbye as Kit slowly disappeared in her rearview mirror.

• • •

Monica pulled into the driveway of the Cranberry Cove Inn and drove around back to the service entrance. A young man in jeans and a T-shirt with *Cranberry Cove Inn* written across the front was waiting for her. His sandy hair was slicked back and looked wet, as if he'd just gotten out of the shower. He hefted the carton of cranberry salsa from Monica's trunk with ease, handed her a receipt and headed back inside.

Monica put the car in Drive and wended her way back down the driveway. She hesitated when she reached the road, but finally turned in the direction of Cranberry Cove Realty. She might as well start collecting for Gus's medical fund now. And while she was there, it wouldn't hurt to see what other information she could glean about Rip Taylor.

As Monica drove down Beach Hollow Road, she practiced what she was going to say when she arrived at the real estate office. If Vera was there, she was bound to ask if Monica had made a decision about the house she'd been shown. She needed to have an answer ready.

She mentally crossed her fingers. With any luck, Vera wouldn't be in the office but out showing a house, and whoever was there would be the chatty, gossipy sort.

Monica pulled into a parking space in front of Cranberry Cove Realty and had to back out twice to straighten the car. She was frustrated with herself. She was allowing her nerves to get the better of her and they were making her clumsy.

She was pleased to note that Vera's BMW was nowhere in sight and she didn't appear to be in the office when Monica peered through the window while pretending to study the real estate listings displayed there.

She pushed open the door with a feeling of apprehension.

There was a youngish man seated behind one of the desks—she judged him to be in his early thirties—his long legs stretched out and his fingers on his computer keys. He jumped when Monica entered and quickly closed his browser window, but not before she had seen the screen. It looked as if he had been playing some sort of game—online poker perhaps?

He stood up and was even taller and lankier than Monica had at first realized. His smile was crooked on one side and he had a dimple in his right cheek.

"Tyler Peterson." He smiled and held out a hand. "What can I do for you?"

Monica shook his hand. His palm was rough—as if he had been doing some sort of manual labor before becoming a real estate agent.

Monica explained about Gus and how she was going to be collecting money for his medical bills.

"If Cranberry Cove Realty is willing, I can drop off a canister to put out on the reception desk along with a poster for your window. Would that be okay, do you think?"

Tyler shrugged. "Yeah, sure. Last month we collected money for the Cranberry Cove High School band. They're raising funds to pay for a trip to Disneyland to compete in a competition."

"Do you think Cranberry Cove Realty would consider a corporate donation?" Monica said.

Tyler screwed up his face. "I can ask. I'll talk to Barbara. She's the owner."

Monica was wracking her brain trying to think of a way to bring Rip Taylor and his murder into the conversation when Tyler beat her to it.

"I'm a big fan of Gus's chili," Tyler said. "I have Rip Taylor to thank for that. I never would have known about it if Rip hadn't clued me in the time we went to the diner for lunch." He shook his head. "Leave it to Gus to have a secret menu for his regulars. He's quite the character, isn't he?"

Monica nodded. "You must miss Rip. What a terrible tragedy," she said in a somber voice.

Tyler looked down and began plucking at a piece of lint on his jacket. "Yes. A tragedy," he said without looking up.

"I've heard he was a good guy," Monica, who had heard no such thing, said.

Tyler shrugged. "Sure." He said it as if there was a question mark at the end.

"I've always imagined real estate to be a cutthroat business." Monica kept her eyes on Tyler's face. "Were you and Rip good friends? I suppose there's a lot of competition in this business."

She knew she was pushing it by asking so many questions, but Tyler didn't seem to be at all suspicious.

"I don't know that we were friends," Tyler said, perching on the edge of his desk. "Buddies is more like it. We'd go out for the odd beer together and complain about the clients." He gave a fleeting smile. "Some of them can be real demanding." He picked up a pen from his desk and began twirling it between his fingers. "There were funny stories, too." He shook his head. "And Rip had a way of telling them that had us all in stitches."

"Oh?"

Tyler leaned toward Monica. "There was this one time Rip told us about when he had an appointment to show a property. Everything was all lined up. The homeowner knew he was bringing his client and had agreed to be out of the house. Like I said, it was all set up just the way we normally do it."

He chuckled. "So, Rip gets there and there's a strange car in the driveway. He doesn't think much of it—maybe the owner has two cars, you know?"

Monica nodded.

"He gives his spiel about the property and then takes his client inside. Almost immediately they hear some strange noises that sound like they're coming from the bedroom. Rip isn't sure what to do. The owner said they would be out of the house. He thinks maybe the owner has a dog in a crate in the bedroom. He's seen some pretty wild stuff, including a boa constrictor in a tank in someone's living room. He's a bit hesitant but he decides to investigate. He doesn't want to spring any unwelcome surprises on his client. He heads down the hall to the bedroom and what does he find?"

Monica assumed that was a rhetorical question and didn't answer.

"He finds the owner of the house in bed with some man and Rip was pretty sure it wasn't her husband. Apparently, she'd forgotten that Rip had made an appointment to show the place!"

Monica didn't know what to say. Of all the things she'd expected, that wasn't one of them.

"The poor guy was horrified. Not Rip, though. He thought it was hilarious, but the poor sucker in the bed didn't find it all that funny. It would have been embarrassing enough but apparently, the guy was married. And not to the woman he was in bed with."

"Who was it? Did Rip recognize him?"

Tyler hesitated and Monica thought he might refuse to answer, but he was so caught up in his story it apparently didn't even occur to him to be a little discreet.

"I can't remember his name. I think he worked for Lakeside Realty. They're one of our biggest competitors. Rip said the man's father-in-law owns this real fancy car dealership—Jaguars, I think he said—out on the Blue Star Highway somewhere. I guess he was a real screwup and his father-in-law didn't want him in the business."

It didn't appear as if Tyler was going to stop talking any time soon. He began to tell Monica a story about someone he used to work with and when that ended, segued into yet another tale. Monica was getting tired from standing and finally managed to extricate herself by claiming to have another appointment.

She'd gotten more than she'd bargained for, she thought as she headed out to her car. What if the man Rip had accidentally surprised was afraid Rip might spill the beans on him? It would give him a good reason to want to shut Rip up permanently.

The question was, who was he?

Chapter 8

Monica was stopped at a traffic light when her cell phone rang. She quickly grabbed it off the passenger seat and glanced at the number. It was Deirdre Swanson, their architect. As soon as she was able, she pulled over to the side of the road and listened to the voicemail Deirdre had left. She hoped nothing was wrong.

As it turned out, there were a few minor details Deirdre wanted to discuss with her. Monica agreed to meet Deirdre at her office since she was already halfway there.

Deirdre was hanging up the telephone when Monica arrived. She took off her glasses, laid them down on the papers unrolled on her desk and wiped her eyes.

"Is everything okay?" Monica said as she took a seat across from Deirdre.

Deirdre sighed. "Yes . . . no, not really. The murder of that real estate agent Richard Taylor is so distressing. And it's hitting a little too close to home." She pinched the bridge of her nose.

Monica tilted her head inquiringly.

"I told you and Greg how Taylor pulled a fast one on my niece, Emily. It cost her her house along with a lot of money." Deirdre bit her lip. "It seems some detective got hold of that information and actually showed up at the hospital where Emily works to interview her."

"Was it Detective Tammy Stevens?"

"Yes. I think that was the name. Emily did say it was a woman. She said she was mortified when her supervisor came up to her and announced that the police were there to talk to her."

"I'm sure Detective Stevens soon realized that your niece was entirely innocent."

Deirdre leaned on her desk and put her head in her hands.

"That's the problem. Emily can't prove she didn't do it. She said she can't tell the police where she was or what she was doing or it would get her in trouble." Deirdre looked up. "She assured me it had nothing to do with that real estate agent's death but she wouldn't tell me what it was either. If it was really so innocent, why is she keeping it a secret?" Deirdre groaned. "Especially if it would clear her of a murder charge."

Monica wasn't sure what to say. "I'm sure it *is* something innocent," she said finally. "People are often embarrassed to admit the most ordinary things—things most other people wouldn't care about." She cast around for an example and a neighbor she'd once had popped into her head. "Some women don't want anyone to know they dye their hair. Or that they watch soap operas or reality TV."

"That doesn't sound like Emily, but I suppose you could be right." Deirdre straightened up. She shook her head. "It has to be something worse than that." She ran a hand through her hair. "What could be worse than being a suspect in a murder?" She sighed. "Sorry to unload on you like this."

She forced a smile. "It just hit me all of a sudden. Obviously, that's not why I wanted to see you." She pointed to the plans on her desk. "I was wondering if you wanted the washer and dryer that we're putting in the laundry room off the kitchen elevated and if you would like a built-in toy box in the second bedroom. It would work perfectly in the nook by the dormer window."

Monica had an immediate vision of herself filling the toy box with dolls or stuffed animals. She couldn't control the smile that spread across her face. "The toy box would be lovely."

• • •

Monica was about to start her car when her cell phone rang. She pulled it from her purse and answered the call. It was her mother.

"Hello?"

"Are you on your way back?" Nancy said on the other end of the line.

"I'm about to be. Why? Is something wrong? Is everything going okay?" Monica felt a sharp pang of worry. Her mother wasn't getting any younger and she'd been complaining about back pains lately.

"Everything is just fine, dear. And that's why I'm calling. Janice, Kit and I are managing perfectly well and we thought you might want to take the afternoon off. You can put your feet up and rest. Pregnant women need their rest, you know."

"I feel fine," Monica insisted, feeling slightly annoyed. "I'm not in the least bit tired."

To her dismay, she had to stifle a sudden yawn that would have put paid to that statement.

"Janice says that not getting enough rest contributes to premature births."

Monica thought it was fortunate that her mother couldn't see her roll her eyes.

"I'm perfectly rested, I assure you." Monica put her key in the ignition.

"But there's simply no need. We're managing fine. You'll have plenty to do after the baby is born."

Monica felt her eyes well up with tears. Basically, what her mother had said was that she wasn't needed. She sniffed and reached into her purse for a tissue. She knew it was ridiculous to feel rejected, but she couldn't help it. No doubt Janice would put her sudden rush of emotions down to pregnancy hormones, she thought wryly. But in this case, she would probably be right.

Monica ended the call and started the car. What to do now? She realized that for the past several years she had been working so incessantly that she no longer had any idea what to do with free time.

Perhaps she'd make a nice dinner for Greg. She could go to Bart's Butcher Shop and pick out something special—a steak or some lamb chops.

She drove slowly down Beach Hollow Road, glancing left and right for an empty parking, space and finally found one a door down from Gina's shop and two doors down from Bart's. She pulled in and turned off the engine. The pickup truck that had been on her tail waiting impatiently for her to pull off the road sped past, kicking up dust and crumbled bits of loose macadam.

A brisk breeze was sending dried leaves swirling down the gutter and eddying at Monica's feet. Soon snow would be piling up along the edge of the sidewalk. The thought made Monica shiver. She pulled her collar up and stuck her hands in her pockets.

She peered into the window as she passed Gina's shop. Gina was behind the counter, and when she saw Monica, she waved for her to come in.

The air inside the shop was perfumed with a variety of scents—lavender, patchouli and sandalwood among many others. Monica took a deep breath and felt the tension in her shoulders and neck relax.

"What brings you downtown?" Gina said, leaning her elbows on the counter.

Monica made a sad face. "Apparently I'm not needed in the kitchen today."

"That's good, isn't it? Gives you a chance to rest."

"I suppose. It does make me feel a bit unwanted though."

"Not needed and unwanted are two different things," Gina said briskly, shaking a finger at Monica.

"True. It's just such an odd feeling." Monica sighed. "To be at loose ends all of a sudden." She rubbed her cold hands together.

"How about some tea? That will warm you up."

"That sounds heavenly. The wind has a real edge to it today."

"Milk? Sugar?"

"Just some sugar, thanks."

"I'll be right back." Gina disappeared through a door behind the sales counter.

Moments later she reappeared with two steaming mugs, which she put down on the counter. She reached down and pulled out a blue and white tin from a shelf underneath.

"Windmill cookies," she said, opening the box and holding it out toward Monica.

Monica took one of the windmill-shaped cookies and put it next to her mug. She picked up her mug of tea and blew on it, sending ripples across the surface. She took a sip and sighed. The warmth felt heavenly.

She studied Gina's face for a minute. "How are you? Are you holding up okay?"

Gina shrugged. "All this worrying is giving me wrinkles." She put both hands on either side of her face and lifted the skin. "I'm thinking of getting Botox. It's done wonders for your mother. She looks ten years younger."

"What does Mickey think? I'm sure he loves you just the way you are."

Gina waved a hand dismissively. "Oh, you know men. They never notice anything. He says I look fine the way I am."

Monica couldn't help but notice that the thought made Gina glow with pleasure.

"So why bother then? Mickey thinks you already look great. He loves you. Why go through all that?"

"A girl has to have standards," Gina said. "Besides, Mickey's not totally blind. What if some beautiful young thing comes along and he casts me aside?"

"I doubt he'd do that," Monica said. "But please yourself." She pushed her hair behind her ears. "Isn't it expensive, though?"

Gina fiddled with the gold and topaz ring on her right hand. "It can be pricey, that's for sure. But your mother seems to have found someone who is quite reasonable."

Monica raised her eyebrows. "Are they qualified?"

Gina nodded her head. "Yes. The woman is a nurse so I'm sure she knows what she's doing."

Monica wasn't sure that being a nurse qualified someone to administer Botox, but then she really knew very little about it.

"I'm going to give this Meyer woman a call and make an appointment. I need something to cheer myself up."

Monica's ears pricked up. "Meyer?"

"Yes." Gina reached under the counter and pulled out a scrap of paper. "Emily Meyer, RN. I wrote down her information. She does it on the side. That's why it's less expensive. It's not exactly legal, but like I said, she's a nurse so I doubt there's any harm in it."

Was it a coincidence? Monica wondered. Were there two Emily Meyers who happened to be nurses? It didn't seem likely.

And if Emily Meyer was running some sort of underground Botox clinic, she certainly wouldn't advertise that fact. Could that be the alibi that she refused to share with the police and her aunt Deirdre? If so, she certainly couldn't be the murderer.

• • •

Before heading to her doctor's appointment, Monica stopped at Bart's Butcher Shop, where Bart eyed her stomach curiously, one eyebrow raised. She was beginning to understand how Kate Middleton must have felt being scrutinized by the media for any sign of pregnancy practically before the ink on the marriage certificate was dry.

Bart agreed to put a porterhouse steak aside for Monica until after her appointment.

"Red meat is good for you," he said as he wrapped the steak in butcher paper. "Builds red blood cells. We can't have you getting anemic." He smiled at Monica. "That happened to my sister when she was expecting her third. She ended up having to go for an iron infusion."

Monica tamped down the sigh that rose to her lips, thanked Bart and went back to her car. Was every person she met from now on going to think they were an expert on pregnancy and birth?

Her doctor's office wasn't far and within minutes, Monica was pulling into the parking lot. A row of spaces right in front of the building had signs that read *Expectant Mothers Parking*. Monica felt a bit absurd pulling into one of them — she was perfectly capable of walking the extra few feet from the second and third rows of spaces, but she suspected she would appreciate it as she approached the nine-month mark.

The wind whipped her hair across her face as she got out of the car and clouds were moving rapidly across the sky. Cold air made its way down the back of her neck and she shivered. She and Greg would have to light a fire in the fireplace that evening. Just thinking of the cozy warmth of the leaping and dancing flames made her anxious to get home.

The walls of the waiting room of doctors Fitzgibbons, Van Raalte and Garcia were painted a neutral beige with generic framed prints hanging around the room. Only one of the other expectant mothers in the waiting room had chosen to sit on the sagging green sofa under the window. Monica plopped down on it, and it gave a loud sigh like a bellows letting out air. It immediately swallowed her in its depths. No wonder most of the women had chosen the straight-backed chairs. She imagined that anyone past four months of pregnancy would have difficulty getting up from its enveloping cushions.

A woman with dark hair and blunt bangs was sitting at the other end of the sofa. Monica looked over as the woman pulled a copy of *OMG!* magazine from her tote bag. The cover was bright with lurid colors and bold black headlines advertising the usual tabloid fare — a story about an unspecified scandal in the royal family — what else was new, Monica thought — as well as the usual celebrity gossip — who had been spotted out with whom, which couples had broken up or were about to according to an "inside source," and who was having financial problems.

The woman thumbed through the pages, occasionally stopping to read an article. She was near the end of the magazine when she gasped.

Monica looked over at her, her eyebrows raised. "Is everything okay?"

"Yes. I'm just surprised, that's all. That's my sister-in-law's ex-husband," she said, pointing a manicured finger at a grainy black-and-white photograph.

Monica peered at the magazine. The picture was of Rip Taylor and the heading read *The Mystery Continues.*

"What do you know? I never thought that cheating creep's murder would make a national tabloid." She turned to Monica. "I'm Pamela Van Der Zee, by the way. I'm married to Lacey Van Der Zee's brother, Tom. Lacey is Rip Taylor's ex-wife."

"Monica Albertson," Monica said.

Pamela brandished the magazine. "I know it's wrong to speak ill of the dead, but I can't find it in myself to be sorry that rotter is gone." She pinched her lips together. "He ended up cheating on Lacey with the woman who drew up their prenuptial agreement."

Monica's ears perked up. "Oh?"

Pamela nodded. "Thank goodness Lacey had that prenup. Tom insisted on it. He told her she had to protect her money. Of course, Lacey fancied herself to be in love"—she put air quotes around the word *love*—"and had stars in her eyes. Lawrence—that was her first husband, the one who left her all that money—hadn't been gone even three months when she took up with that Rip character. He wasn't happy about the prenup, I can tell you that. Lacey was afraid he was going to call off the engagement, but he did go through with it. As it was, he certainly enjoyed living off Lacey's money while he could."

"Who ended the relationship?" If Lacey had been that much in love it seemed unlikely that she would have been the one, Monica thought.

"Lacey did." Pamela bobbed her head briskly. "She finally came to her senses when she found out he was cheating on her with that lawyer, Kayla Moore." Pamela let the magazine drop into her lap. "Lacey is such a softie. So many of her friends are all about getting their hair and nails done, going shopping and out to lunch. But not Lacey. Do you know she volunteers?" Pamela nodded her head as if to emphasize the point. "She helps put together sack dinners for kids who otherwise might not get anything to eat. What's that organization called?" She tapped her lips with a well-manicured index finger. Suddenly she clapped her hands. "Food for Kids. That's it."

Monica was surprised to hear about the prenup and the fact that it had been Kayla who had drawn it up. She wondered what had been in it. Certainly the terms were meant to protect Lacey's money, but had there been anything in it for Rip? From the sound of things, he hadn't gotten much

"Did Rip get anything in the divorce?" she said, thinking of the Jaguar Gina said Rip had been driving.

Pamela shook her head. "Not a thing. It was ironclad. He barely got away with the clothes on his back."

"He got nothing? Not even a car?"

"Nope. Nada. Zilch." Pamela glanced at the magazine article again. "I wonder if they've found out who killed him yet. I haven't seen anything in the papers recently."

"Unfortunately, I don't think they have," Monica said. "At least I haven't heard anything either."

Pamela snorted. "Frankly, I don't care if they never find out who did it. Serves him right."

Chapter 9

Monica smiled to herself as she drove home after picking up her steak from the butcher shop. The doctor's appointment had gone well. It was too early yet to hear the baby's heartbeat but the doctor had assured her that both she and the baby were healthy and the pregnancy was progressing as it should. She couldn't wait to tell Greg the good news.

She turned down the dirt road that led to her cottage, bouncing over the ruts that had been frozen into the dirt. She was about to turn into her driveway when she noticed several cars parked ahead of her and a group of people clustered around a stand of trees near one of the bogs. The trees were nearly bare now, with only the odd shriveled brown leaf still clinging to the branches.

One of the vehicles looked like a police car, she noticed, and another looked just like the car Detective Stevens normally drove.

What was going on? She quickly pulled into her driveway, shut off the engine, got out and began walking toward the bog. Jeff was standing with Stevens, who was wearing a black parka with a knit scarf around her neck. Jeff was gesticulating wildly with his hand as he talked. Monica noticed that he had tucked the hand of his injured arm in his pocket. The broad navy blue back of a policeman was visible as he bent over. He appeared to be examining something in the tall grass.

Monica started to walk faster. She hoped nothing was wrong but it had to be something serious if Stevens and the police were there. It couldn't be another body. It just couldn't be. That was a nightmare she never wanted to relive.

She passed Stevens's car and noticed a crumpled bag from a fast food restaurant on the passenger seat and a foam cup in the cupholder. There was a smudge of pale pink lipstick on the plastic lid.

"What on earth?" Monica said when she reached the group and saw what they were staring so intently at. Half hidden in the tall grass was a white porcelain toilet tank.

"That must be the one that was stolen," she said, pointing at it. She turned to Detective Stevens. "But surely it hardly warrants investigating. I saw on the news that the thief had already been caught."

A loon, rising from the shores of the bog, rent the air with its cry. The sudden sound made Monica jump and she felt her heart speed up. She'd been awfully jittery lately. Was that another pregnancy symptom?

Stevens cleared her throat and fingered the scarf around her neck. "Why steal a toilet tank?" she said. "We figure something had to have been hidden in it. If it was drugs, we might find some lingering traces that will confirm it." She rolled her eyes. "Johnson claims that all he took was the tank itself but that just doesn't hold water." She smiled. "Pardon the pun."

The sound of a car approaching caused them all to turn and look. Stevens groaned.

It was a red and white van with *WZZZ News* written on the side.

"The press is here," Stevens said, making a face. "Right on cue. You wouldn't think that a stolen toilet tank would be newsworthy."

"Small town," Jeff said laconically. "Every little thing is a big deal."

"I guess I still haven't gotten used to that." Stevens shrugged and peered into the distance. "Looks like the *Cranberry Cove Chronicle* is right behind them." She jerked a thumb toward a dusty Kia that had pulled up behind the WZZZ van.

She scowled as a young woman with a camera perched on her shoulder began to make her way toward them with the reporter who had interviewed Mrs. Lombardi hastening to catch up.

The reporter from the *Chronicle* continued to move toward them at a trot. He caught the toe of his shoe on a tree root and nearly fell, cartwheeling his arms to regain his balance.

Stevens squared her shoulders and braced herself as the duo raced to see who would get to her first. The reporter from WZZZ spoke briefly with the cameraman and then got into position next to Stevens, his lips stretched into a broad smile. The cameraman nodded and the reporter began talking. He introduced the story, panting slightly, then shoved the microphone at Stevens. Her answers were curt and clipped.

"Why a toilet tank?" the reporter asked with a smirk. "What do the police feel is so important about this case?"

"All cases are important," Stevens said, tight-lipped, her cheeks slightly flushed.

But the reporter was not satisfied. "Did you find anything inside the tank?"

"No."

The reporter was obviously becoming frustrated by Stevens's terse answers.

"Do the police suspect something was in the tank at one time? Something important perhaps?"

Stevens waved a hand. "I'm afraid that's all. Now, if you'll excuse me, I have work to do."

The WZZZ camera continued to roll as the reporter wrapped up the segment.

"Stay tuned for more on this breaking story," he said somberly.

Stevens pulled a pair of gloves from her jacket pocket and with the help of the uniformed patrolman began to secure the toilet tank in a large plastic bag. The tank was unwieldy and the patrolman grunted with the effort. Stevens gritted her teeth as the wind continued to snatch the bag from her hands.

Finally, the tank was secured. Stevens stood up. Her face was red and she put a hand to her back. The patrolman wrapped his arms around the tank and carted it toward Stevens's car. Monica watched as he tucked it into the trunk.

The reporter from the *Cranberry Cove Chronicle* looked disappointed as he stuck his notebook and pencil in his back pocket.

The two reporters were already on the way to their respective vehicles when Stevens said goodbye and headed toward hers.

Monica watched as the vehicles started up, turned around and drove back down the road. She turned to Jeff. "I wonder what the police expect to find in the tank? And why did Johnson choose to dump it here?"

Jeff grinned. "Like the man said, stay tuned for more information. I'm sure we haven't heard the last of this. We'll probably find out soon enough."

Monica said goodbye to Jeff and walked back to her cottage, shuffling through the leaves that had blown up against her trellis and were scattered on her front walkway. The *Cranberry Cove Chronicle* was lying on the doormat. She picked it up and tucked it under her arm. She opened the door a crack and had to shoo Hercule away from it so she could open it all the way. His tail was wagging so fast it was a blur. He sniffed vigorously at the package of meat in Monica's hand and tried to nudge it with his snout. She ruffled the fur on top of his head and bent down to receive his enthusiastic doggie kisses.

Mittens was more aloof, swishing in and out between Monica's legs and arching her back as Monica scratched under her chin.

Monica put the meat in the refrigerator and stood massaging her temples. She was more tired than she'd realized, which was alarming. She hadn't actually done all that much. Maybe her anxiety about the doctor's visit had compounded her fatigue. Fortunately, she could relax now knowing that everything was fine.

She bent, untied her sneakers and kicked them off by the door. She leaned against the wall and rubbed her arches. Her feet had begun to ache. She couldn't help but wonder how they were going to feel when she was nine months pregnant.

The urge to take a nap was nearly irresistible but she fought it off and put a mug of water in the microwave. She peered into the cookie jar on the counter. She was disappointed to find that it was empty. She suddenly laughed, immediately thinking of that old saying about the shoemaker's children always going barefoot. Tomorrow she would make a tray of cranberry walnut chocolate chunk cookies to take home for her and Greg.

The microwave dinged, she removed the mug of hot water, added an herbal tea bag and some sugar and carried it over to the kitchen table, where she'd dropped the newspaper. She would drink her tea, catch up on the news and hopefully get a second wind in time to cook dinner.

Monica unfolded the paper and scanned the front page. She skipped over most of the stories until she saw the headline *Jax Johnson Hires Prominent Local Attorney*. She leaned her elbows on the table and started to read. The article began with a recap of Jax Johnson's crime, although since the paper had gone to press before Jeff found the toilet tank on the farm property, there was no mention of it.

After the summary of previous events, the article delved into information about Johnson's lawyer, Kayla Moore, referring to her as a "prominent local attorney." Apparently, she was making a name for herself having recently won a very complicated case—a bitter custody battle—that had briefly catapulted her into the national news. Monica vaguely remembered seeing something about it on television and the mention of Kayla Moore's name. What was she like? Monica wondered. Obviously, she was a hard-driving career woman. She went after what she wanted—she stole Rip away from his wife, after all—but did she have a softer side as well? According to her maid, she was the one who filled Rip's thermos with fresh coffee every morning. Was she capable of murder? She certainly had the opportunity. But did she even have a reason to want Rip dead?

Monica continued thinking about Kayla as she flipped through the rest of the paper, stopping to look at an advertisement for a baby stroller that was on sale at a nearby store.

Perhaps if she knew more about Kayla she could either uncover a motive for her wanting Rip dead or she could completely eliminate her as a suspect. She'd gleaned a lot by visiting Rip's office and perhaps that would work to learn more about Kayla as well. But she didn't want to talk to Kayla herself. It was unlikely that would reveal much of anything. She'd learn a lot more from her associates. But first she would have to make sure that Kayla would be out of the office. She looked up the number for Kayla's firm and quickly dialed it.

Monica's voice faltered slightly as she asked for Kayla Moore. She had no idea what she would say if she was actually connected and breathed a sigh of relief when the receptionist told her that Kayla was out. She declined to leave a message and hung up.

She put her mug in the dishwasher, slipped on her jacket and grabbed her purse.

Now was the perfect time to visit Kayla's office.

• • •

More clouds had moved in, darkening the sky and making it look like dusk even though the sun wasn't due to set for another hour. It started to rain as Monica headed through town toward Kayla's office and she turned on the windshield wipers. Soon the rain began to turn to sleet, the drops pinging against her windows.

She parked the car in front of a nondescript four-story brick building. She ran toward the entrance, pulling her collar up and ducking her head against the icy rain. The small lobby was just large enough to house a signboard with the tenants' names on it, an elevator and an unused stand ashtray.

Kayla's office was a flight up. Monica pressed the button for the elevator and the door opened immediately. It jerked and rumbled as it made its way to the second floor, where the doors opened with a harsh squeal. A familiar smell greeted Monica as she stepped out and she wasn't surprised to see that the plaque on the nearest door read *Walter Postma DDS.*

Kayla's office was sandwiched between the dental office and one belonging to a financial planner. Monica tapped on the frosted glass door and then slowly turned the knob.

The reception area was the stereotypical idea of an attorney's office with wood-paneled walls, an old-fashioned maple desk where the very modern computer looked out of place, and bookshelves filled with leather-bound law tomes.

The receptionist sitting behind the desk had headphones in her ears and was focused on her computer screen. She was wearing dark-rimmed glasses, had her hair cut in a short bob that ended just below her ears, and was wearing black slacks and a mauve cable-knit sweater. A wooden name plate with *Betty Draisma* written on it in gold letters was positioned facing Monica.

Betty pulled the headphones out of her ears and looked up at Monica expectantly. "Can I help you?"

Monica cleared her throat. "I would like to speak to Kayla Moore." She hoped the woman wouldn't recognize her voice from her earlier telephone call.

"I'm afraid she isn't in at the moment." Betty frowned. "Did you have an appointment?" She flipped through the pages of a planner on her desk.

"No, no," Monica hastened to reassure her. "I . . . someone recommended her. I understand she won that custody case they talked about on the news a while ago."

Betty smiled, leaned forward and put her elbows on the desk. "Yes. That case made the national news. It was quite exciting. They even came to film the office for that special they did."

"Does Ms. Moore have a lot of cases like that?"

Betty tilted her head. "Not exactly. I mean, most of them are somewhat routine. Bankruptcies, DUIs, property disputes. Things like that."

"I read that she's handling the Jax Johnson case. That's been getting some coverage on the news."

"Oh, that." Betty dismissed it with a wave of her hand. "It's a novelty. Who would steal a toilet tank?"

Well, Jax Johnson for one, Monica thought.

"Ms. Moore was fairly certain the absurd nature of the case would lead to a fair amount of press coverage."

"It sounds like she's very ambitious."

"Very." Betty picked up a pencil and began tapping it on her desk. "She has her sights set on bigger things than this." She swept a hand around the office.

"Oh?"

Betty nodded. "She has her eye on the district attorney's office someday. And from there?" She shrugged. "Who knows?"

That was interesting, Monica thought as she left the office. But being hard-driving and determined to get ahead didn't automatically make you capable of killing.

Besides, Monica had yet to uncover a reason why Kayla would want Rip dead.

• • •

Monica was surprised to find Greg at home when she opened the back door.

"You're home early," she said.

"I have to go back to the store again but I thought maybe we could have an early dinner," he said as Monica hung up her jacket.

"I'm glad. I bought us a porterhouse steak from Bart's."

Greg grinned. "I wouldn't want to miss that." He kissed Monica on the cheek. "What are we having with it?"

"I thought a salad and some potatoes."

"Mashed?" Greg said eagerly.

"Sure. Would you mind peeling them while I go change? I accidentally stepped in a puddle and my jeans are all wet on the bottom."

"Not a bit. You go get into some dry clothes and I'll start on the spuds."

Monica went upstairs, grabbed a fresh pair of jeans out of the closet and pulled them on. She paused in front of the mirror and ran a brush through her dark hair, which had been tossed about by the wind.

Less than five minutes later, she was back in the kitchen, where Greg was at the counter, a pile of potato peels in front of him.

He put down the potato peeler and turned to Monica. "I heard something peculiar on the radio as I was on my way home," he said.

"Oh?" Monica reached for her apron and tied it around her waist.

"You remember the story about the fellow who stole that toilet tank?"

"Mmhmm," Monica said as she turned on the broiler.

"The news report said it was found here—at the farm. Is that true? Do you know anything about it?"

"Yes, it was, as a matter of fact. The tank was hidden in some tall grass down by the bogs. Jeff came across it and called the police. Detective Stevens showed up and the press wasn't far behind." Monica opened the refrigerator and retrieved a head of lettuce. "It seemed like an awful lot of fuss over a stolen toilet tank. How much could the thing be worth, anyway? Unless something was hidden in it."

"That's just it. According to the news report, the police apparently found the remains of some powder in the tank. It appears to be cocaine, although they won't know for sure until they get the lab results back."

Monica drew in her breath. "Cocaine? Hidden in the tank?"

"That's what the reporter said. That must be why that Johnson character stole it."

"But why not simply take the cocaine? Why steal the whole tank?"

"The police think that some of the plastic wrapping around the drugs must have ripped and the cocaine would have spilled if he'd tried to take the packages out. I guess even a couple of grams can be worth thousands. He didn't want to lose any of it if he could help it so he stole the tank itself."

Chapter 10

Janice was already on a second batch of cranberry streusel bread when Monica arrived at the farm kitchen the next morning. The air was redolent with the scent of sugar, vanilla and cinnamon and a row of golden-brown loaves sat out on a tray ready to be delivered.

"Those smell delicious," Monica said as she tied an apron around her waist.

"I added a touch of orange zest to the dough." Janice dusted flour off her hands. "I thought the bread was lacking something and that added the little extra something it needed."

"Oh." Monica felt somewhat deflated. She thought the bread had tasted perfectly fine the way she always made it.

Janice cut a slice off the end of one of the loaves. "Here," she said, handing it to Monica. "I think you'll see I'm right."

Monica broke a piece off and popped it in her mouth. She had to admit Janice was right. The addition of the orange zest took the taste to a whole new level.

"It's good, isn't it?" Janice stood with her hands on her hips waiting for an answer.

Monica had to admit it was, as much as it pained her. "Yes. Excellent. Let's add that to the recipe from now on."

She stood on her tiptoes and reached for the new roll of paper towels on the shelf above the dispenser.

"Don't!" Janice yelled.

Monica stopped with her hand halfway above her head. "What's wrong?"

Janice tut-tutted. "Don't you know a pregnant woman should never lift her arms above her head?"

Monica frowned. Not another one of Janice's pregnancy myths. "Whyever not?"

"The umbilical cord can get tangled and strangle the baby."

Monica felt a moment of panic but then common sense took over.

"That's got to be an old wives' tale. My doctor would have told me if that was the case."

Janice gave her a dark look. "Don't say I didn't warn you."

The door opened and a shaft of light slanted across the kitchen floor. Lauren breezed in bringing with her the scent of fresh air and sunshine. She had her arms around a large cardboard box. Several rolled-up posters were sticking out of the top.

Monica smiled at her. "Good morning. It looks like you've been busy. What do you have there?" Monica pointed at the box.

"These are all the materials you'll need for the fundraiser for Gus." She plunked the carton down on the table and yanked off her mittens. "Here are the posters." She pulled one from the box and unfurled it.

"It's perfect," Monica said. "I hope the shopkeepers will agree to hang them in their windows."

"I've got these as well." Lauren reached into the box and took out a canister wrapped in paper printed with the same information as the posters. "These can be put by the cash registers for people to toss in their spare change."

"These are all wonderful," Monica said, holding up the poster again. "I'll take them around this afternoon." She put the poster back in the box.

A look of distress crossed Lauren's face. "I can do it for you. No need for you to go to all that trouble."

"It's no trouble." Monica smiled to show she meant it. "Really. I'll be glad to get out for a bit." She turned to Janice. "Can you manage without me this afternoon? Kit will be here shortly. He went to check out the new café in the bookstore."

Monica felt a bit guilty because what she didn't say was that distributing the posters and canisters would give her the chance to talk to more people and possibly pick up some vital clues.

• • •

The noon whistle blew as Monica was hanging up her apron. She'd spent the morning baking, and the farm store was now well-stocked with goodies for their afternoon customers. Janice was sitting at the table unwrapping a bologna sandwich and Nancy, who had arrived shortly after Lauren left, was tying ribbons around jars of cranberry salsa.

Monica said goodbye, picked up the box Lauren had delivered and headed back to her cottage. She put the box in the trunk of her car and went inside. She stood at the kitchen counter and quickly downed a bowl of lentil soup she'd heated in the microwave.

Hercule looked disappointed when he saw her putting on her jacket again.

"Don't worry, boy." Monica bent down to ruffle the fur on the top of his head. "I'll be back before you know it."

The drive into town didn't take long. Most of the parking spots along Beach Hollow Road were taken but Monica was finally able to pull into one in front of the hardware store. She might as well start at that end of town, she thought, as she pulled a poster and canister from the trunk of her car.

The owner of the store was startled to hear about Gus's accident and readily agreed to hang a poster in the window and place the canister by the cash register.

That was easy, Monica thought as she headed to Bart's. Bart was equally happy to help and even wrapped up a large knucklebone for Hercule.

The sounds of clinking crockery and foods sizzling on the grill washed over Monica as she opened the door to the diner. The restaurant was packed with the lunch crowd—a mix of salesmen dressed in business casual and farmers in overalls and work boots.

The waitress who had told Monica about Gus's accident took the poster and cannister from Monica and as Monica left, she noticed the waitress was already taping the poster to the window.

She made her way down the street, stopping in at Twilight and Danielle's Boutique before finally arriving at Gumdrops, where Hennie and Gerda VanVelsen, the identical twin sisters who owned the shop, greeted her with a smile. As usual, they were dressed alike in lavender plaid skirts and matching sweaters.

At first, Monica had found it impossible to tell them apart, but over time she'd noticed subtle differences in their personalities—Hennie was the forthright one while Gerda tended to hang back and let her sister take the lead. Both were as charming as their shop with its selection of Dutch treats as well as what used to be called penny candy stored in glass containers that created a kaleidoscope of vivid colors along one wall.

"How are you feeling, dear?" Hennie said with a slight frown wrinkling her forehead.

"Perfectly fine," Monica assured her.

"That's good to hear," Hennie and Gerda said in unison.

"Promise you'll take care of yourself and not work too hard," Hennie said, raising an eyebrow and fixing Monica with a stare.

Monica put her hand over her heart. "I promise."

"Good," Hennie said decisively. "Now, what can I do for you?"

Monica explained about Gus and his accident and the fund to collect money for his medical bills.

"The poor man." Gerda wrung her hands. "We'd heard about the accident but didn't realize it was that serious." She looked to Hennie. "Of course, we'd be glad to help in any way we can."

Hennie took the canister from Monica and placed it by the cash register. "Our handyman, Al, is coming by later to change one of the lightbulbs. A delightful man, always so prompt and so helpful. I'll ask him to hang the poster for us."

Monica continued to lean against the counter. This seemed like as good an opening as any. She knew the VanVelsens could never resist a bit of gossip. "Have you heard about the murder of that realtor?"

"We certainly have." Hennie straightened her shoulders. "Dreadfully shocking, wasn't it, Gerda?"

"Oh, my, yes. When we heard the news, I felt quite faint and had to sit down. Hennie made me a strong cup of tea, and that put me to rights again. Isn't that true, Hennie?"

Hennie looked slightly irritated by her sister's lengthy interruption. She nodded briskly.

"Richard Taylor was quite the star back in his younger days, playing football for Cranberry Cove High School. That's when people began to call him Rip, because of how fast he could run."

"The sports reporters used to say he ripped across the field and that's how he got his nickname," Gerda added.

Hennie gave her sister a sharp look. "He went on to play for Michigan State after he graduated." She put her hand on her chest. "Not that I know much about sports, mind you. I've always found football to be quite tedious with all that stopping and starting. But even though I didn't follow the sport, you couldn't help hearing all the stories. Rip was the talk of the town."

"That he was." Gerda bobbed her head up and down. "And they don't seem to know who killed him, do they?"

"I don't think so," Monica said. "At least I haven't heard anything.

There hasn't been anything on the news recently."

"I don't know what the world is coming to." Gerda fingered the yellowing pearls around her neck. "Another murder in Cranberry Cove." Her forehead creased in concern. "And theft," she exclaimed, her cheeks beginning to flush. "There was that man who stole a toilet tank. Can you imagine? What on earth would he want with one of those? No one is safe." She pulled her cardigan sweater around her more closely. She turned to Hennie. "I seem to recall there was some story about Richard Taylor and that fellow they caught stealing the toilet tank. Do you remember, Hennie?"

"Of course I do. His name is Jax Johnson and he and Rip were in high school together, although I believe Rip was a grade behind him." Hennie tapped her forehead with her finger. "I do have a good memory if I must say so myself." She looked quite pleased.

Gerda frowned. "Wasn't there some sort of accident?"

Monica's ears perked up. "An accident? Like a car accident?"

Hennie cleared her throat. "No, no, nothing like that. It was a terrible accident nonetheless. It was during the football game when Cranberry Cove High played South Harbor High. There's always been a bitter rivalry between those two schools so this was the most important game of the year. Gerda and I were there, weren't we, Gerda?"

Gerda nodded. "Not that we're in the habit of attending football games, mind you, but we had a concession selling candy. Hopjes— coffee-flavored caramels—and Droste pastilles were the most popular." She trailed off when Hennie gave her a stern look.

"Rip Taylor was playing for Cranberry Cove and Jax Johnson was playing for South Harbor High." Hennie leaned on the counter and steepled her fingers. "The score was tied when Jax got the ball. He ran down the field so fast he was almost a blur and was clearly headed for a touchdown when Rip tackled him. Everyone on the South Harbor side of the field groaned in disappointment. We fully expected Jax to get up, but when he didn't immediately spring to his feet, the coach and the team doctor rushed over. The crowd was hushed as they waited nervously to see what was going to happen."

"We assumed Jax was fine and the game would go on," Gerda said. "But Jax was taking so long. He was still lying on the ground even though several minutes had gone by. People began to get worried."

Hennie's eyes were wide. "But he never did get to his feet. A group of people were surrounding him by then and when they parted briefly, we could see poor Jax lying on the ground, his leg bent at an impossible angle."

"I'll never forget the sight. It was gruesome." Gerda shuddered. "I had to look away."

Hennie cleared her throat. "The accident ended Jax's career. He was set to go to the University of Michigan on an athletic scholarship and there were even rumors that he would be drafted into the pros before he finished college, but he was never able to play again."

"How awful!" Monica said.

"Rip went on to become captain of the Michigan State football team and Jax? We heard he dropped out of school and got mixed up with an unsavory group of people." Gerda shook her head.

"It's so sad to see that Jax has fallen into a life of crime, although why anyone would want to steal a toilet tank is beyond me." Hennie sniffed.

She could always count on the VanVelsens to provide interesting information, Monica thought as she said goodbye and left the shop.

And in this case, they'd provided a new suspect as well. From the sound of things, Jax had every reason to hate Rip Taylor. But did he still harbor a grudge over something that had happened years ago? And had it led him to murder?

• • •

Monica decided to make another stop at Cranberry Cove Realty. This time she had the posters to use as an excuse for visiting them so there would be no need to pretend she was in the market for a house. If Vera was there, she'd simply say that she and her husband had changed their minds about buying a house and had decided to build a new one instead.

She pulled up in front of the real estate office and took a poster and canister from her trunk. The office looked deserted when she peered through the window, but when she stepped inside, a woman walked out of a door at the rear of the office.

"Can I help you?" she said when she saw Monica.

She had a round white face that was totally lacking in angles and reminded Monica of a lump of dough. Her gray hair was set in waves and she was wearing a skirt that was too long to be fashionable and a black cardigan over a plain white blouse.

"I'm afraid all of our agents are out with clients at the moment." She waved a hand toward the empty desks. "But I'd be happy to take down your name and number and have one of them call you to make an appointment when they get back."

"Actually, I'm not here to buy a house," Monica said, taking the poster out from under her arm.

The woman looked confused and Monica hastened to explain about Gus, his accident and the collection she was taking up to help pay his medical bills.

"I'd be more than happy to put a poster in our window," the woman said with a smile. "I'm Pat, by the way."

"Monica Albertson." Monica handed over the poster.

"Our family has been going to the Cranberry Cove Diner ever since I can remember." A wistful look passed over Pat's face. "My father used to take us for breakfast on Saturday mornings to get us out of the house and give our mother some precious peace and quiet. I always ordered the same thing, blueberry pancakes with a side of crispy bacon, and every time my father suggested I try something new, I refused." She smiled. "Gus wasn't there back then but I remember when he started. It would be a terrible shame if he had to close the diner."

"I guess we all have our stories. I remember the first time I discovered the diner had chili even though it wasn't on the menu."

Pat laughed. "It's our little secret."

Monica gestured toward the empty desks. "You must be a bit shorthanded with Rip Taylor gone."

Pat pursed her lips. "We are, a bit. Although Tyler has been working overtime to make up for it. It's ironic, really." She gave a small smile. "Rip was known for stealing the other agents' business. He and Tyler were having an enormous row one day when I got back from lunch. Rip's face was so red I feared for his heart and I could see that Tyler's jaw was tightly clenched. They pretended as if nothing was going on but I suspect they were arguing about Rip's pocket listings."

"Pocket listings?" Monica said.

"Off-market listings," Pat said. "Meaning they're not listed on the MLS, the multiple listing service. The agent contacts a few people he knows who are in the market for a house to see if they're interested.

Then if the property sells, the agent doesn't have to split the commission with the buyer's agent but gets the entire amount for himself."

"Is that illegal?"

Pat tilted her head. "Not exactly, but the National Association of Realtors has banned the practice for its members. Listings must be posted to the MLS within one day."

"And that's what Rip was doing — pocket listings?"

"I'm quite certain it was and it wasn't fair to the other agents. I suspect that's what Rip and Tyler had been arguing about."

The trip had been worthwhile, Monica thought as she said goodbye to Pat and went out to her car. Delivering the posters and canisters for her fundraising campaign was proving more fruitful than she had expected.

It now sounded as if Tyler Peterson also had a potential motive for killing Rip Taylor. The question was, had he?

Chapter 11

Monica was about to get into her car, when it began to sprinkle lightly. She checked the backseat for an umbrella but then realized she'd left her umbrella in the trunk. She hesitated but the rain was picking up in intensity and she decided she'd better get it now.

She'd opened the trunk and was reaching inside when another car pulled into the lot, parking in the space beside her. Monica used the trunk lid to shield herself from view as best she could in case the new arrival was Vera. She glanced over at the car that had just arrived and noticed that Tyler was getting out of the driver's seat. Moments later, the passenger-side door opened and Kayla joined him. Even though Monica had never met her, she recognized her from the photograph in the newspaper.

The two of them were standing awfully close together, Monica noticed, and she was surprised when Kayla reached out and straightened Tyler's tie. The gesture seemed so . . . intimate. They spoke in muted tones and Monica couldn't hear what they were saying until Tyler raised his voice slightly.

"I'll be back in a minute," he said. He touched Kayla's cheek. "Although every minute away from you is a minute too long." He leaned toward Kayla and gave her a lingering kiss.

So Tyler and Kayla were what Monica's mother would call an *item.* When had that started? Rip hadn't been dead all that long—less than a week.

Monica thought back to her conversation with Kayla's maid, Joan. She'd said that Kayla's boyfriends didn't last long and had hinted that Rip would probably be gone soon as well. And she'd admitted that Kayla and Rip sometimes fought. Had Rip caught Kayla cheating and had that been what they'd fought about?

Did that give Kayla a motive? She could have simply thrown Rip out. It's not like they were married. But what if he'd refused to go? He was living a fairly luxurious life and Kayla was financing it by all accounts. Perhaps Rip had discovered Kayla had a secret that she didn't want known. Perhaps he'd used the knowledge to ensure that she didn't dare break up with him.

If so, had Tyler decided to take matters into his own hands and rid

Kayla of Rip once and for all? There was already animosity between the two of them. Had that simply poured fuel on the fire?

Kayla got back in the car and Monica quickly slid into her own driver's seat. She hoped Kayla hadn't seen her—not that it really mattered. Pat could vouch for the fact that her presence at the real estate office had been perfectly innocent.

Almost innocent, Monica thought as she pulled out of the parking lot. The fact that she'd picked up some interesting gossip had been a bonus.

• • •

As Monica headed back toward town and Beach Hollow Road, the rain became fiercer, pounding against her windshield and almost immediately flooding the gutters. She flicked on her windshield wipers and then her headlights. The skies had darkened considerably since she'd left the Cranberry Cove Realty office.

Rip's murder was never far from her mind, suspects and motives swirling in her head as she tried to make sense of it. There were so many people who had a reason to want Rip dead—Emily Meyer because Rip had cheated her in the sale of the house she'd inherited; Tyler Peterson because Rip had cheated him with his pocket listings, and on top of that, Tyler obviously wanted Rip's girlfriend for himself; Kayla Moore because she wanted to be rid of Rip; Jax Johnson because Rip had ended his dreams of becoming a pro football player; even the fellow from Lakeside Realty who might fear that Rip would reveal he'd been in bed with another woman. Could Rip's ex-wife, Lacey Van der Zee, also have a motive? Monica couldn't imagine what it might be. It wasn't as if Rip had taken her to the cleaners in the divorce. Just the opposite. Rip was the one who had been left with nothing.

Except a Jaguar, Monica thought. How on earth had Rip been able to afford a Jaguar when he couldn't even come up with the cash to buy an officemate a baby present? Maybe he stole the money, but from where? If he'd stolen the car itself, surely the police would have caught up with him long before now.

She was waiting at a traffic light when a thought came to her so swiftly, she said *oh!* out loud. The light turned green but Monica was still lost in thought and didn't step on the gas until the driver behind her leaned on his horn.

There was one way Rip might have made that money. Blackmail. And that fellow from Lakeside Realty would have made the perfect victim. Had Rip threatened to tell the man's wife about his being caught in the act, so to speak? Tyler had said the fellow's father-in-law owned a Jaguar dealership and Rip had driven a Jaguar. Was there a connection?

Since she had the afternoon off, Monica decided to drive by Lakeside Realty. She didn't know what that was going to accomplish but she hoped something would come to her.

She pulled over, grabbed her phone and looked up the address. She groaned when she saw it was at the other end of Beach Hollow Road. She turned around in the parking lot of the Cranberry Cove Inn and headed back in the direction from which she'd come. She didn't have far to go. Lakeside Realty was housed in a small brick building set back from the road. Monica pulled into the driveway and followed it to a small parking lot behind the building. She drove slowly down the row and scanned the line of cars.

Parked closest to the back entrance of the building was a shiny brand-new Jaguar. It stood out like a sore thumb among the ordinary Fords and Chevrolets, many of which could have used a run through the car wash. If Monica's hunch was correct, that car most likely belonged to the fellow whose father-in-law owned the Jaguar dealership. Now she just had to figure out a way to get his name.

The idea came to her as she was walking around to the front entrance of Lakeside Realty. It was a bit iffy but if it worked, she'd soon know who the man was.

The office was set up much like Cranberry Cove Realty, with desks in a row and one out front where the receptionist sat. She was a young woman with long blond hair, dressed in a rather severe black pantsuit and pale blue blouse. Her fingers were flying over the computer keys but she immediately stopped when she heard Monica enter.

"Can I help you?"

Monica pretended to wring her hands. "I hope so. I'm afraid there's been a bit of an accident. Well, more like a fender bender really. Nothing all that serious. I'm afraid I bumped a car out there in the parking lot." She gestured toward the back of the office. "I think it's a Jaguar."

The receptionist's eyes widened and Monica heard her indrawn breath.

"There's no damage that I can see but I thought I'd better tell the owner. It seemed the right thing to do." Monica gave a timid smile. "Is he or she here by any chance?"

The receptionist swiveled her chair around and yelled "Marty," so loudly Monica jumped. "Someone's here to see you."

Marty appeared through the door at the rear of the office. He had light brown hair combed over a large bald spot at the crown of his head and his stomach strained the front of his rather rumpled white shirt. He looked at Monica quizzically.

"Are you buying or selling?" he said as he approached her.

"Neither, actually." Monica pretended to wring her hands again. "I'm afraid there's been a bit of an accident."

Marty's eyes bulged and he put a hand on his chest. "Not the Jaguar?"

Monica held up a hand. "There's no damage." She hastened to reassure him. The poor man looked as if he was about to have a stroke. "But I thought it was only right to have you take a look for yourself."

Marty yanked his suit coat off the back of one of the chairs, sending it spinning, and put it on as he followed Monica out of the building and to the parking lot. He was breathing heavily and there were sweat stains under the arms of his white shirt.

"I'm Monica Albertson," Monica said as they headed toward where the Jaguar was parked.

"Marty Fisher," Marty called over his shoulder as he hastened toward the car. "Where did you say you hit her?" He ran a hand lovingly over the rear fender.

"Right there." Monica pointed vaguely to a spot.

Marty's face was glistening with sweat as he examined the car. He pulled a handkerchief from his pocket and wiped his forehead.

"I don't see anything. Are you sure you hit it?" He looked at Monica.

Monica shrugged. "I thought so."

"You must have just tapped it." He wiped his forehead again. "Don't worry about it."

Monica decided to go for broke. "You knew Rip Taylor, didn't you?" she said to Marty.

Marty's face turned bright red and then the color slowly receded until he was as white as the flour Monica used for baking. Droplets of sweat ran down the side of his face and he brushed at them impatiently.

"That piece of garbage? Yeah, I knew him. And I'm not sorry he's dead." His eyes narrowed as he stared at Monica. "Why are you asking me that anyway? Are you a reporter or something?"

Monica put her hands up in surrender. "No. I was just curious."

Marty clenched his fists and for a minute Monica thought he was going to punch her. Relief washed over her when the receptionist stuck her head out the back door of the building.

"Marty," she yelled. "Telephone."

• • •

Monica pulled out of the Lakeside Realty parking lot so abruptly, her car tires kicked up bits of loose gravel in her wake. She was beginning to wonder if she should leave well enough alone and stop investigating. She had to admit that encounter with Marty had scared her.

She kept looking behind her as she drove and was relieved when no Jaguars appeared in her rearview mirror. She was even more relieved when she pulled onto the dirt road leading to her cottage.

Lauren was waiting by Monica's back door, ready to ambush her when Monica pulled into her driveway.

"Is something wrong?" Monica said as she got out of her car. She had visions of Jeff injured in an accident or worse.

The rain had stopped and dusk was slowly settling.

Lauren brandished her phone. "TikTok," she said.

"Tick tock?" Monica repeated, wondering if she had forgotten something and was late.

Lauren waved her phone again. "TikTok," she repeated. "Promo for the farm and the farm store."

"Ah," Monica said as understanding dawned. "I hope you haven't been waiting out here long. It's freezing." She put her key in the lock and opened the door.

"Nah." Lauren looked up at the sky. "At least the rain has stopped. I thought I would take a chance I might catch you. I thought maybe you were home resting because of . . . you know." She gestured in the vague direction of Monica's abdomen.

Was everyone on the planet going to tell her to rest? Monica wondered as she led Lauren inside and flicked on the lights in the kitchen.

Hercule greeted them lavishly, spending a good minute sniffing Lauren as if he was trying to remember whether or not he'd met her before. Mittens peered around the corner from the living room to see what the commotion was about but then, uninterested, retreated back to her spot on the sofa.

"Would you like a cup of tea?" Monica held up a hand. "And before you start to worry, yes, it is decaffeinated."

Lauren laughed. "I wasn't going to say anything, honest. When I'm pregnant I'm not going to tell anyway until I can't hide it anymore. I don't know how you can stand having all these people tell you what to do."

So Lauren and Jeff were thinking of having children. Monica had a momentary vision of her child and Jeff's playing together on the swing set she and Greg were going to put in the backyard of their new house.

"So, about that tea?"

"I'd love some." Lauren pulled out a kitchen chair, sat down and began to scroll through something on her phone.

Monica made the tea and carried the two mugs to the table.

"So, how do you make one of these TikToks?" she asked after setting the tea down.

"We film something with my camera." Lauren pointed to a symbol on her phone. "That's the TikTok app."

"What sort of thing would we film?" Monica couldn't imagine anyone being interested in the workings of Sassamanash Farm, let alone her baking a batch of cookies.

"I thought we'd show you baking and then we can do a voice-over. I've already made a couple of TikToks with Jeff giving a tour of the cranberry bogs."

"Shouldn't we do that at the farm kitchen then?"

"Yes," Lauren said. "Do you want to do it now or do you need to rest?"

"I'm perfectly fine," Monica said with emphasis on the word *fine*. She took a last sip of her tea. "Let's go then."

She grabbed her jacket, which she'd hung over the back of one of the kitchen chairs and put it on. She turned out the lights, closed the door and led Lauren down the path toward the farm kitchen.

Janice was cleaning the counters when they got there.

Lauren explained about the video. "I want to film Monica baking something."

Janice's mouth tightened. "But I've already cleaned up." She waved a hand toward the counters and the gleaming oven.

"Don't worry. We won't make a mess, and if we do, I'll take care of it," Monica said. "You go on home. You must be beat."

Janice's mouth tightened further. "You should be getting some rest," she admonished Monica. "Not filming things for one of those places they've got on the Internet these days."

She made it sound as if Monica was doing something illegal or, at the very least, highly suspicious.

Monica sighed in exasperation. "We're not filming porn, for goodness sake."

"No, it's food porn." Lauren giggled and Janice shot her a dirty look.

"What?" Lauren said. "Food porn is simply pictures of artfully arranged food."

Janice grunted but she didn't look convinced. She finally relented, put on her jacket and left, however reluctantly, and Monica let her shoulders sag with relief. If help wasn't so hard to find . . .

"So, what do we do?" She turned to Lauren. Suddenly she did feel tired and the thought of sitting down with her feet up was tantalizing. "I can't even remember the last time I combed my hair." She put a hand to her head.

"Don't worry. You won't be in the video. We'll do a voice-over off camera." She held up her phone. "Let's do a trial run. Why don't we start with filming a display of the farm products? Then we'll record the narration and you can describe them and talk a bit about how you make them."

That sounded easy enough. Monica arranged a pyramid of cranberry preserves on the counter. She had to admit the jars looked very appealing with the ribbons Nancy had insisted on tying around them. She added a few containers of salsa and put a wooden crate with *Sassamanash Farm* stamped on it in the background.

While Lauren filmed the scene, Monica sat down with a groan and stretched out her legs.

Several minutes later, Lauren bustled over to show her the video.

Monica was surprised at how professional it looked.

"It looks wonderful," she said. "Everything looks very appealing. What do we do next?"

"Now we'll record the voice-over. Have you decided what you want to say? It doesn't have to be anything fancy."

"Maybe I should rehearse first," Monica said.

Lauren shook her head. "No. It's better if it sounds natural. TikTok is all about spontaneity."

Monica stifled another groan. She never liked being on stage or in the limelight in any way, but she didn't want to disappoint Lauren.

After several tries, they both agreed that the voice-over was as good as it was going to get. Monica cringed when she heard her voice on the recording, but Lauren assured her she'd done just fine.

"What do we do with this now?" Monica plopped into a chair again.

"I'll upload it to TikTok and then we'll keep our fingers crossed. Hopefully it will go viral. We'll see how it does and then I'll plan the next one."

Another one? Monica groaned inwardly for the third time. At least this one was *in the can*, as the expression went.

Lauren left and Monica was about to turn out the lights over the counter when the door opened so abruptly it bounced off the wall. *What on earth . . .*

Monica spun around to see Gina standing in the doorway. Her customary updo was coming down and she was panting slightly.

"Gina! What is it? Is something wrong?"

Gina stepped into the room. It took her a moment to catch her breath. "I don't know what to do."

Monica led her over to a chair and convinced her to sit down but Gina immediately sprang up again and began to pace back and forth. Monica thought she looked shaky. The last thing she needed was for Gina to faint. The kitchen floor was tile and if she hit her head on it . . .

"That detective Stevens has been to see me again. I think she knows I was in the car with Rip when he was killed."

"You still haven't told her the truth?" Monica's jaw nearly dropped. "You have to. You're innocent. You have nothing to be afraid of."

Gina shook her head and her updo wobbled precariously.

"They're getting desperate. They want to pin the murder on someone and close the case so why not me? I'd make the perfect scapegoat."

"Detective Stevens wouldn't do that," Monica said. "I know her and that's not how she works."

Gina looked at Monica, her eyes imploring. "You have to do something."

"What can I do?" Monica held her hands out, palms up. Just because she'd solved a few murder cases in the past didn't mean she would be able to solve this one.

"You can find out who really murdered Rip. You're good at it. You've done it before."

And almost gotten myself killed, Monica thought. After her hostile encounter with Marty, she'd all but decided to hang up her Sherlock Holmes cap.

"I think we'd best leave the investigating to the police," Monica said firmly.

"We can't." Gina grabbed Monica's arm. "They're drawing the wrong conclusions. You've got to help me."

Monica looked at Gina. She was obviously in great distress.

So, against her better judgment, Monica agreed.

Chapter 12

Monica woke up Friday morning feeling surprisingly energetic. Hercule lifted his head from his dog bed when he heard her feet hit the floor, but when he saw she was headed toward the bathroom, he let it drop back down again.

Mittens was waiting outside the bathroom door when Monica came out wrapped in her terry-cloth robe. She meowed loudly and brushed up against Monica, her tail swishing back and forth, as Monica slipped on a pair of jeans and a warm sweater. A peek outside the window showed her that the day was clear with a bright blue sky. The bare branches of the tree behind the house swayed slightly in what must be a brisk wind.

When Monica got downstairs, there was a note from Greg propped up against the salt and pepper shakers on the kitchen table saying he had already left for the bookstore. With the opening of the second floor and the new café only days away now, he was busier than ever.

Monica made a cup of tea and ate a quick breakfast before leashing up Hercule for his morning walk.

It felt good to stretch her legs, and before she realized it she'd passed the cranberry bogs, the farm kitchen and was nearly to the maintenance shed where Jeff kept the farm equipment. Hercule pulled her toward the open door of the shed and Monica stuck her head in. Jeff was working on one of the water reels, which were affectionately known as egg beaters to cranberry growers. They were used to beat the berries off the vines during the harvest.

Jeff was sitting on the floor. His good hand was covered in grease and he had various bits and pieces of machinery spread out around him.

He smiled when he saw Monica. "Good morning."

Hercule ran to him, his tail wagging. He put his paws on Jeff's shoulders and began to vigorously lick his face.

"Okay, boy, okay," Jeff said, laughing.

"Hercule!" Monica snapped her fingers and he turned to look at her, his head cocked to one side.

Jeff got to his feet and brushed off his overalls. He reached for a folded newspaper that was sitting on his workbench.

"Have you seen this?" He unfolded the paper and thumbed

through the pages. He handed it to Monica and pointed to one of the articles.

The article was focused on Jax Johnson's trial and there was a picture of Jax and his attorney, Kayla Moore, leaving the courthouse.

"That woman." Jeff tapped the paper with a finger. "I saw her here at the farm one day. I don't remember when exactly."

"At the farm store?"

Jeff shook his head. "No."

"What was she doing here then?"

Jeff shrugged. "I don't know. It was rather odd. She was coming from the direction of the bogs. I thought perhaps she was lost and was looking for the store. I asked her if she needed help and she said no—she just wanted to see the bogs." Jeff scratched his forehead, leaving a smudge of grease on it. "That's not unusual. It's happened before, but at this time of year there isn't much to see. The cranberries have all been harvested and the bogs are frozen over. Besides, it was bitterly cold that day and the drizzle was turning to sleet."

"Hardly the sort of weather you want to take a stroll in," Monica said. She pointed at Jeff. "You've got a bit of grease right there." She touched his forehead.

Jeff grabbed a rag off his workbench and wiped it off. "Better?"

"Much."

"I can't help but wonder if that woman had anything to do with the toilet tank I found in the weeds." Jeff shifted from one foot to the other.

"Wouldn't it have been awfully heavy for a woman to carry, especially all that distance?"

"She wasn't alone." Jeff balled up the greasy rag and threw it back on his workbench. "There was a man with her."

"Any idea who he was?"

"Nah. He had a baseball cap pulled down low on his forehead and I didn't get a good look at his face."

By now, Hercule was getting impatient with this conversation. He'd sniffed the entire premises, found nothing of interest and was anxious to move on.

Monica said goodbye to Jeff. She had some trouble convincing Hercule to turn back toward home but eventually he gave up the struggle and trotted more or less obediently beside her. That whole incident Jeff told her about was very odd. Why would Kayla be hiding the toilet tank her client stole? It was evidence in his trial. If the woman Jeff had seen had indeed been Kayla, it could get her disbarred . . . or worse.

And the man she was with—could that have been Rip? If so, he must have known Kayla was breaking the law. That would have given him something to hold over her head to guarantee she wouldn't—couldn't really—break up with him.

The police still hadn't located the cocaine that had supposedly been hidden in the toilet tank. If it had been in Jax's possession, surely the police would have found it by now. Maybe Kayla and Rip had taken it? It was apparently worth a lot of money. It must have been very tempting. Maybe even impossible to resist. Rip, at least, needed money. But if Kayla had wanted the money for herself, that would have given her another reason to want to get rid of Rip. Permanently.

But it was all speculation on her part, Monica thought as she opened her back door and unhooked Hercule's leash. He dashed inside and immediately began to roll on his back on the living room carpet.

Monica didn't have anything she should go to the police with at this stage. They'd probably laugh her out of the station. She was embarrassed just thinking about it. Still, she couldn't put her ideas out of her mind as she headed toward the farm kitchen to begin baking.

• • •

The morning went smoothly and soon Monica had a full cart to wheel down to the farm store. She had been surprised when Nancy had suggested a recipe of her own—cranberry orange cream cheese Danish. Nancy had baked up a batch and Monica had had one with a cup of tea midmorning. She had to admit it was delicious. Now they would see if the patrons of the farm store agreed.

Despite Monica's protests that she was fine, Nancy, Janice and Kit had all been in agreement that she should take the afternoon off after delivering the baked goods. She finally decided it was pointless to argue in light of their united front.

Hercule was thrilled to see her when she returned home and Monica immediately leashed him up and took him on a brief walk. When she looked back at the cottage, she saw Mittens had pushed the curtains aside and was peering out the window. Monica made a mental note to pay some special attention to her that afternoon.

Hercule made a mad dash for his water bowl the minute they got back to the house, and after several big gulps, flopped onto the floor with his tongue hanging out.

Monica reached into the pantry for a bag of cat treats and handed one to Mittens, who was weaving in and out between her feet. Mittens devoured the treat, meowed her thanks and then began to groom her back leg.

Monica's stomach growled and she set about making her own lunch. She had some leftover soup in the refrigerator, which she heated up in the microwave. She took the bowl to the table, and while she ate, jotted down all the facts of Rip's murder she was keeping in her head.

She thought back to her conversation with Lacey's sister-in-law. She had made it clear that Rip had left the marriage with nothing thanks to the prenup. So where did he get that fancy car? Blackmail seemed to be a definite possibility.

Maybe Lacey knew, Monica thought as she carried her empty soup bowl to the sink, rinsed it out and put it in the dishwasher.

How could she meet Lacey in a way that wouldn't look too forward or like she was prying? She was wiping down the counter when she remembered that Pamela had said Lacey volunteered at Feed the Kids. That might be one way to get close to her without arousing suspicion. And surely they could always use another volunteer?

· · ·

The Feed the Kids volunteers met in a large structure that looked like a warehouse from the outside. It was off the Blue Star Highway and Monica had no trouble finding it. A dozen cars were parked out front, including a sporty-looking Lamborghini. Monica didn't know all that much about cars but she did know that a car like a Lamborghini cost more than she made in a decade. It had to belong to Lacey. Who else could afford something like that?

The interior of the facility was spare but very clean. The concrete floor had obviously been well swept and the windows were smudge-free. Monica stood by the door for a moment to take it all in. A long stainless-steel counter ran the length of the space. It was lined with open cardboard cartons with a woman standing in front of each one.

She had no trouble picking out Lacey. She was younger than most of the other volunteers and had a huge emerald-cut diamond ring on the ring finger of her right hand that winked and sparkled in the light from the fixtures above.

One of the women looked up, and when she saw Monica she smiled and began to walk toward her. She was middle-aged, in black slacks and a white sweater with red polka-dots, and reminded Monica of her second-grade teacher.

"Can I help you?" she said. "Are you here to volunteer?"

"Yes," Monica said somewhat sheepishly, knowing that wasn't entirely the case. All of these ladies were giving their time to aid a charity and she was only there to snoop.

"That's wonderful. I'm Tricia, by the way." She held out her hand.

Monica shook it and introduced herself.

"We're short a volunteer today," Tricia said, motioning toward the line of women. "Bethany is down with a cold and couldn't make it, poor thing."

Tricia tilted her head as she looked at Monica. "Have you volunteered for Feed the Kids before?"

"No, I haven't."

"Then let me explain what we do here. Our mission is to provide a sack dinner for children who are food insecure and won't be getting dinner at home. We fill the lunch bags with a sandwich, a piece of fruit, some cut-up vegetables, a carton of milk and a wholesome snack." She waved toward the women again. "We set up an assembly line to fill the bags. There's really nothing to it." She smiled encouragingly at Monica.

Monica nodded.

Tricia took Monica by the arm and began to steer her toward the long counter. "You'll take Bethany's place between Lacey and Paula.

Monica couldn't believe her luck as she stepped into an open space between the two women.

"Lacey, can you explain to Monica what she needs to do?"

"Sure, no problem." Lacey pointed to the carton in front of Monica. "You're on bananas," she said. When the sack is passed to you, you'll add one banana and then pass it on to Paula on your right."

Paula smiled at Monica.

"Then the bag goes on down the line and is filled with the rest of the meal. The last person on the line closes the bag and places it into a carton ready to be delivered. We have two assembly lines going. More and more kids don't get enough to eat. It's a crime."

Monica couldn't help but wonder how many hungry mouths Lacey's diamond ring and expensive sports car could feed but didn't say anything. For all she knew, Lacey donated generously to worthy causes.

"We have a special treat for the kids today. The company that manufactures those chocolate bars the kids love so much has donated enough of them to put one in every sack. It will be a nice surprise."

Lacey handed Monica a bag. "How long have you been doing this?" Monica said as she took it and added a banana from the carton.

Lacey looked on approvingly. "A couple of months. I wanted to give back to the community and the thought of kids going to bed hungry breaks my heart." She put a hand to her chest. "I never had any kids myself. Lawrence and I were talking about it when he was killed in that dreadful accident."

"I remember reading about it. I'm sorry," Monica said as she grabbed another banana from the carton.

"Don't be," Lacey said. "It was his own fault speeding like that. He never thought about the people he could have killed. Or the people he would leave behind, you know?"

Monica nodded agreement.

"Is that your car in the parking lot? The Lamborghini?"

"Yeah. But don't worry. I drive responsibly. Those cars can go up to I-don't-even-know how many miles an hour but I have no desire to find out." She reached for a plastic-wrapped sandwich from the box in front of her and dropped it into a bag. "My ex always wanted to test it but I refused to let him have the keys. After seeing what had happened to Lawrence . . ." She shuddered.

"Rip Taylor?" Monica said. "Was that your ex?"

"The one and only." Lacey tossed her head. "Good riddance, although I don't suppose even he deserved to be shot in the head like that."

"I gather he had a pretty fancy car of his own," Monica said, passing her bag to Paula.

"Yeah. That Jag. I have no idea where he got the money for it. He certainly didn't get it from me." She leaned close enough for Monica to smell her perfume. "If you ask me, I think he was blackmailing someone. How else could he have gotten that kind of money? His commissions didn't amount to anywhere near enough to afford a brand-new Jaguar."

They were on the same page about that, Monica thought. It was the only answer. And she had a pretty good idea who Rip had been blackmailing.

Chapter 13

By the time Monica had finished filling all the paper sacks with bananas, she had formulated a plan. She didn't know if it would work but it was worth trying. Hopefully it wouldn't even take her too far out of her way.

The other volunteers stood in a cluster chatting and drinking coffee from the urn someone had put out while they were working, but Monica didn't join them. Instead, she headed immediately to her car. She put the key in the ignition but didn't turn it. Instead, she pulled her phone from her pocket and looked up Jaguar dealerships. As she had suspected, they were few and far between. Tyler had mentioned that Marty Fisher's father-in-law's place was just off the Blue Star Highway. Monica found it easily enough, and when she plugged the address into her GPS, she was pleased to see that it was actually on her way home.

Traffic on the highway was moderate. Monica supposed most people hadn't gotten out of work yet. She made good time, and after driving for ten minutes she turned right onto the exit ramp and followed the directions, which took her to Visser's Jaguars. She pulled into their parking lot and found an empty space. She was beginning to think that all car dealerships looked alike — rows of shiny new cars with price stickers on them, flags or balloons waving from their antennas, and in their midst a modern glass and steel structure housing the offices and showroom.

The big difference was the cost of the cars themselves. Monica glanced at one of the stickers and inhaled sharply. At first, she thought she was mistaken and actually counted the zeros to be sure she was reading the number correctly. She couldn't imagine paying that much for a car that would decrease in value the minute it was driven off the lot and that would one day be virtually worthless.

A salesman was hovering between the cars. The tips of his ears were red and he was blowing on his hands to warm them. He was sharply dressed in a well-tailored suit, starched white shirt and silk tie. He glided over toward Monica and looked her up and down doubtfully.

He gave a nearly imperceptible shrug. No doubt he was reminding himself that rich people could be eccentric, and for all he knew she was worth millions.

"Can I help you?" he said in tones as smooth as silk.

Monica regretted not crafting her opening lines while driving down the highway. She cleared her throat nervously.

"I'm a friend of Marty Fisher's," she said, hoping she sounded convincing. "He said that this was the place to come if I wanted a Jaguar."

The salesman broke into a smile. "Indeed, it is. Marty owns one of our cars — a Jaguar F-type coupe in Velocity Blue."

Monica widened her eyes. "That sounds like a very expensive car."

The salesman stuck his hand in his pocket and began jingling his change. "It is. But Mrs. Fisher drives a much more expensive car," he added with a smug expression. "A 2021 Jaguar XJ in Yulong White Metallic." He leaned toward Monica conspiratorially. "Mrs. Fisher's father owns Visser's Jaguar."

Monica thanked the man for his help and returned to her car. She sat for a moment without turning the key. The red Jaguar Rip had been driving had to have come from Marty, because by all accounts it wasn't something he would have been able to afford himself. How had Marty afforded it? Even if his father-in-law had given it to him at cost, it was still a lot of money.

Could he possibly have stolen the car? Marty must have been willing to do almost anything to keep his wife from finding out about his affair. It seemed obvious that she was the one holding the purse strings. Monica couldn't remember reading about the theft of a Jaguar in the *Cranberry Cove Chronicle* but she could easily look it up.

• • •

As soon as Monica got home, she took Hercule out for a walk. He was tempted to dawdle but it was beginning to drizzle and the air had taken on a raw edge that made her shiver despite her warm jacket. She was glad when he finally finished his business and they could go back inside.

She made herself a cup of tea and set up her laptop on the kitchen table. Her fingers were crossed that she was right and that she would find an article about a Jaguar having been stolen from Visser's lot. Of course, the *Cranberry Cove Chronicle* might not have covered it, but something like a stolen car was what generally passed for news in their small town. If there was any information out there, she should be able to find it. Nothing ever completely disappeared from the Internet.

Mittens jumped on the table and sat next to Monica's laptop, purring loudly. She reached out a paw and rather delicately hit one of the keys.

"You know you're not allowed on the table," Monica said as she picked Mittens up and placed the cat in her lap, where Mittens curled up in contentment and continued to purr loudly. "You just wanted some attention, didn't you?" Monica stroked her glossy fur.

By now her computer was powered up. She opened her favorite search engine and after several frustrating tries, where the only entries popping up were ads for Jaguars and Jaguar dealerships, she finally landed on something that looked promising.

It was a surprisingly small article in the *Cranberry Cove Chronicle* about a Jaguar going missing from the lot of Visser's dealership. The police had been stumped. The showroom hadn't been broken into. Where did the thief get the key? All the cars had been locked, and thanks to increased safety controls by manufacturers, it was no longer possible to hot-wire a car. If the thief had broken a window, most of the shattered glass would have fallen inside the car, but it was reasonable to assume that a tiny speck of glass might have been found on the pavement outside the vehicle. The police had been unable to find a single trace of a broken window, nor had any garages or repair shops within a reasonable vicinity reported replacing any windows on a late-model Jaguar.

Monica found it interesting that the case had been dropped shortly after the theft occurred. The article contained a quote from the police chief, who had indicated that all possible avenues had been explored yet they had still come up empty-handed.

That was curious, Monica thought. Why hadn't the police pursued it further and why hadn't Visser insisted upon it? One thought came to mind—Visser had simply pocketed the insurance money and no longer had any interest in finding the stolen car or the thief.

Especially if the thief had been his son-in-law. Did Visser suspect that Marty was the culprit and that was why he hadn't put up a fuss when the police had failed to solve the case? People like Visser who had influence and money usually got what they wanted, and perhaps what he had wanted was for the whole thing to blow over.

• • •

"I hope you can make my party this morning," Nancy said when Monica picked up the telephone the next morning.

"What party?" Monica rubbed the sleep out of her eyes. Did pregnancy cause forgetfulness? she wondered.

"Don't tell me you've already forgotten."

Monica searched her memory for any flicker of information she could dredge up.

"Oh! You mean your candle party."

Monica suddenly remembered that her mother had told her she'd signed on with Glow Lights to sell candles at at-home parties.

"Well, you do remember." Nancy's tone was sharp. "Yes, my candle party. Glow Lights is introducing a brand-new scent and I'll have a preview sample. They're calling it Pecan Pie Spice."

Monica wondered what on earth Pecan Pie Spice smelled like. Pecans? Cinnamon and nutmeg? It sounded revolting but she didn't tell her mother that.

As soon as Nancy hung up, Monica slid out of bed and headed for the shower. She took the time to blow dry her hair because she knew her mother would comment on it otherwise. She also chose her outfit with care. She wasn't terribly interested in fashion—the styles they showed in most magazines looked ridiculous to her—but she did have a good pair of black pants and a lovely silk blouse she'd bought on sale at Danielle's Boutique in town.

Once dressed, she looked herself over in the mirror and was pleased with the results. She thought her mother would be pleased as well.

Monica made herself a quick cup of tea and fed Mittens and Hercule. She was about to leash up Hercule when she noticed a note propped up on the kitchen table. It was from Greg saying that he had already taken Hercule on a long walk before leaving for Book 'Em. He ended the note with a row of Xs.

Hercule watched Monica as she crumpled the note and tossed it in the trash.

"You've already been out, buddy. You can't fool me." Monica scratched the top of his head. He sighed and slunk off to curl up in a beam of sunlight coming through the window.

Monica glanced at the clock. She'd be late if she didn't hurry. She had promised her mother she would help set things up for the party.

It was a fine day, with the pale sunshine typical of November and a breeze that was barely perceptible. Monica enjoyed the drive to Nancy's house—a tiny Cape Cod–style home a few blocks from Beach Hollow Road, near the Cranberry Cove library and the church. In the summer it was shaded by large beech trees, but now the branches were bare and a scattering of leaves dotted the front lawn.

Monica parked in the driveway and walked up the slate front path. She knocked briefly and then turned the doorknob and let herself in.

"Hello?" she called out as she hung her coat in the closet in the foyer.

"In the kitchen, dear," Nancy called back.

"What smells so good?" Monica gave her mother a quick hug.

"I'm baking a loaf of cranberry bread and I've got the coffee going." She pointed to a machine on the counter, which was burbling and hissing. "There's tea as well for anyone who wants it. I put aside some decaf for you." She smiled at Monica.

"What do you need me to do?" Monica looked around the kitchen.

"If you could take that tray"—Nancy pointed to the table behind her—"out to the living room and arrange the plates and napkins on the sideboard, that would be a big help."

Monica carried the tray into the living room and set it down. The room was small but cheerful with a chintz-covered sofa and armchair, a slightly faded Oriental rug and a brick fireplace flanked by bookcases. A fat candle in a glass jar was burning on the coffee table. Monica sniffed. Pecan Pie Spice? White boxes with *Glow Light* written on them in gold script were stacked next to the table.

Monica was fanning the napkins out on the sideboard when the doorbell rang.

"Would you get that?" Nancy appeared briefly in the kitchen doorway.

Monica opened the door and a sudden gust of wind nearly snatched it from her hand.

"I thought Nancy might need some help," Gina said, stepping into the foyer and slipping out of her purple fake fur coat. She must have noticed Monica looking at it.

She put a hand on Monica's arm. "Fake fur in vivid colors is very in this year. The latest issue of *Vogue* was filled with them."

Gina followed Monica out to the kitchen. Monica was grateful that her mother and her stepmother had achieved a truce of sorts. It didn't stop them from criticizing each other in private, but it did keep them from each other's throats in public. Monica's father dumping Gina for a younger model after he'd left Nancy for Gina had created a fragile bond between them.

The doorbell rang and both Monica and Nancy headed toward it at the same time. Nancy plastered a smile on her face and opened it.

"Tiffany, please come in," she said as she ushered a woman over the threshold. "Let me introduce you." She gestured toward Monica. "This is my daughter, Monica. Monica, this is Tiffany Stewart, my hairstylist. She's an absolute genius. You should make an appointment with her sometime."

Monica was tempted to scowl but she managed to keep a smile glued to her face as she greeted Tiffany.

Tiffany appeared to be in her late thirties with dark hair in a blunt chin-length cut and long mauve-colored nails. Small white flowers were painted on her index fingernails. She was wearing skinny jeans tucked into ankle boots and a chunky knit sweater that slipped off one shoulder.

Gina came out of the kitchen and Nancy was introducing her when the bell rang again. Monica felt the blast of cold air as her mother opened the door. She recognized Lauren's voice but not the voice of the girl who was with her.

Once again, Nancy made the introductions. She introduced Lauren and then said, "And this is Emily Meyer."

Monica was startled. The last person she'd expected to meet was her architect's niece. Obviously, Emily and Nancy must have become friendly while Emily was administering Nancy's Botox treatments.

Once again, Monica noticed how fragile Emily looked with her pale complexion and slight build. She was wearing a rather shapeless dress printed with tiny white flowers and a pair of dark tights. Her outfit reminded Monica of something women would have worn on the prairie.

Once everyone had been introduced, Nancy waved them over to the sideboard, where the refreshments were set out. They chatted somewhat awkwardly as they helped themselves to tea or coffee and slices of cranberry bread.

As soon as everyone was settled, Nancy introduced Glow Lights' newest candle. "This is our new fall scent . . ." She paused and everyone froze as if they were hanging on her every word. "Pecan Pie Spice." She held up a candle the color of nutmeg and passed it around for her guests to smell. "It comes in small, medium and large as well votives suitable for your fall table." She tapped each of four boxes in turn that were set out on the coffee table.

Nancy waited while each of the women had a chance to sniff the Pecan Pie Spice candle before reaching for another box and opening it. "And with Christmas practically around the corner, I am thrilled to give you a sneak preview of our December scent, Candy Cane," she said as she removed a red-and-white-striped candle from the box. "It will be available by the first of December."

Her guests oohed and aahed appropriately and Nancy flushed with pleasure.

After introducing several other nonseasonal scents, Nancy passed around pens and order forms and the guests began to fill them out. The chatter turned general as they finished up and Nancy collected the papers.

"How is that new man of yours?" Tiffany leaned back in her seat and winked at Nancy. "Are you still going out?"

"What?" Monica couldn't stifle her exclamation. She glanced at her mother, who was looking rather pink. "How long has this been going on?"

"Oh . . ." Nancy waved a hand in the air. "Not long. Only a couple of weeks."

"Why didn't you tell me?" Monica stared at her mother as if she had metamorphized into some alien creature or had sprouted two heads.

"I didn't want to say anything until . . ." Nancy picked up one of the boxes and began to fiddle with it.

"Until what? Until you were heading down the aisle?" Monica felt her face flushing.

Nancy put the box down. "Please. Let's not make a big deal out of it. I met him at the library. I was scanning the best-seller section when we both reached for the same book at the same time. We both laughed and he asked me if I wanted to go for coffee. One thing led to another and we've gone out a couple of times since."

"See?" Gina said, pointing at Monica. "It was the Botox. It's turned your mother into a new woman and given her confidence." She turned to Emily. "By the way, I've been meaning to call you. I'm thinking about some Botox myself." She glanced pointedly at Monica.

Emily leaned closer to Gina and squinted. "Botox would do wonders for you. It would get rid of these." She traced a finger across Gina's forehead. "I can schedule an appointment for you right now." She reached for her handbag and pulled out a leather-covered planner with the year stamped in gold on the cover.

Lauren gestured toward Emily's datebook. "That's a bit old school, isn't it?" She smiled to show she was only teasing.

Emily's face tightened. "It is. But I worry about keeping things confidential if I'm using an online calendar. You hear so much about hackers and stolen data these days. It makes me nervous. My clients don't want anyone to know they've been to see me."

Of course she would worry, Monica thought. By all accounts, Emily wasn't licensed to provide Botox. She didn't know what the penalty would be if she was found out, but she could understand why Emily didn't want to risk it and possibly jeopardize her job at the hospital as well.

"I wonder if I should make another appointment myself," Nancy said. She ran a hand over her forehead and frowned. "It really does make such a difference."

Emily looked startled. She thumbed through her appointment book. "I just saw you last Friday."

"That can't be." Nancy looked slightly crestfallen. "Has it really only been just over a week?"

Emily nodded and pointed to an entry in her planner. "Yes. I saw you Friday at ten a.m."

Monica was startled and hastened to cover up her reaction. Friday at ten a.m. was about the time Rip Taylor had been shot. And that meant Emily Meyer had an alibi.

And that meant she couldn't have been the murderer.

Chapter 14

After the guests finally left, Monica stayed behind to help her mother clean up.

They were standing in the kitchen with dirty dishes piled on the counter. Monica snatched one of the few remaining slices of cranberry bread and broke off a piece.

"I'll wash if you'll dry," Nancy said, squeezing detergent into a dishpan. Bubbles formed and steam rose as hot water from the tap poured into the sink.

The one amenity the cottage was lacking was a dishwasher. Not that they would have used it for Monica's grandmother's porcelain tea service. It had been in the family for multiple generations even before her grandmother's time. It was brought out for special occasions and always treated with exceptional care.

Monica picked up the first delicate teacup and began to dry it. "So, tell me about this man of yours."

Nancy made a face. "He's not *my man*. At least not yet. But I do like him. He's a retired history professor. But he's not dry and musty as you'd expect. He has quite a sense of humor."

"No jacket with elbow patches, no pipe-smoking walking cliché then?"

Nancy laughed. "Hardly. When I met him, he was wearing jeans and a flannel shirt." Nancy scraped at a spot on one of the dishes with her fingernail. "I think he might be a bit younger than me."

Monica whistled. "A younger man!"

She didn't know why she was teasing her mother like this. It wasn't as if there was any chance her parents would get back together. Nor did she want that. It just made her uneasy and she wasn't sure she wanted to figure out why.

"You probably think I'm foolish." Nancy handed the plate to Monica to dry. "But I'm lonely. You must understand. You have Greg now and soon you'll have a family. I've seen the difference that's made in you." She dabbed at her eyes, leaving a cluster of soap bubbles on the bridge of her nose. "Sometimes I wonder if anyone would even notice if I was gone."

"Mother! Don't say things like that. Of course we'd notice."

"Don't mind me." Nancy sighed. "There's something about the change of season that always gets to me."

"Does this professor have a name?"

"Jimmy Stewart. Like the actor." Nancy smiled. "He rather reminds me of him."

"Any chance we'll get to meet him?"

Nancy pursed her lips. "Maybe. Someday. It's too early to impose the whole family on him. I can't imagine what he'd think."

He'd probably run for the hills, Monica thought.

It looked as if she'd have to be content to wait. She finished drying the last teacup and tried not to think about it, but she had to admit her curiosity was killing her.

• • •

Greg called as Monica was leaving Nancy's. She stopped at the end of the driveway and put the car in Park.

"What's up?" She hoped there wasn't some catastrophe at the bookstore.

Greg cleared his throat. "How was the party at Nancy's? Did you buy anything?"

"I got a holiday-themed candle called Pumpkin Pie Spice and a couple of votive lights for our Thanksgiving table."

Greg cleared his throat again. "I hate to ask but I was wondering if you could stop by the diner and bring me something for lunch? I'm going to be tied up here for hours. The painters brought the wrong color paint for the restrooms and the carpet installers are due any minute." He hesitated for a moment. "As long as you're not too tired."

"I'm fine and it's no problem at all," Monica said. She put her hand on the gear shift. "Anything in particular?"

Greg's voice sounded slightly sheepish. "A burger and fries. Oh, and a chocolate milkshake. I know that's not the healthiest lunch but I'm starving."

Monica smiled as she hung up the call. Greg had taken her for milkshakes on one of their earliest dates. At first, she'd felt like she was back in high school, but in the end, she had enjoyed it tremendously. After all, who doesn't like a delicious milkshake?

Greg had offered to join her in sticking to a healthy diet during her pregnancy. Misery loves company, he'd said. But certainly, there was no harm in the occasional indulgence. As long as it remained that—occasional.

Monica put the car in gear, waited while a navy blue SUV meandered by, carefully backed out of the driveway and headed down the street. She reached Beach Hollow Road in minutes, and despite the fact that it was Saturday, normally the busiest day in town, she snagged a parking spot not too far from the diner.

It was a typical Saturday at the diner with people standing three deep at the counter waiting to order and the lone waitress flying up and down the narrow space with a tray rattling with dishes. Monica glanced at the grill. It seemed so odd without Gus in his accustomed spot behind the counter cracking eggs onto the sizzling griddle and flipping burgers with practiced ease.

The delicious smells were making her hungry so Monica decided to get some lunch for herself as well. The leftover pea soup in the refrigerator could wait for another day. When she finally reached the counter, she placed her order and then went to stand near the door so she would be out of the way. While she waited, she scrolled through the email messages on her phone. She looked up in alarm when there was a loud crash and she felt hot liquid splash onto her trousers.

"I'm so sorry," the harried waitress said as she groaned and bent to pick up the coffee cup she'd dropped. Her face was beet red and she was breathing heavily.

"Let me help you," Monica said.

"No, no," the waitress insisted. "Leave it while I get you a towel." She tucked her tray under her arm and disappeared behind the counter, returning moments later with a roll of paper towels, a trash bag and a dustpan and broom.

Monica insisted on helping and began to pick up the larger pieces of thick white crockery that had scattered all over the floor.

"I don't know what came over me," the waitress said, blotting up some of the coffee. "I've been run off my feet all morning and I guess I got a bit careless. My tray tilted, and well, you know the rest." She put a hand to her back. "I think I'm getting too old for this."

"It happens to everyone," Monica assured her. "How is Gus, by the way? Have you heard anything?"

The waitress straightened and blew a lock of hair out of her eyes.

"I'm told he's doing better. He might be released from the hospital soon and then he'll go to rehab for a bit." She took a tissue out of her uniform pocket and wiped her forehead, which was damp with perspiration. "Brenda—she's the gal who works the evening shift—went to see him. She said he was quite touched when he heard there was a collection being taken up for him."

"We couldn't let him lose the diner," Monica said. "Cranberry Cove wouldn't be the same without it or Gus."

She watched as the waitress walked away with the bag of broken dishes and the wad of sopping wet paper towels. The conversation had reminded Monica that she'd have to begin collecting the cannisters soon. Hopefully they would be stuffed full of contributions.

The diner door opened and she quickly scooted out of the way as Tyler Peterson walked in. He gave her a brief nod of recognition and went to stand in the line at the counter.

Monica glanced at her watch. Her order ought to be ready soon. The place was bustling and the replacement chef clearly wasn't as quick as Gus.

She was putting her phone in her purse when Tyler squeezed into the space beside her. He had his phone in his hand and was playing some sort of game on it. He looked up when a customer walked in, waved and called his name.

He was dressed in ragged clothes—not the distressed and ripped jeans that were so in vogue, but pants that looked as if they'd been worn nearly through. The cuffs of his flannel shirt were frayed, his hair needed cutting and he had a scruffy beard that didn't look intentional. Monica wondered how Tyler knew him. Based on his appearance, she doubted the man had been to see Tyler about buying a house.

"I'll see you at the meeting," he called to Tyler as he made his way toward the counter.

Monica glanced at Tyler. He'd lowered his phone momentarily and she saw that he was playing some sort of card game. Poker, maybe?

She wondered what sort of meeting the two men were attending. It certainly couldn't have anything to do with Tyler's job. There was no way that other man was a real estate agent.

The cook placed a brown paper bag on the counter and called Monica's name. When she went to retrieve it, she noticed that the fellow who had spoken to Tyler had gotten a cup of coffee. She let him go ahead of her in the line by the cashier and watched as he dug around in his pocket and pulled out some change, slowly counting out the pennies.

"Excuse me," Tyler said as he stepped in front of Monica. He pulled a couple of singles from his pocket and handed them to the cashier. The man grinned and thanked Tyler profusely.

Tyler shrugged. "No problem, man."

Very odd, Monica thought as she eased her way through the crowd to the door. The fellow was clearly living on the edge and yet he and Tyler had something in common—a meeting they were both attending. Her curiosity was aroused and she decided to find out just what it was.

She followed the man as he walked down Beach Hollow Road. He pulled the cup of coffee out of the bag from the diner and tossed the bag in a trash can in front of the hardware store.

They passed the last store along the commercial part of Beach Hollow Road and Monica began to wonder where they were headed, when the fellow turned onto the path in front of St. Andrew's Church. Things were getting more and more curious, Monica thought.

She followed him into the building and down a corridor to an open door that led into a small room where a dozen or so folding chairs were set up in a circle. A sign taped to the wall outside the room read *Gamblers Anonymous Meeting*.

Monica heard footsteps coming down the hall and moved swiftly toward the door marked *Exit*. The last thing she wanted was to run into Tyler here.

So, Tyler had a gambling problem, Monica thought as the door eased closed behind her. Had he been playing one of those online poker games on his phone when she'd run into him at the diner? She heard those games got a lot of people in trouble, leaving them owing money they couldn't possibly pay.

Did Tyler's gambling tie into Rip's murder in any way? She didn't know—at least not yet.

• • •

Monica dropped Greg's hamburger, fries and milkshake off at Book 'Em and drove back to the farm. She'd ordered a cup of chili for herself. She glanced at the paper bag on the seat beside her. A large grease stain was spreading across the front and the aromas emanating from it were making her stomach growl.

She decided she would go to the farm kitchen immediately. She'd neglected it long enough—it was time to see how Janice, Nancy and Kit were making out. Fingers crossed, everything was running smoothly.

Everyone was hard at work when Monica arrived. Janice was rolling out dough, Kit was mixing batter and Nancy was unpacking a carton of sugar.

Monica took off her coat, hung it up and put her lunch on the table. By now, she was officially starving. She grabbed some utensils and a couple of paper towels, removed her cup of chili from the bag and pried the lid off. She inhaled deeply. It smelled heavenly.

Janice walked over and stood staring at Monica. She frowned and pointed at the forkful of chili Monica was poised to put in her mouth.

"What's that?"

"This?" Monica indicated the cup of chili. "It's chili from the diner."

"Chili!" Janice threw her arms in the air. "You're expecting. You shouldn't be eating that."

"I don't see what my being pregnant has to do with—"

"Don't you know? Eating spicy foods while you're expecting can burn the baby's eyes."

Monica heard Kit give a faint groan and Nancy shook her head, an expression of frustration on her face.

Nancy put her hands on her hips. "Janice, don't you realize that those pregnancy myths are just that? Myths. No one takes those things seriously in this day and age. They're old wives' tales."

Monica had to admit, she felt equally exasperated. She knew Janice meant well, but it was still upsetting to hear all these dire warnings even though she knew perfectly well they weren't true.

A thunderous look crossed Janice's face.

Uh-oh, Monica thought. She felt a moment of panic. What if Janice quit? What if she just walked out with no notice at all? Kit was going to be running Monica's Café at the bookstore as soon as it opened, Nancy would help, but her idea of helping wasn't always the same as hers, and Monica would be left on her own. She felt exhausted thinking of all the work it would take to handle the massive amount of baking by herself.

Tears pricked the back of her eyelids and she blamed the pregnancy for making her so emotional.

Nancy and Janice were glaring at each other like two dogs circling each other before a fight. Suddenly Janice ripped off her apron, tossed it on the counter and headed toward the door. She grabbed her jacket from the hook and began to put it on.

Monica ran up to her and put a hand on her arm.

"Please don't go. My mother didn't mean to upset you." She glanced at her mother, whose lips were compressed into a thin, tight line. "Isn't that right, Mom?"

Nancy must have seen the panic on Monica's face.

She shrugged. "I'm sorry," she said, sounding as sincere as a kid apologizing for eating all the cookies in the cookie jar.

Kit and Monica looked at each other and Kit rolled his eyes.

Monica held her breath while Janice seemed to waver, one arm half in and half out of her sleeve. Finally, she pulled her jacket off and hung it back on the hook.

Monica breathed a huge sigh of relief. Nancy didn't look particularly happy but there wasn't anything Monica could do about that.

"Okay," Monica said, more firmly than she felt. "Let's get back to work. There's still a lot to do."

• • •

Monica was tidying up the farm kitchen—wiping flour off the counters, cleaning the mixer as well as a stack of cookie sheets—when her cell phone rang. It was Greg.

"How do you feel about dinner out tonight?" he said.

"That sounds wonderful. I have to admit I'm a bit tired."

"Would you rather do take-out? I can bring something home."

"No, I'll be fine. I just need to put my feet up for a bit."

"I'll make a reservation at the Pepper Pot. Does that sound good?"

"Yes."

Monica hung up the phone with a smile on her face. Greg took such good care of her. She'd never dreamed that being married could be so . . . wonderful. She'd been engaged once before but the relationship hadn't been like the one she had with Greg, where she could be herself. She'd been sad when her fiancé had been killed in a swimming accident, but in the end, she'd realized she barely missed him. Marrying him would have been a mistake.

Monica dried the last cookie sheet, put it away and reached for her jacket. She flicked out the lights and opened the door, wincing at the biting cold that greeted her. She pulled her collar up around her ears, stuck her hands in her pockets and began the walk back to her cottage.

Hercule wagged his tail furiously and Mittens wound in and out between Hercule's paws when Monica opened the door. She knelt down to pet them both. Hercule rolled onto his back hoping to have his stomach scratched, and Mittens arched her back as Monica ran a hand over her head.

She grabbed Hercule's leash, but he tried to make a game of it, dancing around as she tried to clip it to his collar. She finally had to tell him to sit in order to complete the job. She wasn't anxious to go back out into the cold, but Hercule showed no such reservations as he pulled her out the open door.

As soon as he finished his business, Monica managed to persuade him to come back inside by luring him with the promise of a treat. Hercule never passed up a chance to get a dog biscuit.

The animals now taken care of, Monica collapsed into an armchair in the living room and flicked on the television. She barely heard the beginning of the newscast before her eyes began to close. When she opened them again, she was startled to see the time. She'd better hurry up and get ready. Greg would be home at any minute.

The Pepper Pot wasn't a particularly fancy restaurant but it was nice enough to warrant a change of clothes. Monica put on her best pair of slacks along with the cashmere sweater she saved for special occasions. She even put a spritz of the perfume Greg had given her for Christmas behind her ears. She was brushing her hair when she heard the crunch of gravel as Greg's car pulled into the driveway.

Greg was waiting in the kitchen when she got downstairs. Hercule was leaning against Greg's leg as he scratched the dog's ears. He smiled when he saw Monica.

Monica hugged him and felt the cold coming off his jacket.

"It's quite raw out there," Greg said, retrieving Monica's good coat from the closet. "You'd better take your scarf and some gloves."

Monica bundled up as she followed Greg out to the car. The night sky was sprinkled with stars and the skeletal branches of the trees swayed slightly in the wind.

The road was dark with impenetrable shadows along either side until they reached the rise that led into town. From that vantage point, Monica noticed several pinpricks of light from cargo ships plying the inky black waters of the lake and the twinkling lights of Beach Hollow Road in the distance.

They found a parking space easily enough. They didn't have far to walk but Monica was still grateful for the flood of warmth that greeted her when they pulled open the door to the Pepper Pot.

The low buzz of voices mingled with the sounds of rattling crockery, and the scent of onions, garlic and herbs in the air made Monica's stomach growl.

"Two?" the hostess said, tucking some menus under her arm.

Monica and Greg followed her to a small table along the wall and Greg pulled out Monica's chair as the hostess placed the menus on the table.

"I'm starved." Monica opened hers and began scanning the entrées. Mickey, the owner of the restaurant and Gina's beau, changed the menu with the seasons—lighter dishes in the summer and heartier stews and soups in the winter.

Monica thought she would begin to drool as she considered the selections, finally deciding on the cassoulet. Greg chose the Irish stew and they gave their orders to the waitress when she appeared at their table.

"This was a good idea," Monica said as she looked around. She'd been working so hard lately she'd nearly forgotten how to relax. Now with the delicious aromas and the enveloping warmth of the restaurant she felt herself begin to unwind.

They'd been served and were starting in on their meals when Monica noticed Mickey emerge from the kitchen. He made his way through the tables, smiling and stopping to say hello. Mickey's personal touch was one of the reasons the patrons liked the Pepper Pot and probably why the restaurant had immediately become a hit.

Monica noticed Mickey had stopped at one of the patron's tables, where he stood with his hand on the man's shoulder. The woman seated opposite him was middle-aged with short hair, a white sweater with snowflakes on it and impressive diamond stud earrings.

Mickey shifted slightly and Monica recognized Marty Fisher as the man he was standing behind. Her first instinct was to hide. Would he recognize her? She was sorry the waitress had taken the menus away—she could have held one up to her face.

Fortunately, Marty wasn't looking in her direction and Monica forced herself to relax. Her last run-in with Marty had been less than cordial and she wasn't anxious to encounter him again.

Micky spent several minutes at Marty's table talking and laughing before clapping Marty on the shoulder again and heading to Monica and Greg's table.

He pulled over an empty chair and straddled it, leaning his arms on the back. His sleeves were pushed up, baring his muscular forearms.

"How are two of my favorite people?"

"We're fine," Monica said.

Mickey shook his head. "I'm afraid Gina's not doing so well. Every time there's a knock on the door, she's convinced she's going to be arrested for that Rip Taylor's death."

Monica raised her eyebrows. "I told her to go to the police."

Mickey laughed. "So did I. But you know Gina. She has a mind of her own. It's one of the things I love about her."

"Was that Marty Fisher you were talking to over there?" Monica tilted her head toward the other table.

"Yeah. He's a good customer—comes in regularly. He always orders the pot roast in winter and walleye in summer." Mickey leaned forward. "As a matter of fact, I met Rip when Marty brought him for lunch one day. I asked him to show us some houses—that's how Gina came to be in his car that morning." He shook his head. "Now I wish I'd never met him. If I hadn't, Gina wouldn't be in this mess."

"So, Marty and Rip were friends?" Monica said, knowing full well that wasn't the case.

Mickey raised an eyebrow. "You know Marty?"

Monica felt her face getting red. "Not really, but I know who he is."

Mickey shook his head. "Something was up between the two of them. That time they met here for lunch, Marty looked very uncomfortable—he barely touched his pot roast but he downed two martinis almost as fast as the waitress could bring them."

No wonder, Monica thought. Rip had information that could really put Marty in the hot seat.

Mickey leaned closer. "And when the lunch was over, I saw Marty hand Rip a wad of cash." He held up his thumb and index finger to indicate the thickness. "And it wasn't to pay for his share of the lunch either because Rip stuffed the whole lot into his pocket."

A woman appeared in the doorway at the back of the restaurant and motioned for Mickey.

"I've got to go." He squeezed Monica's shoulder and nodded at Greg. "Enjoy your meal."

Greg raised his eyebrows. "How do you know this Marty fellow Mickey was talking about?"

Monica looked down at her lap. "Someone told me about him."

"Is he one of your suspects?" A small smile played around Greg's lips.

"He could be. I think Rip was blackmailing him."

"Given what Mickey just told us, that sounds logical, but don't you think there might be other reasons why Marty was giving Rip money? Maybe Marty owed him for something? Or they had a bet and Marty lost."

"Could be," Monica said. "But somehow I don't think so."

"Why do I get the feeling there's something you're not telling me?" Greg helped Monica into her coat.

Monica exhaled loudly. "Rip went to show a client a house and he caught Marty in a . . . compromising position. I think he'd been taking advantage of that to blackmail Marty."

Greg whistled. "That could be. If that's the case, I doubt Marty is mourning Rip's demise."

"Definitely not," Monica said as she made her way to the entrance of the restaurant.

"So that's what makes him a suspect?" Greg held the door open for her.

"Yes."

• • •

Later that night Monica dreamt she was at the police station looking at a lineup of suspects in Rip's murder. They were a ragtag bunch, three men—Marty, Jax and Tyler—along with Kayla, Lacey and Gina. Gina! Monica bolted upright in bed, her eyes flying open. Her forehead was sweaty and her heart pounding.

"Are you okay?" Greg mumbled.

"Just a bad dream."

Greg grunted, patted Monica's arm and rolled over.

Monica felt something wet against her hand. Hercule was poking his nose at her to check on her. She rubbed the top of his head and, reassured, he went back to his bed, where he plopped down with a sigh.

Monica couldn't immediately go back to sleep. *Gina isn't a suspect* kept going through her head like a mantra. Gina couldn't be. The very idea was ridiculous. She forced herself to put it out of her mind and concentrated on who else had a reason to want Rip dead.

Marty certainly had a good motive for killing Rip. Monica was quite certain he was being blackmailed. Then there was Tyler, who might harbor a grudge against Rip for stealing some of his real estate listings. Especially if Tyler desperately needed money to pay off gambling debts.

Kayla wanted to break up with Rip. Did he have information he could blackmail her with? Was he hoping to force her into letting him stay and she killed him to free herself? Or, what if Tyler had done it so he and Kayla could be together.

It was even possible that Jax was still harboring resentment over the football injury Rip had caused that dashed his dreams of eventually being drafted by the NFL.

Monica was about to drift off when she thought of Lacey. Wasn't the spouse always the prime suspect in a murder? But Lacey had no reason to kill Rip. She'd gotten the divorce she wanted, and thanks to the prenup, it hadn't cost her a dime.

Monica felt her eyes growing heavy. She turned on her side and pulled up the covers. She'd think about it in the morning.

Chapter 15

Monica slept a bit later than usual Sunday morning but Greg was up early and off to the bookstore. With the opening of the café coming closer every day, there was no time to waste.

Normally one or the other of them made a special breakfast on Sundays — waffles or pancakes topped with cranberry preserves or scrambled or fried eggs with cranberry scones on the side. Monica yawned as she contemplated her choices. She didn't have the energy to make something just for herself so she settled for popping slices of cranberry bread in the toaster oven and lavishly spreading them with butter.

She carried her toast and cup of decaf coffee to the kitchen table, where Greg had left the Sunday paper. Monica was idly thumbing through it when the phone rang.

"Are you busy?" It was Greg.

"Just finishing my breakfast." Monica cradled the phone between her ear and her shoulder as she picked at the last of the crumbs on her plate.

"We've hit a snag. We need a special sort of molly bolt according to the carpenter. I've called around and there's a place outside of town that has what I need," Greg said. "I hate to ask, but would you mind picking it up for me? I can't leave the store at the moment. Wilma is out with a bad case of strep throat so I'm all alone."

"Of course," Monica said. "I'll head out as soon as I give Hercule a walk."

"Thanks." Monica heard Greg sigh with relief as he ended the call.

She glanced out the kitchen window. Frost glistened in the pale winter sunshine and the bare branches of the trees whipped back and forth. It was time to get out her heavy winter parka.

Hercule didn't mind the cold in the least, although it nipped at Monica's nose and cheeks. As soon as he was finished with his business, she convinced him to go back inside, where she gave him a treat. She checked Hercule's and Mittens's water bowls, and a few minutes later she was on her way.

She shivered as she glanced at Lake Michigan from the rise by the abandoned Shell station. How could water that looked so enticing in the middle of summer look so cold and uninviting now?

Monica followed the directions Greg had given her. The big box store was several miles out of town near the highway that headed north toward Grand Rapids.

The parking lot was busy when Monica pulled in. People streamed out the sliding doors pushing carts loaded with lumber, plumbing supplies and cans of paint. She felt a bit intimidated by the enormity of the store, but a kind clerk helped her find the exact bolt Greg needed and she was on her way back to Cranberry Cove faster than she had anticipated.

Her route took her past the street where Kayla lived and, on an impulse, she turned down it. Maybe the house would speak to her or something, not that she really believed in that sort of thing. That was more up Tempest's alley.

The front lawns of the homes on the block were raked clean of fallen leaves and many of the doors were festooned with clusters of Indian corn or grapevine wreaths dotted with colorful gourds. Monica had a shock when she pulled up in front of Kayla's house. Dried leaves were scattered on the grass and the sun shining on the windows revealed smudges and fingerprints. It looked as if the landscapers hadn't made a visit in quite a while and as if the windows hadn't been washed recently either.

Monica was about to drive away when the front door opened and Kayla's maid, Joan, walked out. She was carrying a large suitcase. Her coat was open and she was wearing black slacks and a red sweater. Was she going somewhere on her week off? Monica wondered.

Monica waved as she quickly got out of the car. Joan didn't appear to remember her at first but then gave a timid smile.

"It's Joan, isn't it?" Monica said. The wind whipped her hair across her face and she brushed it out of her eyes.

"Yes." Joan's tone was wary and she eyed Monica suspiciously.

Monica gave her a reassuring smile. "Are you going on vacation?"

Joan's lips tightened and she shook her head. "I'm leaving. But I don't see what business that is of yours."

"Oh," Monica said. "I'm sorry to hear that."

Joan bit her lower lip. Monica suspected she was struggling with her feelings, but in the end the urge to vent won out. "I've been with this family for many years and I never expected this." Her mouth clamped shut into a thin line.

"What's happened?"

"There's no money. The check Miss Moore gave me on Friday bounced." Her lips tightened further. "And not for the first time, either. But she's always made good on it before. But this time . . ." She shrugged.

"I thought she'd inherited the family fortune. Plus, there's her salary as a lawyer. What has she spent it all on?"

Joan leaned closer to Monica and lowered her voice. "Gambling, that's what I think." She sniffed. "That new fellow who has been coming around is a bad influence. Always playing those poker games on his phone."

"Did Miss Moore gamble as well?"

"I don't know." Joan pointed a finger at Monica. "But I know she loaned him money."

"It must have been a lot." Monica turned her collar up as the wind whistled past them.

"It had to have been. Miss Moore's parents left her quite well off. And now?"

"Do you know who he is?" Monica said, although she knew the answer already.

Joan wrinkled her brow. "I think his name is Tyler something-or-other." She shrugged. "None of them last very long. Besides, it's not my concern anymore." She picked up her suitcase. "I'm off to my sister's in Indiana." She sighed deeply. "It's probably time for me to retire anyway. My back's been bothering me for years and I deserve a rest." She sniffed and tilted her head in the direction of the house. "Unlike some of them, I've been careful with my money. I have a nice little nest egg put away. I was only staying because I'd been with the family so long." She sighed. "I've known Miss Moore since she was a child."

"I wish you well," Monica said.

Joan snorted but didn't respond.

Monica said goodbye and got back into her car. It sounded as if Tyler was in deep when it came to gambling. But if so, why was he attending Gamblers Anonymous meetings?

• • •

Monica pulled into her driveway and parked her car. She walked up the path that led to the back door, past the garden that had bloomed all summer but was now shriveled and colorless. She couldn't wait for spring when the perennials would sprout and she could begin to plant some colorful annuals.

She received an ecstatic greeting from Hercule and a slightly cooler welcome from Mittens when she stepped inside. She didn't stay long—just long enough to top up Mittens's water bowl and take Hercule on a quick walk.

She said goodbye to the animals, closed the door and began to walk back down the path. She was nearing the farm kitchen when she heard a rumble in the distance. A large white truck, streaked with mud and with *Harvest Fruit* painted in red on the side, was approaching the building, where crates of cranberries were stacked, ready to be shipped. That was odd, Monica thought. They didn't usually pick up on Sundays. As a matter of fact, she couldn't remember it ever happening before. She'd have to ask Jeff about it later.

When she opened the door to the farm kitchen, cranberries were popping in a large pot on the stove, giving off the scent of berries, oranges and warming spices. It smelled like Christmas to Monica. Too bad Glow Lights didn't make a scent like that. They could call it A Cranberry Christmas. Monica giggled at the thought.

"What's so funny?" Janice looked up from the pot she was stirring.

Monica waved a hand. "Oh, nothing. Just a silly thought that popped into my head."

Monica got busy measuring sugar into the mixer. She was going to make a batch of cranberry orange white chocolate chunk cookies. They were popular with their customers, who said they enjoyed them as a special treat after Sunday dinner.

Janice continued to stir the bubbling cranberry sauce, her face red from the rising steam. Damp tendrils of hair clung to her narrow forehead.

"Where's Kit today?" She looked up from the pot briefly, her spoon momentarily still.

"He's helping Greg set things up at the new café in Book 'Em. The opening isn't far off now."

"Hmmph," Janice sniffed. "Are you sure he's going to be able to handle it?"

"Kit?" Monica stopped the mixer and turned to face Janice. "Yes, of course. Why?"

But Janice didn't answer. She simply shrugged.

Was Janice angling for Kit's job? Monica wondered. She blew out a breath. Hopefully Janice wasn't going to be more trouble than she was worth. It had taken months to find her, and Monica couldn't handle the work alone. It would be difficult enough on Monday when Janice had her first day off.

Lauren opened the door and a gust of cold air swept through the kitchen. Her eyes were glowing and she was smiling widely. She held up her cell phone as she walked toward Monica.

"We've gotten thousands of hits," she said, nearly tripping over the words in her excitement.

Monica frowned. "What on earth are hits? Is that something good?"

"Yes." Lauren was practically bouncing on the balls of her feet. "On TikTok."

"What?" Monica said in disbelief. "Because of that video you made of me showing off our products?"

Lauren nodded. "The very same."

"But why . . . how?"

"You're not going to believe it." Lauren pulled off her mittens and unbuttoned her coat. "This fellow made a TikTok video of himself on his longboard drinking from a bottle of cranberry juice. It went viral. And since our video also came up when anyone searched for cranberries, we began to get hits as well."

Janice made a disapproving noise and banged the lid on the pot she'd been stirring. Lauren turned to look at her, her eyebrows raised, but Monica shook her head and mouthed *Just ignore her.*

Lauren pulled out a chair, sat down and stretched out her legs. "And get this. Lots and lots of people are recreating the video and it's caused a run on cranberry juice. Apparently entire shelves are empty in any number of grocery stores." She tapped a few keys on her phone and handed it to Monica.

On the screen was a news article with the headline *Unusually High Demand for Cranberry Juice Forces Companies to Increase Production and Hire Staff.* According to the first line of the article, cranberry farmers harvested more than a hundred billion cranberries in just six weeks.

Monica shook her head and handed the phone back to Lauren.

Perhaps that was why the truck from Harvest Fruit was doing a pickup on a Sunday.

Before Lauren buttoned her coat, donned her mittens and headed back out the door, Lauren made Monica promise she would record some more TikTok videos and Monica reluctantly agreed.

She found it hard to believe that something like a video on TikTok could spark a run on cranberries, but it obviously proved the power of social media. She sighed. She'd made Lauren a promise and she'd have to honor her commitment. She'd protested that she hated the way she looked and sounded on tape but Lauren had assured her that everyone felt that way. But if it helped the farm, she was willing to do it.

• • •

Janice had gone home and Monica was cleaning up when there was another knock on the door.

"Come in," she yelled as she swept up flour that had drifted onto the flour.

"I thought I'd find you here," Nancy said, shrugging off her coat and hanging it over a chair.

"You look upset." Monica leaned her broom in the corner and pulled out a chair for herself. She sank into it gratefully.

Nancy frowned but then quickly smoothed out her expression, as if she was afraid the movement might create new wrinkles.

"It's this candle business," Nancy said. "It's not going the way I'd expected. Or at least not the way Diane—she's my manager—said it would."

"What's not going the way you'd hoped?" Monica kicked off her right shoe and began to rub the arch of her foot. "You sold a lot of candles yesterday, didn't you? I even bought one myself."

Nancy's lip curled. "And I appreciate that but I didn't sell as many as I would have liked. But that's not all. Diane just called me and said I have to buy samples of the new merchandise that's going to debut in December for the holiday season."

Monica stopped rubbing her foot and raised her eyebrows. "But why do you have to buy it? Don't they just give it to you?"

Nancy shook her head. "No, they make us pay for the samples. I need them to show customers the new holiday line at my next party."

She drummed her fingers on the table. "And the merchandise isn't cheap, either. All the sales I made yesterday won't even cover the cost."

"What are you going to do?"

Nancy straightened up. "I'm going to tell Glow Lights they can keep their candles. I'm done." She brushed her hands together.

Monica felt a wave of guilt. "I might be able to pay you for helping out in the kitchen." She hadn't asked for her mother's help, but she'd certainly welcomed it. But the budget was tight and she wasn't sure she could swing it.

Nancy reached out and patted Monica's hand. "That's okay, dear. I don't really need the cash. It was just something to do. I thought it might bring me a little mad money." She grimaced. "It turns out that the people making the money are the ones at the top. People like Diane who have dozens of women working for them and earning them commissions."

"A pyramid scheme?" Monica slipped her foot back into her shoe.

"I suppose you could call it that. Although I'm sure it's perfectly legitimate." Nancy picked up her handbag. "Well, I gave it a try and I have to admit it was rather fun hosting that party. It's been too long since I've done anything like that. I was afraid I might be losing my touch."

"Never," Monica said, smiling.

• • •

Woodsmoke was in the air as Monica walked back to her cottage. She inhaled deeply. She loved the scent. It brought visions of cozy rooms lit by firelight with invitingly plump sofas and chairs. She shivered, feeling goose bumps forming on her arms. Fortunately, her own cozy cottage was visible in the distance and she quickened her step.

Hercule was wild with glee at seeing Monica, as if she'd been gone for days and not just a couple of hours. She snapped on his leash and took him for a quick walk. She'd thought of buying him an adorable sweater she'd seen online but it was apparent that his thick wiry coat kept him warm enough.

Mittens was waiting for them when they went back in. Monica peeled off her gloves and rubbed her hands briskly. She touched her cheeks, which were even colder than her hands.

Mittens meowed and swished back and forth between Monica's legs. She checked the cat's bowl, which was half empty. She retrieved the bag of cat food from the pantry and topped off the dish. Mittens gave a contented sigh and began to groom herself.

Monica was boiling water for some tea when there was a knock on the door.

"Hello!" a voice called out. "It's me, Gina."

"Come in," Monica said as she pulled open the door.

"It's freezing out there," Gina stomped her feet and rubbed her hands together.

Monica looked at her stepmother. She was wearing a cropped moto jacket that was open at the neck, revealing a gold choker, and her hands and head were bare. No wonder she was cold, Monica thought.

"You need to dress for Michigan weather," Monica said. "A hat, gloves, scarf, warm sweater."

Gina groaned. "Next you'll have me in thermal shirts and flannel-lined jeans." She pulled out a chair and sat down. "You can take the girl out of the city, but you can't take the city out of the girl, I'm afraid."

Gina splayed her hands on the table. "Listen, I came to ask if you'd do me a favor and come look at a house with me." She rubbed her forehead. "I'm kind of spooked after what happened with Rip but Mickey is anxious to find something. His place is beginning to feel a bit crowded. My clothes barely fit in the closet and he's had to store his in the guest room, poor thing."

"Sure. I'd be glad to go with you."

Gina's shoulders relaxed. "Great. I have an appointment in . . ." She looked at her watch. "Half an hour."

"Time for a cup of tea then." Monica got two mugs from the cabinet, filled them with water and put them in the microwave.

Monica leaned against the kitchen counter. "How is Mickey these days? We saw him at the restaurant the other night."

"I'm worried about him." Gina wrapped her hands around the mug Monica handed her. "He's working like crazy. It's too much. The doctor said if he didn't slow down and take better care of himself, he was headed for a heart attack." She put her head in her hands. "The problem is, he won't listen."

Monica wasn't surprised. Mickey didn't seem like the type to take orders from anyone — not even his doctor.

Monica glanced at the clock on the wall. "We'd better get going."

"Let's take my car. I'll drive," Gina said as she pulled on her jacket.

• • •

Monica breathed a sigh of relief when Gina pulled up in front of Cranberry Cove Realty. She swore that despite the frigid temperatures outside, she'd actually begun perspiring when Gina scooted through a light that had just turned red. Her driving had gone downhill from there and Monica's palms were slick as she reached for the door handle.

They were headed toward the front door of Cranberry Cove Realty when Monica suddenly came to a complete stop. What if Vera Roth, the agent who'd shown her that house, was there? Would she even remember Monica? Surely, she saw lots of clients every day. Monica didn't think there was anything about her to make her stand out. She'd been lucky once. Would her luck hold out?

Gina gave her a little poke. "What's wrong."

Monica opened her mouth and then closed it again. "Nothing. Nothing at all," she said, reaching for the door handle.

As luck would have it, the woman sitting behind the desk was Vera Roth, the very person Monica had hoped wouldn't be there. She felt her face color and she ducked her head quickly.

"Can I help you?" Vera gave Monica an odd look and Monica was relieved when she didn't say anything. "What exactly are you looking for?" She looked from Monica to Gina and back again.

"I'm looking for a house," Gina said.

"That I'd guessed." Vera stood up and smoothed the skirt of her navy blue suit. "What sort of house? Large? Small?" She sounded slightly exasperated.

"I had been working with Rip Taylor —" Gina began.

"You're the woman," Vera exclaimed. She quickly resumed a neutral expression, as if suddenly realizing her outburst had been unprofessional. "We were all very sad to hear about Rip's death." She touched a hand to her heart briefly.

Gina paused respectfully before continuing. "He showed me a house on Bradford Street. I was quite keen on it, but now I'm not so sure. Given everything that's happened, the place sort of gives me the creeps." She gave an exaggerated shiver. "But I saw there's another house for sale down the block that looks promising. It was just listed today."

Vera's face lit up—no doubt at the prospect of a sale. She went behind her desk again, put on a pair of reading glasses and began tapping on her computer.

"Sunday is the worst day to list a house, you know. But sometimes it's hard to talk a client out of it. They're so determined to get their house on the market and refuse to wait." She peered at Monica and Gina over the rim of her glasses. "And houses listed on Sunday often go for less than list price, so you might be in luck." She turned back to the computer. "Ah, yes, here it is. Seventeen Bradford Street. It says it's a lovely three-bedroom on a quiet street."

Gina snorted and poked Monica in the side. "The street wasn't so quiet the day Rip was murdered."

Vera ignored her and peered at the screen. She scribbled down the address on a piece of paper and waved it at them. "Let's go. This house sounds perfect for you." She gave Gina a professional smile. "We can take my car." She got up from her chair and steered them toward the door.

Monica and Gina waited while Vera buttoned her tweed coat and wrapped a scarf around her neck.

"After you," she said as she held the door open.

She beeped open the doors to her BMW and waited while Monica and Gina got settled.

Riding with Vera was considerably less hair-raising than with Gina, and as they turned onto Bradford Street Monica realized she hadn't once clutched at the door handle.

Vera pulled up in front of a tidy white house with black shutters and a welcoming-looking red front door with a brass knocker in the shape of a pineapple. Monica didn't think the house looked like Gina at all. She had pictured her stepmother in something less conservative—modern with lots of glass, steel and concrete—like the house she'd had Monica's father buy when they were first married. Perhaps Gina was settling down and her tastes were changing, although that change certainly hadn't yet made itself evident in her wardrobe choices.

The house was as traditional on the inside as it was on the outside, a center-hall colonial that held no secrets and nothing unexpected but had plenty of space and light.

Gina seemed to like it. She was smiling as Vera led them from room to room, pointing out the obvious like the multipaned windows and the polished wood floors.

Finally, they had seen everything including the crawl space in the basement.

"Well?" Vera said, her hands clasped in front of her chest.

"I like it," Gina said. "But my significant other needs to take a look at it as well."

Vera's smile tightened into a thin line. "Shall we go?" She was obviously eager to get rid of them now that an immediate sale wasn't on the table.

They stepped outside and waited while Vera locked the house up. Monica glanced around, noticing the trees, now bare, that lined both sides of the street and the lawns all neatly raked clean of fallen leaves.

Monica noticed the front door of the house across the street opening. The house was larger than its neighbor and set well back from the sidewalk on what appeared to be at least an acre of property. A woman stepped out the door with an elaborately groomed French poodle on a leash. She looked familiar and Monica squinted, trying to make out her features.

The woman led the poodle down the driveway toward the sidewalk, and as she got closer, Monica realized why she looked familiar. It was Lacey Van Der Zee, Rip Taylor's ex-wife.

How interesting, Monica thought, that she lived on the very street where Rip was killed. Monica would have expected her to live in a much fancier neighborhood, but she had to admit that Lacey's house was quite lovely with its Southern colonial façade and the white columns framing its front door.

Monica couldn't help wondering if Lacey had seen anything the day Rip was killed. And if she had, did that put her in danger as well?

Chapter 16

Monica and Gina were quiet on the way back to the real estate office but Vera kept up a continuous spate of chatter extolling the virtues of the house they'd just toured. They were almost to their destination when Vera suddenly stopped talking and they heard her indrawn breath.

Monica looked out the window. She blinked twice and was tempted to rub her eyes. Several police cars, their flashers blinking red and blue, were pulled up outside Cranberry Cove Realty. It looked as if every policeman in Cranberry Cove was at the scene.

But the scene of what? Monica wondered. Had someone else been killed? The thought made her mouth go dry and her hands begin to shake. She couldn't imagine what, short of murder, would require such a strong police presence. What if the killer had come by thirty minutes earlier when she and Gina were there? The thought made her nearly gasp.

She was jumping to conclusions, she told herself. It might be nothing, a false alarm, but when she looked out the window again, she noticed two policemen carrying out paper-wrapped bundles.

Vera hastily pulled into an empty parking spot. Her BMW was slightly over the yellow line, but she didn't seem to notice in her haste to get out of the car.

"What do you think is up?" Gina said in hushed tones.

"I don't know. But I see Detective Stevens. I'll go ask her."

Vera was already standing at the door to the real estate office. She appeared to be arguing with one of the policemen and it looked as if she was trying to persuade him to allow her inside the building, but he kept shaking his head. She tried to go around him, but he put out an arm and stopped her. She stamped her foot in frustration and walked back toward her car, her fists balled at her sides.

Monica slipped out of the car before Vera reached it and headed toward Stevens, who was leaning against one of the patrol cars. She had her hands stuffed in the pockets of her parka and her shoulders were hunched against the cold.

"What's going on?" Monica said, somewhat breathlessly.

Stevens spun around, startled, but then smiled when she saw it was Monica. She frowned and gestured toward the Cranberry Cove Realty sign. "Are you looking for a new house? I thought you were building one."

"We are," Monica said. "My stepmother, Gina, is looking for a place."

Stevens nodded and Monica noticed the deep purple shadows under her eyes.

"What's going on?" Monica repeated, tipping her head toward the door of the building.

Stevens hesitated. Just then the red and white van from WZZZ pulled up and double-parked by Vera's car.

"I guess the word will be out soon enough." Stevens sighed and ran her hands through her hair, leaving it in disarray. "You know that toilet tank we found out at Sassamanash Farm?"

Monica nodded.

"As you have probably heard, the lab results from the residue in it came back indicating it had contained cocaine at one time." Her mouth quirked to the side. "Everyone wondered why Jax Johnson would steal a toilet tank. Now we know why." She stifled a yawn. "Sorry. It was a late night yesterday." She rubbed her hands over her face. "The tank was empty when we found it so the cocaine had to have gone somewhere." She pointed toward Cranberry Cove Realty. "We had a tip that we might find it here."

Monica's eyebrows shot up. "Here?"

"Yes. It seems that Tyler Peterson, one of the agents, has something of a gambling problem and desperately needs money."

Monica frowned. "How on earth did Tyler find out about the cocaine? Did he know Jax Johnson?"

Stevens picked at a spot on her parka. "That's what we are trying to find out. Hopefully we can convince him to enlighten us."

Just then the door to the building opened and Tyler emerged bracketed by two policemen.

"Did you find out anything?" Gina said when Monica joined her where she was leaning against her Mercedes. Her teeth were chattering and she pulled her leather jacket around her more closely.

"Let's get in the car." Monica opened the passenger door.

"Well?" Gina said as soon as she'd started the car and turned up the heat.

"According to Detective Stevens, the cocaine that was missing from the toilet tank that was thrown away at Sassamanash Farm was found here at Cranberry Cove Realty. They think Tyler Peterson is responsible. Apparently, he owes a lot of money — gambling debts."

Gina whistled. "But how did Tyler know about the coke? Was he friends with that fellow who stole the tank?"

"I don't know," Monica said as she fastened her seat belt. "And neither do the police. But I'm going to find out."

• • •

Greg was home when Monica got back to her cottage. He was sitting in the living room, his feet on an ottoman and Hercule lying by him, the dog's pink tongue lolling out the side of its mouth.

"You both look exhausted," Monica said as she leaned down to kiss her husband.

"We are." Greg pointed to Hercule. "Hercule slipped out the back door as I was coming in and thought we were playing a wonderful game when I attempted to catch him. Isn't that right, boy?" He reached down and scratched Hercule's head. Hercule slowly flopped onto his side with a grunt of satisfaction.

Greg took Monica's hand in his. "Where were you? I hope you weren't still working all this time."

"No. Gina and I went to look at a house she's interested in." Greg moved his feet and Monica perched on the ottoman.

"Was that the one she was looking at when . . ."

Monica shook her head. "No, but it's on the same street." She brushed her hair off her face. "Interestingly enough, Lacey Van Der Zee lives right across the street. Of course, her house is considerably bigger than the one Gina was looking at."

"Lacey . . . ?"

"Rip Taylor's ex-wife." Monica rubbed her temples. "I wonder if Lacey and Rip had known Kayla before Rip became involved with her. They only lived a block away from each other. Monica drummed her fingers on her knee. "Maybe that's how Lacey ended up choosing Kayla to draw up their prenuptial agreement."

"It must have been awkward for Lacey to have her ex-husband living so close by with his new lover." Greg shifted in the chair. "She must have felt resentful."

"Possibly." Monica reached down to pet Hercule. "But she didn't seem bitter when I talked to her. On the contrary, I got the impression she was actually quite relieved. She got everything she wanted in the divorce, after all. She got rid of Rip and it didn't cost her a thing."

Greg grunted. "Is Gina going to put in an offer on the house?"

"She wants Mickey to see it first. Besides, she forgot all about it when we got back to the real estate office. We both did."

Greg tilted his head. "I thought realtors were like vultures. Once they got you in their clutches, they didn't let go."

"I am sure that would have been the case if the place hadn't been surrounded by police when we got there."

Greg's eyebrows shot up. "The police? What on earth were they doing there?"

Monica tucked one foot under her. "It turns out that Tyler Peterson, who is one of the agents at Cranberry Cove Realty, was the person who stole the cocaine that was hidden in that toilet tank Jeff found here on the farm." Monica fingered her gold wedding band. "What I can't figure out is how did Tyler know about the cocaine? As far as I've been able to tell, he's not acquainted with Jax Johnson, so it's not as if Jax told him about the drugs either on purpose or by letting it slip accidentally." Monica sighed. "But he had to have found out somehow."

"Maybe he overheard someone talking about it?"

"I doubt it." Monica suddenly sat up straighter. "But Kayla must have known about it. Kayla is Jax's lawyer, so Jax had to have told her he'd stolen cocaine along with the toilet tank. But would she have told Tyler about it? Isn't that unethical or something?"

"Pillow talk." Greg smiled. "A lot of secrets get revealed that way."

"Tyler has a gambling problem and owes a lot of money, so I can see how he'd be tempted to steal the drugs." Monica drummed her fingers on the ottoman. "Kayla needs money as well according to her maid, so maybe they were in it together." Monica rubbed her forehead. "Jax tells Kayla about the coke. Maybe she was the one who counseled him to hide it. And then she tells Tyler and he convinces her they should steal it."

"Hmmm," Greg said, nodding.

"The coke is worth a lot of money. Maybe Rip found out about it and wanted a cut." Monica paused and ran her hands through her hair. "Maybe Rip blackmailed Kayla—telling her that he'd report her to the bar association if she didn't give him a share."

Monica jumped to her feet and began to pace back and forth across the living room carpet. "It would put her career on the line, and from what I've heard, her career is all she really cares about. She's gunning for the district attorney's job."

Monica stopped and turned to face Greg. "Frankly, I wouldn't put it past Kayla to resort to murder to protect her position."

• • •

Monica was in the kitchen heating up a pot of the curried butternut squash soup she'd taken out of the freezer, when Greg called to her from the living room.

"What's up," Monica said, drying her hands on her apron.

Greg pointed at the television, where the WZZZ news broadcast was on.

"They've arrested Ralph Lombardi, who owned the toilet tank that was stolen."

Monica glanced at the screen, where the reporter, a young woman in a blue sheath dress and matching coat, was yelling into the microphone, nearly drowned out by the sound of a leaf blower further down the street. She was standing in front of the house where Mrs. Lombardi had been interviewed earlier after the theft of the toilet tank.

"It looks as if Jax Johnson was in some sort of minor drug ring with this Lombardi fellow," Greg said, shifting in his seat. "I guess Johnson tried to cut Lombardi out by stealing the tank. Obviously, he was really after the cocaine."

"I guess he wanted all the money for himself." Monica perched on the edge of the sofa.

The scene on the television changed and the cameras were now focused on the news desk, where the two anchors regarded the audience with grave expressions.

"In related news," the young man began. His hair was slicked back and he was wearing round tortoiseshell glasses that made him look like an owl. "Tyler Peterson, accused of receiving the stolen cocaine, has been released on bail."

The camera cut to a scene outside the courthouse, where a weary-looking Tyler paused on the steps, shielding his eyes from the lights flashing from the cameras of the reporters assembled below. Kayla was at his side holding his elbow, as if to guide him.

"That was quick." Monica watched Tyler and Kayla duck into a waiting car. "I wonder if Kayla will be acting as Tyler's attorney?"

Greg shrugged. "You said they're an item, didn't you? She might be too emotionally involved."

Monica thought for a minute. She turned to Greg. "Or she might be involved — period."

• • •

The alarm rang shrilly on Monday morning and Monica reached out a hand and slapped it off. She snuggled under the covers and drifted back to sleep. It was late by the time she woke up again and she jumped out of bed in a panic.

She showered quickly, dressed in jeans and a warm sweater and pulled a comb through her hair. She grimaced as it caught on a snarl at the back of her head. Hercule's walk was going to have to be cut a bit short that morning, she thought as she hurried down the stairs. She vowed to make it up to him later in the day, but when she walked into the kitchen, she noticed a note propped against the salt and pepper shakers saying that Greg had already taken Hercule out.

Monica felt her shoulders relax in relief. She made a quick bowl of instant oatmeal, topped it off with some dried cranberries and ate it standing at the counter.

She checked the animals' water and food bowls, gave them each a treat and yanked her coat off the hook.

The farm kitchen was already filled with the aromas of bread and cookies baking when Monica finally arrived. She tossed her coat toward the hook by the door and reached for her apron.

Kit was busy kneading a batch of dough and Nancy was packing a large cardboard carton with jars of cranberry sauce.

Kit jerked his head toward the box. "The manager of the Cranberry Cove Inn called first thing. Their new menu is Thanksgiving themed and he asked for all the cranberry sauce we had in stock."

"I can run it into town if you'd like," Monica said, beginning to untie her apron. "Unless you need my help here . . ."

The thought of sitting in her car rather than standing behind the counter was enticing. Her back muscles were beginning to cramp and her feet hurt even though the day had barely begun.

"If you don't mind," Kit said, swiping at some flour on the front of his shirt.

"Not at all." Monica tried to hide her relief, reflexively putting a hand to her aching back.

Nancy finished packing the carton while Monica pulled on her coat. She glanced at Monica and Monica could have sworn she looked slightly embarrassed. Her cheeks had turned pink and she was fiddling with the charms on her bracelet.

"While you're in town would you mind doing me a favor?"

"Sure," Monica said as she buttoned her coat and pulled her gloves from her pocket.

"I ordered a special crystal from Tempest's shop and it just came in. Would you mind picking it up for me?"

"What sort of crystal?" Monica had always thought her mother didn't go in for things she often referred to as that ridiculous *woo-woo* stuff. What had suddenly changed her mind?

Nancy's face flushed further. She waved a hand in the air. "It's nothing really. Simply something I thought was pretty and that I might turn into a necklace."

Monica didn't believe a word her mother was saying but she decided to let it slide. She'd find out soon enough.

"Ready?" Kit hefted the box onto one hip and headed toward the door. He followed Monica outside and down the path, where the ruts were now frozen solid. He was wearing a T-shirt in rainbow colors and there were goose bumps blossoming up and down his arms.

Monica bit her lip. "You must be freezing. We're almost there." She pointed to her cottage in the distance.

"I'm fine." Kit shifted the carton to the other hip as they approached Monica's driveway. "The fresh air feels good. It gets pretty hot standing next to that oven when it's going full blast."

The day was as cold as the previous ones had been but despite the sun being rather pale, it felt good on Monica's face. Hercule must have gotten wind of their arrival because she heard him barking at the back door.

Kit put the carton in Monica's trunk and closed the lid with a loud thump as Monica got behind the wheel and started the engine. She waved to him as she backed out of the driveway and Kit gave her a sketchy salute.

Monica kept her eyes on the road but spared a quick glance at the scenery when Lake Michigan came into view off to her left. There was very little wind and the water was relatively calm, with small foam-topped waves licking at the shore.

Beach Hollow Road was bustling as if with pent-up energy as Monica drove down it toward the Cranberry Cove Inn. She pulled into the parking lot and followed the drive around to the service entrance at the back. A busboy with dark hair buzzed into a crew cut and a T-shirt that had *Pure Michigan* written on it immediately appeared. He grabbed the carton of cranberry sauce as soon as Monica popped open the trunk.

"The Inn's going all out for Thanksgiving," he said as he tightened his arms around the box. "From now until the big day there will be turkey, stuffing and all the trimmings on the menu. And you can't have Thanksgiving dinner without cranberry sauce." He grinned and rapped the carton with his knuckles.

Monica thanked him, got back in her car and was heading out of the parking lot when she remembered that Lauren's birthday was coming up. It was the day before Thanksgiving and she'd promised Jeff she would pick out a gift for him to give her. The poor guy had no idea what to buy and had appealed to Monica to help him out. She debated various ideas as she drove down Beach Hollow Road. There weren't a lot of shopping options in Cranberry Cove — Danielle's was a pricey boutique and Monica didn't think the items they sold looked to be Lauren's style. The hardware store carried souvenirs for the summer visitors but those were hardly appropriate. She thought of Gumdrops and a box of chocolates but then abandoned the idea.

Maybe a small piece of jewelry? That was romantic and something that would be a keepsake. Monica had read somewhere that young girls were into wearing delicate necklaces and earrings. Perhaps Bijoux would have something in Jeff's price range.

She found a parking space in front of Twilight and dashed across the street to the jewelry store. She paused and glanced in the window, where modest gold chains were displayed on necklace stands covered in rich blue velvet. Something like that would be perfect for Lauren.

A bell jingled melodically as Monica pushed open the door. The salesman, dressed in a somber black suit more befitting an undertaker, was at the counter reverently arranging a bracelet on a black velvet cloth for two customers. He fiddled with it until he was finally satisfied and then stepped back and waved his hand over it like a magician conjuring up a trick.

His customers leaned over the counter and examined the bracelet carefully. The man was wearing a black overcoat and had a pair of black leather gloves tucked under his arm. The wind had tousled the thin brown hair that he had combed over his head to hide his bald spot, leaving one piece dangling below his left ear.

A woman was snuggled up against him. She had hair dyed an improbable shade of red teased into a bouffant flip. She was wearing a short fur jacket with a cashmere sweater tight enough to show off her substantial curves along with black leggings and suede ankle boots.

The man reached out and fingered the bracelet on the cloth, turning it this way and that, and watching as the diamonds encircling it set off shards of light.

The piece must cost a fortune, Monica thought as she bent to examine the more modest items in the case in front of her. There were more gold chains like the ones displayed in the store window along with bracelets fashioned of impossibly delicate links and gold stud earrings hardly bigger than a freckle. They all looked like something Lauren would wear.

"It comes with matching earrings," Monica heard the salesman say to his customers.

The woman could barely contain a squeal. "Can we see them?" she purred to the salesman. "You do want to see them, don't you, baby," she said to the man, gripping his arm.

The salesman pulled a stand from the case on which two diamond chandelier earrings hung and placed it in front of his customers. "Two carats total," he said, running a finger lovingly over the gems.

Monica glanced at her watch, wondering how much longer the other customers were going to linger. Was the man going to buy the woman the items or was he still trying to decide? Certainly, something as pricey as a diamond bracelet and diamond earrings weren't a spur-of-the-moment purchase. She was about to leave and come back at another time when the clerk appeared to be finalizing the sale. The man reached into his pocket and pulled out a checkbook while the salesman fussed over the wrapping of the bracelet and earrings.

The woman with him was nearly jumping up and down in her excitement. She kept throwing her arms around the man and reaching up to kiss his cheek.

The man glanced in Monica's direction and she had to stifle the gasp that rose to her lips. It was Marty Fisher. And the woman he was with was definitely not Mrs. Fisher. He didn't appear to recognize Monica and she quickly ducked her head, letting her hair fall forward over her face like a curtain.

The salesman slipped the rose-colored jewelry box into a bag with *Bijou Jewelers* written on it and handed it to the woman. She looked as if she was about to burst from excitement.

The woman had to be Marty's mistress, Monica thought. She certainly didn't appear to be a relative and a man doesn't buy jewelry like that for his sister or cousin.

It certainly looked as if Marty was going all out now that Rip was dead and he was no longer paying blackmail money. He was now free to spend his cash on anything he wanted. Wouldn't that give him a pretty strong motive for murder?

Chapter 17

In the end, Monica chose a delicate gold chain with a tiny heart at its center. She was quite pleased with it. It was within Jeff's budget and she was sure Lauren would be delighted with it.

She had been relieved when Marty had finished his purchase and had left Bijoux without appearing to recognize her. If her suspicions about him were correct, she might have found herself caught in the crosshairs of a killer!

The salesman placed the chain in Bijoux's signature rose-colored box, slipped it into a similarly colored bag and handed it to Monica with a flourish. She put the bag in her tote and left the shop. Twilight, her next destination, was right across the street, and after a red pickup truck had made its way down the road, she looked both ways and then dashed to the other side.

Twilight always had an oddly soothing aura about it. Tempest said it was because of all the crystals arranged in the display case. According to her, crystals were capable of bringing a sense of calm and serenity to the atmosphere. Monica wasn't so sure about that. She thought it was Tempest herself and her fluid movements and flowing clothes that gave the place its tranquil air.

Today Tempest was behind the counter arranging some sage smudge candles into a pleasing display. She was wearing a purple velvet top with batwing sleeves and a keyhole neckline and there was a light green crystal hanging from a silk cord around her neck.

She smiled and fingered it as Monica approached the counter.

"Peridot," she said, holding the crystal in the palm of her hand. "It brings positive energy and abundance."

"I could do with some of that myself," Monica said, leaning her elbows on the counter. "The energy part at least." She ran a hand through her hair.

Tempest gave a knowing smile. "Once you're past the first trimester of pregnancy, the fatigue should lessen."

"I hope so."

It suddenly occurred to Monica that she knew very little about Tempest's past. Did she have grown children somewhere? She did know that Tempest lived alone, but had she been married at some point?

Tempest reached into the display case and removed a clear stone. She handed it to Monica.

"This is crystal quartz. It amplifies energy."

She could certainly use that, Monica thought. "What do I do with it?"

"Hold it in your hand for a few minutes and set your intention."

Monica raised her eyebrows. "Intention?"

"What you hope the crystal will bring you. In this case, you might want to ask for energy to carry you through your pregnancy."

Monica gripped the stone in her right hand, shut her eyes and set her intention, as Tempest called it. She couldn't begin to imagine what Janice would think of all this. Then again, Janice seemed to believe in the most ridiculous pregnancy myths, so anything was possible.

She opened her eyes. "Now what do I do?"

Tempest pointed at her. "Put it in your pocket and keep it close."

"Anything else?"

"And," Tempest said, "put it in the sun for an hour or two every day to recharge the crystal with the sun's energy."

Feeling very foolish, Monica slipped the stone into her pocket. "What do I owe you?" She had no idea what crystals cost and hoped it wasn't a lot.

"Oh, pooh. It's my gift to you." Tempest waved a hand as Monica began to reach into her purse. "And now I imagine you've come in for the crystal your mother ordered," she said with raised eyebrows.

Monica nodded and Tempest reached under the counter and pulled out a small box. She took off the top and held it out toward Monica.

"Rose quartz," she said.

The stone was pale pink and very pretty. Had her mother ordered it because she liked the color?

"Rose quartz is strongly attached to the heart chakra," Tempest said with a coy smile. "It speaks of love and romance."

Monica was taken aback. First her mother had dropped the bomb that she was seeing someone and now she was buying crystals related to romance. How serious was this relationship?

Tempest picked up a bag and slipped the box into it. She handed it to Monica.

"I'm glad you came by. I'm about to start jury duty tomorrow and Daryl will be minding the shop for me." She scowled. "I suppose it's my civic responsibility. Anyway, that lawyer came by the other day."

Monica frowned. "What lawyer?"

"The lawyer who's representing the fellow who stole the toilet tank. Although I gather he actually stole more than just the tank."

"Kayla Moore? Is that who you mean?"

Tempest reached under the counter and pulled out a business card. She grabbed a pair of purple-framed reading glasses sitting on the counter and perched them on her nose.

She glanced at the card in her hand. "Yes. Kayla Moore." She looked at Monica over the rim of her eyeglasses. "And she wasn't here to buy something."

"What did she want then?"

"She wanted me to vote to acquit the fellow who's going on trial." Tempest drew her eyebrows together. "Is that allowed? It seems to me it ought to be illegal."

"It is illegal," Monica said. She was shocked.

"Should I report it?" Tempest squeezed the bridge of her nose. She frowned. "But to whom?"

"I would go down to the courthouse. Someone should be able to tell you who to talk to—the judge maybe."

It looked as if Kayla was even more determined to get ahead than anybody realized, Monica thought as she said goodbye to Tempest and left the shop. That certainly made her ambitious, but did it make her a killer as well?

• • •

Clouds were moving in as Monica left Twilight and the sky was slowly darkening. Was it snow or rain on the way? she wondered. She was walking toward her car when someone grabbed her arm.

It was Gina.

"Do you have time for a quick bite? Sandra's minding the shop for me for an hour."

Monica hesitated. There was work to do back at the farm. But surely another half hour wouldn't make all that much difference.

"Sure. The diner? I don't have time for the Pepper Pot or the Inn."

"The diner is fine." Gina linked her arm through Monica's as they strolled next door.

Monica's stomach growled the minute Gina pulled open the door to the diner and the smell of frying food enveloped her. So far, she hadn't had any of the odd cravings that she'd read about, like pickles and ice cream. But perhaps they were another myth, like the ones Janice seemed to have in abundance.

There was a long line at the counter for take-out—the new chef couldn't match Gus for speed—but they were able to snare a booth that two men had just vacated. They were silent as the waitress collected the used plates, cutlery and glasses and whisked them away on her tray. She reappeared almost immediately with a cloth and wiped down the table.

"I'll be right back with some ice water," she said as she swiveled on her heel. Moments later she returned with two glasses, dripping with condensation, and plunked them down on the table. She gave Monica and Gina a practiced smile and pulled an order pad from her pocket and a pencil from behind her ear.

"What'll you have?" she said with an air of complete indifference.

"What's the soup of the day?" Gina said, frowning at the menu.

"Tomato."

"I'll have that and a green salad." Gina handed the menu back to the waitress.

Monica was still considering the selection. She'd been to the diner often enough that she ought to have memorized the menu by now. She could feel the waitress staring at her, impatience etched on her face.

"I'll have the Reuben," Monica said finally.

Gina gave her an odd look as the waitress walked away, the menus tucked under her arm.

"You've never ordered the Reuben before. I didn't even know you liked them." Gina reached for her water glass.

"I guess I have a craving for one."

Gina smiled knowingly. "It looks like pregnancy cravings are settling in."

Monica grimaced. Was she about to become a walking cliché?

Gina leaned her elbows on the table. "What did you get in Twilight? I saw you coming out of Tempest's shop."

"Nothing for me, although Tempest gave me a crystal that she said would give me energy." Monica pulled it from her pocket and held it up for Gina to see. "It's crystal quartz, Tempest said."

"Very pretty."

Monica reached into her purse and pulled out the bag from Twilight. "I also picked this up for my mother. She'd ordered it from Twilight." She opened the box and showed Gina the rose quartz crystal nestled in the cotton.

Gina whistled. "Rose quartz? That's for love and romance, isn't it?"

"That's what Tempest said." Monica made a face.

"What's the matter?" Gina leaned back as the waitress slid a bowl of soup and a salad in front of her, then placed a sandwich plate before Monica.

"I don't know. It seems odd — my mother dating." She unfurled her napkin. "I mean at her age . . ."

"People crave love at every age." Gina blew on her soup. "There's no time limit." She picked up her spoon. "I remember when my grandmother was in assisted living. During the time she was there, there were four weddings." She looked at Monica. "Of the residents, not the staff."

"You're right, of course. But when it's your own mother . . . I guess I'm afraid she'll get hurt."

"I think she can take care of herself," Gina said with a twinkle in her eye. She was quiet and her expression turned somber. She sat for a minute staring at her bowl of soup.

"Is something wrong?"

Gina shook herself. "No," she said unconvincingly.

"Is it about Rip's murder?" Monica picked up her sandwich. "You still haven't gone to Detective Stevens yet, have you?" She tried to keep her tone from sounding accusatory.

Gina fiddled with her soup spoon. "No. I don't see what good it would do."

Monica didn't want to scare Gina but she was afraid Gina was leaving herself open to a charge of obstruction.

"It would put your mind at rest. That's something. And there might be . . . consequences if you don't come forward."

Gina looked alarmed. "But there's nothing I can tell her," she said, her voice rising. "I fell asleep, and when I woke up Rip was . . . dead." She shuddered.

"Do you remember anything before you fell asleep?"

Gina put her spoon down and picked up her fork, then wrinkled her brow. "Not really. We were talking, discussing a counteroffer if the owner of the house didn't accept our bid. I remember there was a dog barking somewhere in the distance, which was annoying." She shrugged. "But I don't think it's significant, do you?"

Monica didn't but an idea was stirring in her brain. Unfortunately, she couldn't quite get hold of it.

"You told me you dreamt that you saw someone looking in the car window."

Gina frowned. "I did? I suppose I might have but I could have dreamt it the night before." She rubbed her forehead. "Maybe I got confused. I'm afraid I can't remember."

"Maybe someone really did look in the window and you woke up briefly. Do you remember what they looked like?"

Gina paused with her fork halfway to her mouth. She shook her head.

"No. Everything was . . . blurry, like in a dream." She pointed her fork at Monica. "Maybe it really was a dream."

But what if it wasn't a dream? Monica thought as they finished their meal. What if it was the killer who had been looking in the window? The thought made her shiver. What was to have stopped them from killing Gina as well as Rip?

Chapter 18

Monica arrived back at her cottage hardly knowing how she'd gotten there. She'd been so busy thinking, she'd barely noticed the passing scenery. She had to admit, she was still worried that Gina hadn't gone to the police. She should have notified them immediately, and the longer she waited, the worse it looked.

She'd also been thinking about what Tempest had told her. Kayla would be in big trouble if anyone found out that she had tried to get Tempest to agree to acquit Jax Johnson. Monica was quite certain that was tampering with the jury and she could be disbarred for it.

And then there was seeing Marty Fisher buying expensive jewelry in Bijoux. He was obviously enjoying his freedom from blackmail. At least, Monica assumed Rip had been blackmailing him. How else would he have afforded that expensive car?

All these thoughts had driven her mother's romance straight out of her mind, and when she pulled into her driveway, she was almost surprised to see the bag from Twilight sitting on the passenger seat next to her.

She put it all out of her mind as she locked the car and headed straight to the farm kitchen. The skies were even darker now and the wind tugged at her hair and blew it across her face.

She arrived at the kitchen and was about to unbutton her jacket and hang it up when she noticed that Kit and Nancy had a cartful of cranberry muffins, cookies and bread all ready to take down to the store.

"You've been busy," she said and pointed at the cart laden with cranberry goodies. "I might as well wheel that down to the store while I still have my jacket on. I imagine Nora will be needing to refill the cases by now."

Kit frowned and ran a hand through his hair, flattening the spikes he'd so carefully sculpted with the aid of hair gel.

"But it might rain," he said and frowned. "And in your condition . . ." He let the sentence trail off.

Monica laughed. "I'm not going to melt if I get a bit wet just because I'm pregnant."

Kit didn't look convinced. Monica was glad Janice wasn't there because she would undoubtedly know of some myth that claimed pregnant women actually could melt in the rain.

She didn't wait for any further protests from Kit. She grabbed the handle of the cart, opened the door and pushed it outside. She felt a few drops of rain as she passed the frozen bogs, but the worst of the brewing storm appeared to be holding off.

"You're a sight for sore eyes," Nora said when Monica arrived at the store. She gestured toward the bakery cases.

"We're almost out of everything." She blew a lock of hair off her forehead. "It's been a busy morning." She squeezed Monica's arm. "That's good news for you, I imagine. People can't seem to get enough of your cranberry walnut white chocolate chunk cookies." She laughed. "I have to confess to having had one myself. And here I'm always telling the boys they can't have dessert until after they eat their meal."

Monica put a finger to her mouth. "My lips are sealed. It will be our secret."

The door opened and the bell overhead tinkled. Two older women walked in and began to peruse the selection. They watched as Monica transferred the fresh baked goods to the case and the one in the red coat pointed at the cookies and smiled at Monica.

Her pale blue eyes twinkled. "Those look delicious." She leaned closer to the case and turned to her friend. "Don't they look yummy?"

The other woman nodded in agreement.

"I'll take a dozen of those, please," her friend said.

As Monica reached for a sheet of glassine, the women began to talk. Monica kept a curious ear open to their gossip, and when she heard the words *lawyer*, *Kayla* and *Jax*, she was taken aback.

"They found her body by the side of the road," the woman in the red coat said to her friend in low tones. "Absolutely ghastly."

"Tsk, tsk. How dreadful. What do they think happened?" the other woman whispered back.

"Well, it wasn't natural causes, that's for sure." Her friend laughed. "They're saying it looks as if it could be murder."

The woman in the blue coat gasped. "Murder! We've already had a murder recently — that realtor fellow. Very strange if you ask me." She shook her head and the pom-pom on her hat bobbed up and down with the movement. "Cranberry Cove has always been such a safe town. Things like this didn't happen in our day."

"I know. I don't know what the world is coming to."

Monica cleared her throat. "I couldn't help overhearing." She smiled. "But what's this about another murder?"

"It was on the news," the woman in the red coat said breathlessly. "The lawyer who was defending that fellow who stole the toilet tank" — she put a hand over her mouth to stifle a giggle—"was found murdered, if you can believe it."

"Kayla Moore?"

"That's the one." She beamed at Monica as if Monica was a particularly bright child.

Monica's mind was spinning. So, Kayla Moore was dead. Was it the same killer who'd murdered Rip? If so, that eliminated Kayla as a suspect. But why would someone want to kill her?

Obviously, there were a lot of things she still didn't know, Monica thought. And there was still that thought buzzing around in her head and tantalizing her like an annoying fly, but every time it began to come into focus, it disappeared again.

Her mission accomplished, Monica wheeled the empty cart back to the kitchen. She was itching to go home and turn on the news, hoping there would be more information about Kayla's murder. She sighed. She'd have to wait till the evening to find out.

Kit was leaning forward, his hands on the counter, when Monica walked in. There was a sheen of perspiration on his forehead and his shoulders were slumped. He certainly didn't look like himself—he was always so full of energy and optimism.

Monica hung up her jacket and walked over to Kit. She put a hand on his back.

"Are you okay?"

Kit gave a weary smile before straightening up. "I'm fine. A little tired is all."

Monica immediately felt guilty. "I'm sorry I've been gone so long." She looked around. "Where is Nancy?"

She knew her mother couldn't do half the work that she herself did but she was certainly able to take some of the load off Kit's shoulders.

"She went home." Kit's mouth clamped shut into a tight line.

Monica raised her eyebrows. "Why? Was she ill? She said she'd stay while I was gone."

Kit rubbed his forehead. "I'm afraid I upset her." He looked at

Monica, his eyes sad. "I didn't mean to. I just blurted it out without thinking."

Oh, no. Had Nancy and Kit had some sort of tiff? She knew her mother could be a bit abrasive at times, but Kit seemed to be able to handle it.

"Did you have a fight?"

"No, not exactly." The oven timer dinged. Kit grabbed a pot holder and pulled out a sheet of perfectly golden and flaky cranberry scones.

He put the cookie sheet down and began transferring the scones to a cooling rack.

"So, what happened?" Monica grabbed her apron and tied it around her waist.

"I didn't mean to upset her." Kit's face was flushed from the blast of heat from the oven.

"I'm sure you didn't but something must have happened." Monica retrieved a bowl from the shelf and put it on the counter.

"It's about that man she's been dating. Jimmy Stewart." Kit wrinkled his brow. "Although I suppose dating isn't really the right word to use under the circumstances."

"What about him? What do you mean?" She paused with her hand on the cannister of sugar. "I hope it's nothing serious, like he's escaped from jail, or worse, is wanted for grand larceny or murder."

That made Kit smile. "No, nothing like that." He frowned. "But it still upset your mother."

Monica held her hands out, palms up. "Okay, shoot. What is it?" She mentally braced herself for bad news.

"I know Jimmy Stewart. And no, he's not a criminal. It's just that he's . . ." Kit shrugged. "There's no other way to put it. He's gay."

That was certainly something Monica hadn't been expecting.

"But how can he be? He's dating my mother." She put her hands on her hips. "Isn't that proof of . . . something?"

Kit gave a sad smile. "Jimmy and I ended up sitting next to each other at the bar I go to while I waited for some friends to arrive. We started chatting, and when I told him about how I worked here and was going to manage the bookstore café when it opened, he mentioned your mother."

"Could he have been at that bar to . . ." Monica waved her hands in the air. "To meet a friend who was gay and had suggested it?"

"Nice try." Kit wiped his hands on his apron. "No, I don't think so. I've seen him there plenty of times, although we've never talked before. Besides, he thinks your mother is a friend, someone to occasionally have dinner with. Nothing romantic."

And her mother was thinking the exact opposite, Monica thought. She took a deep breath. "I gather my mother didn't take it well?"

"As well as could be expected. She was disappointed, of course. Then she said she felt foolish for having been fooled. I felt terrible telling her but I didn't know what else to do."

"You did the right thing. It wouldn't be fair to let her think the relationship was going to turn into a romance. Was she mad at you for telling her? Is that why she left?"

Kit shrugged. "I don't know. She said she was tired and she was going to go home and lie down." He shook his head. "I feel so bad."

"Don't. I'm sure she'll have forgotten all about it in a few days."

Monica went back to work, measuring sugar into her bowl and creaming it with butter and vanilla. Something tickled her nose and she thought she was going to sneeze. She reached into her pocket for some tissues and her hand touched the quartz that Tempest had given her. She fingered the rough edges and then held it in her palm for a second, hoping that Tempest was right and it would give her energy.

She couldn't stop worrying about her mother and finally decided she'd better call her. She stopped the mixer and reached for her cell phone. She punched in the number and listened as it rang repeatedly at the other end. She clicked off the call with a sigh. She'd try again later.

She was adding flour to her mixing bowl when she remembered the rose quartz she had picked up for Nancy. Should she give it to her now or would it simply upset her more?

She rubbed her forehead. She was getting a headache. She'd decide later.

• • •

It was raining lightly by the time Monica left the kitchen. She ducked her head, pulled up her collar and walked quickly back to her cottage.

Her jacket was soaked by the time she reached her driveway. She opened the passenger door of her car and retrieved the bag from

Twilight that she'd left on the seat. She was still uncertain about what she should do with it. She decided to think about it later and stuffed it in her jacket pocket.

As soon as she got inside, she shook the droplets of water from her hair and brushed them off the shoulders of her jacket. Hercule was waiting with an expectant expression on his face, his head tilting from side to side as he stared at Monica.

"Okay, come on, boy." She fastened his leash, grabbed an umbrella from the stand by the door and went out.

Hercule seemed to sense Monica's impatience and she was relieved when he quickly got down to business and they were able to go back inside.

She hung up her jacket, made herself a cup of tea and took it into the living room. She glanced at her watch. The news would be starting any minute.

She settled into the armchair, dug the remote out from under the cushion, put her feet up on the ottoman and tuned into WZZZ, the local news station.

The program opened with a story about a car accident on Beach Hollow Road outside Bart's Butcher that was snarling traffic, then segued to a protest against a recent unpopular ruling by the city council and finally a brief weather update. By the time they got to the story about Kayla Moore, Monica was half asleep, but her eyes flew open when she heard the woman's name.

A reporter, the same one who'd given an update on Rip Taylor's murder, was at the scene, standing on a stretch of highway just outside of town. She was beside a shallow ditch with long, light brown reeds topped with feathery plumes swaying behind her in the brisk breeze. Yellow police tape was staked out around the area.

Two patrol cars and a dusty Taurus were pulled up in front of the WZZZ news van, their flashers streaking red and blue across the darkening sky. A woman was talking to one of the patrolmen, her face red from the cold, and Monica recognized Detective Stevens.

As soon as the reporter realized the camera was on her, she gave a wide smile, baring even white teeth, and with her index finger hooked a lock of blond hair that had blown across her face and tucked it behind her ear. There was a brief pause and then she began to speak.

"Cranberry Cove is in shock this evening at the report of a

gruesome second murder within its midst. The murder of Richard Taylor rocked the close-knit community only days ago." Despite the gravity of her words, she continued to smile.

"This afternoon, a passing motorist discovered a body in this ditch beside the road." She swiveled around and pointed behind her. "It appears the victim had been shot but we are waiting for police confirmation." She gave another broad smile. "Meanwhile, with us now is Gunner Birdie, the driver who originally discovered the body."

The camera slowly moved until Gunner came into view. He was standing in front of a black pickup truck with overly large wheels and was wearing a Detroit Tigers baseball cap, jeans worn at the thighs and knees and name-brand sneakers. His hands were stuck in the pockets of a Carhartt camo utility jacket. He appeared nervous, shifting from foot to foot and repeatedly licking his lips.

"Mr. Birdie, tell me about finding the body," the reporter said as she moved to stand by Gunner. "Where were you headed when you came upon the dead woman?" She held the microphone to his lips.

His eyes darted back and forth and he fiddled with the brim of his baseball cap.

"I was on my way home from my shift at the Sunrise Bread factory." He cleared his throat. "I thought I'd seen something peculiar sticking up out of the ditch. I thought maybe it was a deer or something. It made me curious, you know?" He looked at the reporter and scratched the back of his neck. "I wasn't in no hurry and didn't have nowhere special I had to be, so I turned around and came back to investigate."

"And what did you find?" The reporter turned her attention to the camera once again and grinned.

"It wasn't no deer I saw. It was a woman and she was dead."

"How did you know she was dead?"

Gunner looked slightly annoyed. "Well, she wasn't moving or nothing, was she? She was just lying there."

"Can you describe exactly what you saw?" When a blank look settled on Gunner's face, the reporter clarified. "What did the woman look like?"

Gunner scratched the back of his neck again. "Her dress was all bunched up on her thighs." He grabbed the legs of his jeans in both hands to demonstrate. "Her face was real white and, I dunno, I could just tell something was wrong. She wasn't wearing no coat and it's cold out." He gave a shiver as if to prove the point.

The reporter's expression turned suitably grave. "And then what did you do after that?"

Gunner scowled at the reporter. He took a deep breath. "I done what anyone would have done. I called the police." He pulled his cell phone from his pocket and brandished it.

"There you have it, folks," the reporter said as the camera zoomed in on her. "The police are investigating and we hope to bring you more information as soon as we have it, so be sure to stay tuned." She smiled again. "And now back to the newsroom." She bobbed her head. "Over to you, Gary and Tanya."

The WZZZ news desk, where two anchors were seated, notes clutched in their hands, now filled the screen.

"What a tragedy," Tanya said, her expression grave. She picked up a small stack of papers and tapped them on the desk.

Gary agreed and looked directly at the camera, his somber expression lightening until he was smiling broadly. "And now for the nightly traffic report with our very own Bert Bixby." He waved a hand and the camera followed, revealing a large interactive map with a man in a houndstooth sport coat standing in front of it.

Monica switched off the television. So, Kayla had been shot. And Rip had been shot as well. Was it a coincidence or were the murders committed by the same person? Monica couldn't imagine what Kayla had been doing walking along that stretch of highway in this weather, and without so much as a coat, so the murderer must have killed her somewhere else and dumped her body in that ditch. Unless, of course, she'd been driven there and then shot. The police were combing the scene for evidence. Monica was confident they'd find the answers.

She yawned and leaned her head back against the chair as her lids got heavy and her eyes began to close. Her whole body relaxed and within minutes she was asleep and didn't wake up until she heard the back door open when Greg got home from work.

Chapter 19

Monica was up early the next day feeling rested and refreshed. A good sleep had renewed her energy. She had an early morning appointment at the lab. Her doctor wanted to do a blood draw and run some tests, and even though he assured her it was strictly routine, there was that tiny niggling worry at the back of her mind she couldn't completely ignore.

For once Greg hadn't left for work early but was in the kitchen measuring water into the coffeepot.

"Can you have some coffee?" he asked, with the coffee scoop in his hand. "Decaf, of course."

"Yes. Black is okay but the doctor doesn't want me to eat anything until after I visit the lab."

Greg turned back to the coffee machine, but then swiveled around. He studied Monica's face.

"You're not worried, are you?"

"No," Monica fibbed. "The doctor said the tests are strictly routine."

Greg didn't look convinced but he went back to measuring out the coffee and soon the machine was bubbling and gurgling as the steaming brew poured into the carafe.

He handed Monica a cup and she cradled it in her hands. The kitchen was chilly. She checked the thermometer outside the back door. It read twenty degrees and there was a dusting of snow on the ground, as if someone had shaken powdered sugar over everything.

Even the animals sensed the cold. Mittens had taken up residence on the heating vent and Hercule was curled up with his back to her.

Greg reached for his jacket. "I'll clean your car off for you," he said, kissing Monica on the cheek.

Monica felt a rush of gratitude. It still felt so miraculous that she and Greg had met. A small town like Cranberry Cove was the last place she'd expected to find love. Maybe it would work its magic on her mother?

She finished her coffee, and as she was putting her cup in the dishwasher, Greg came back in, stamping his feet to remove any lingering snow and bringing a blast of frigid air with him.

Monica reached for her own jacket and slid into it. "I'm off," she said and kissed him goodbye.

The icy wind cut straight through Monica's jacket and she hurried toward her car. Greg had started the engine for her and she sat for a moment, savoring the warm air pouring from the vents. Finally, she put the car in gear and headed down the driveway.

The roads were clear, the light dusting of snow having already melted in the weak morning sun. Monica headed up the hill and was passing the boarded-up farm stand and the abandoned Shell station at the top of the rise when the car began to make a funny noise. Monica listened carefully as she headed down the hill toward town. The car had seemed fine the last time she'd driven it. She couldn't identify the sound and she hoped it was nothing serious. She'd planned on getting a few more years and a few more miles out of the Taurus.

The clunking sound increased alarmingly as she picked up speed. She sighed. She'd better get it looked at if she wanted the car to last any longer. She'd take it to the garage as soon as her appointment was over.

The lab wasn't busy and Monica was able to get in right away. A quick poke and she was off again, this time to the local garage before heading to the bank to make a deposit in Sassamanash Farm's account.

The garage was under new ownership, the previous owner having retired and moved to Florida to escape the cold. A large sign that read *Mike's Garage* was positioned by the road. The parking lot was empty when Monica pulled in save for a blue van in a space right outside the door to the office.

The garage door was open and both bays were empty. Monica was relieved to see there wasn't a car on the lift either. Hopefully, the mechanic would be able to get to hers right away.

She parked her car and walked toward the open garage door, where the smell of gasoline and oil hit her even before she entered. A young man sat behind a battered wooden desk eating a breakfast sandwich. He had carrot red hair and pale blue eyes and his coverall, with *Mike's Garage* stitched in red over the pocket, was clean except for a permanent grease spot near his elbow.

He put his sandwich down on a piece of waxed paper and swiped a hand across his mouth as Monica approached him.

"My car is making a funny noise," she said. "I wondered if you could take a look at it."

He wrinkled his forehead. "What kind of funny noise?"

Monica sighed. How to explain it? "Oh, I don't know. Like maybe something is loose." She did her best to duplicate the sound the car was making.

"It will need to go up on the lift." He reached for a pad of paper and took down her name. While he was writing, Monica looked around the shop. It was tidy with a variety of tools organized on a bench along the back wall. There was a wire basket holding a stack of papers on the desk and an old coffee can filled with pens and pencils.

Monica glanced at the breakfast sandwich sitting out on the desk. Dark yellow egg yolk dribbled down the side of the biscuit. Monica's mouth watered and her stomach grumbled. She realized she hadn't had any breakfast yet and she was suddenly starved.

She looked away from the tantalizing sandwich and a picture taped to the wall above the desk caught her eye. It was a grainy photocopy of a photograph of a woman in what used to be called a pinup pose. The woman appeared to be nude but there was another piece of paper tacked over the picture covering her from her waist to her toes.

The young man noticed Monica looking at it and his face turned nearly as red as his hair.

"Mike—he's the owner—put that up. He said he got it off the Internet." He gestured toward her car. "I'll let you know what I find. You can wait in the office if you'd like," he said, obviously anxious to be rid of her.

Monica walked around to the front of the building and opened the door to the office. It was a small room with a handful of chairs, a small table between them and a metal desk off to one side. A woman sat behind the desk tapping on a computer. She had on an oversized bulky cardigan sweater and had a space heater aimed at her feet. The room was chilly but not nearly as cold as the garage had been.

Monica took a seat and began to flip through the pile of old magazines scattered on the table, but none of them were of any interest. She pulled out her phone, scrolled through her emails and checked the news but her thoughts kept returning to the picture taped up over the desk in the garage. There was something familiar about the woman but Monica was coming up blank. She would take a second look when she went to get her car.

According to the young man, the owner had printed the picture off the Internet. Had the woman posted the picture herself? Monica supposed some people just liked to get attention—like nearly everyone on Instagram who documented their every move, no matter how mundane.

She finished reading the news and was looking through the videos Lauren had put up on TikTok when the office door opened and the young mechanic stuck his head in.

"Your car's ready."

Monica gathered her things together and followed him back to the garage.

"What was wrong? Were you able to fix it?" she asked.

"It wasn't anything major. A few things needed tightening is all." His expression told Monica that he thought she wouldn't possibly understand the intricacies of what he had done so there was no point in trying to explain it.

She felt her shoulders relax. That was a relief. The last thing she needed was a huge repair bill.

The mechanic sat down at the desk and pulled a pad of invoices toward him. As he was writing up the bill, Monica glanced at the picture on the wall again. The woman was attractive and she looked familiar. Very familiar.

She was digging out her wallet when she realized with a jolt that the woman in the picture was Lacey Van Der Zee.

• • •

Monica was pleased to see that the bank parking lot was nearly empty. Hopefully that meant the bank wasn't busy and she'd be in and out in no time.

A man in jeans and work boots was filling out a deposit slip and one of the tellers was helping a woman with a small white dog tucked under her arm when Monica went inside. The rest of the tellers were free. She'd been to the bank frequently and had gotten to know many of the staff. She went up to the window on the end where Nicole sat. Nicole was always pleasant and efficient and Monica liked dealing with her.

Nicole smiled in recognition as Monica approached her window. "Good morning," she said cheerfully.

Monica returned the greeting, took an envelope out of her purse and pushed it across the counter to Nicole.

Nicole punched some keys on her computer and then turned to Monica.

"How are you feeling?"

Monica was startled. Surely news of her pregnancy couldn't have spread as far as the tellers at the bank?

She smiled wanly. "Fine." Nicole handed Monica her copy of the deposit slip and Monica slipped it into her purse. "Thank you," she said.

Just as Monica was turning to leave, the door opened and a woman walked in. She was startled to see that it was the same woman who had been at the jewelry store with Marty Fisher—his mistress, she assumed. She was carrying a large leopard-print tote and Monica noticed the top of a bag from Bijoux Jewelers sticking out of it. She had a Bluetooth earpiece in her ear and was talking to someone on her phone.

"Stephanie, it's me, Courtney," Monica heard her say as she approached a desk with a sign over it that read *Safe Deposit Boxes*. "Can you hang on a minute? I'm at the bank."

She had a brief few words with the white-haired woman behind the desk, and while the woman was retrieving a set of keys from a drawer, Courtney continued her telephone conversation.

Monica couldn't hear everything she was saying but she heard enough to pique her curiosity—words like *Marty* and *police*.

Did the police suspect Marty of Rip's murder? If Rip really had been blackmailing him, that gave him a solid motive.

Monica edged closer, trying to hear more, as the white-haired woman led Courtney through a door to the bank of safe deposit boxes. Monica looked around but no one seemed to be watching, so she followed them. When they stopped at the last row of boxes, she ducked into one of the curtained cubicles provided for the privacy of the bank's patrons.

After a moment or two, she heard soft footsteps as the bank employee walked past her on her way back to her desk.

Monica peeked around the corner and saw Courtney remove the Bijoux bag from her tote and step into one of the other unoccupied cubicles. She was still talking loud enough for Monica to hear most of her conversation.

"So, I said to him, Marty, the police have been questioning you. I've seen enough cop shows to know that means they suspect you. You've got to tell the police you were with me when that man was murdered. You know you didn't do it." There was a slight screech as she opened the lid to her safe deposit box. "So, he says he can't do it on account of his wife. If she finds out he was cheating on her, she'd cut him off without a penny."

Monica heard a clang as Courtney closed the metal lid of the box.

"So, I said you'd rather be convicted of murder than admitting you were having an affair." There was a pause. "Of course, I wouldn't stay with him if he lost his money. Or to be accurate, I should say lost access to his wife's money. Why should I? That's the only reason I hooked up with him in the first place. You should see the necklace and earrings he bought me. You'll die."

Monica had heard enough. She pushed the curtain aside, tiptoed out of the cubicle and left the bank.

Monica had a lot to think about as she drove back to Sassamanash Farm. It looked as if Marty Fisher had an alibi for Rip's murder so she could rule him out. Kayla was dead and Tyler was in jail. The spouse was the usual suspect but what reason did Lacey have for killing her ex-husband?

Monica looked in her rearview mirror and noticed that the same car had been behind her for quite a while. There was nothing unusual in that—most Cranberry Cove residents went to and from town on that road—but when the car turned and followed her down the dirt road that led to the farm, she became curious. Perhaps it was someone going to see Jeff.

She pulled into the driveway of her cottage, expecting the car to continue down the road toward the bogs, but it pulled in after her. She felt a slight frisson of fear and her breath caught in her throat, but then she recognized it as Detective Stevens's car.

Stevens smiled and gave a small wave as she got out of the car. An empty foam cup tumbled out after her, and as she bent to pick it up, Monica's heartbeat slowed to normal.

"I hope I didn't scare you," Stevens said as she approached Monica. "Especially not with you in your condition."

Goodness, now even Stevens knew? "How did you know . . ."

Stevens laughed. "Bart told me when I stopped by his shop to pick up some pork chops. You can't keep a secret for long in Cranberry Cove."

"Obviously not." Monica dug her keys out of her pocket. "Do you want to come in?"

"Just for a minute if you don't mind."

Hercule was enchanted that Monica had brought a guest with her. He sniffed Stevens vigorously, his tail whipping back and forth in excitement, and he absolutely melted when Stevens bent down and stroked the top of his head. Mittens was more restrained in her greeting but even she arched her back and gave a contented meow when Stevens scratched under her chin.

"Would you like some tea?" Monica said as she hung up her jacket.

"I don't want to be any trouble but frankly, that would be heavenly. I ended up standing around outside for hours at the site of a break-in and I'm frozen."

What did Stevens want? Monica fretted as she prepared the tea. Surely, she hadn't come to bring Monica up-to-date on Rip's murder. That left only one alternative—she knew about Gina and wanted to question Monica about her.

The thought made Monica clumsy, and she sloshed a bit of hot water on her wrist. She put the mug down and turned on the cold water.

"I'm being a bother. I'm sorry," Stevens said.

"Not at all. It's nothing." Monica smiled as she held her hand under the water.

She finished preparing the tea, set the mugs down on the kitchen table and slipped into the seat opposite Stevens. She scanned Stevens's face for any clues as to what this interview was going to be about—and she had no doubt it was an interview—but Stevens's face didn't reveal a thing.

Stevens put her hands around the warm mug. "This is just what I needed. Thank you." She cleared her throat. "I wanted to ask you a few questions."

Monica inclined her head.

Stevens ran her finger around the rim of her mug. "It's about your stepmother, Gina."

"Oh?" Monica tried to act surprised, although she had suspected from the start that that was what Stevens wanted to talk to her about.

"We know that Gina had an appointment with Richard Taylor the day he was killed. It's written in his appointment book and the secretary at Cranberry Cove Realty had it listed on her computer calendar." Stevens took a sip of her tea. "We suspect she was in the car with him when he was killed. We found a cup with a woman's lipstick on it. She paused. "The problem is, Gina won't admit it."

Monica tried to maintain a poker face but she suspected she wasn't particularly successful.

"We would like to rule Gina out in the case. We've sent the cup to be tested but we haven't gotten the results yet. When we do, we'll have to ask her for a sample of her DNA."

"You can't possibly think that Gina —"

"No." Stevens shook her head. "I don't think she had anything to do with it but we have to tie up all the loose ends. All we want to do is talk to her. Did she see the murderer? Even if she didn't, it's possible she saw something — anything — that might be useful to the investigation." Stevens frowned. "She's not doing herself any favors by not coming forward."

She drained the last of her tea. "We're assuming it was Gina in the car with Taylor when he was killed." She looked over the rim of her mug at Monica. "Was it?"

Monica felt her face burn. What to do? She didn't want to betray Gina's confidence, but on the other hand . . .

Fortunately, Stevens continued before Monica had time to answer.

"You don't have to answer that," she said with a sigh. "We already know the answer. I was hoping you would confirm it for us." She pushed her cup away and stood up. "Thank you for the tea." She paused with her hand on the doorknob. "You might want to tell your stepmother that she could be in danger. The killer might think Gina saw something and decide that she needs to be eliminated."

Monica stood stock-still as Stevens shut the door behind her. That last sentence of Stevens's had raised goose bumps on her arms and she began to shiver.

Chapter 20

As much as Monica wanted to sit down and put her feet up after her morning errands, she knew she was probably needed at the farm kitchen. She couldn't keep heaping the responsibility on Janice, Kit and her mother.

She still hadn't eaten breakfast and she was starving but there wasn't time for anything elaborate. She grabbed some homemade cranberry granola and filled a bowl. She ate it standing at the counter in her jacket, then rinsed her dish and put it in the dishwasher.

When Hercule saw that she wasn't going to share her food, he returned to the heating vent, where he'd taken Mittens's place. Monica checked both their food and water bowls and then headed out the door.

"You look very healthy this morning," Nancy said when Monica arrived at the farm kitchen. "Your cheeks are all pink from the cold and your eyes are glowing. Pregnancy seems to agree with you." Nancy rolled her eyes. "Not like me. I was the color of pea soup the whole first trimester. I could barely keep water down."

Janice, who had been kneading some dough, looked over at Nancy and Monica. She clapped her hands together in excitement.

"So, you're having a boy!"

Both Monica and Nancy froze. "What on earth makes you think that?" Nancy said.

"It's too early to tell." Monica patted her stomach. "It will be a few more weeks before they can be certain, the doctor said. Although Greg and I haven't decided yet if we want to find out in advance or wait until the birth."

"Mark my words," Janice said. "It's a boy for sure. Girls steal their mother's beauty. If the mother grows more attractive, on the other hand, she's definitely carrying a boy."

"That's nonsense." Nancy planted her hands palms down on the counter. "It's another myth."

Janice gave a knowing smile. "You'll see I'm right soon enough. Just you wait."

"You do have a fifty-fifty chance of being right," Nancy said. Monica saw the muscle in her jaw clenching. "It won't mean the myth is anything more than just that—a myth."

Janice wagged a finger at them. "It will be a boy. I'm sure of it."

Monica decided it was time to end the conversation. Janice was looking smug and Nancy was fuming and a red flush had crept up her neck. Kit was in the corner quietly going about his business. Monica suspected he was pretending not to hear them.

"How are you coming with the cookies?" Monica asked Janice, eager to change the subject. "Nora said they ran out yesterday and asked if we could make an extra dozen or two."

A hair was clinging to Janice's forehead. She wiped a hand across her brow to dislodge it. "I think we can manage it." She looked at Kit, who nodded briefly.

Monica got to work mixing up some batter and was taking the first batch of cookies out of the oven when the door opened.

"It smells delicious in here." Lauren stood on the doorstep and sniffed. "Am I interrupting? I can come back. I just wanted to say hello and to show you something."

"Not at all," Monica said. She put a hand to her back. "I could use a break." She motioned to Lauren. "Come in."

"Good. I'm excited to show you some of the pictures I just took."

Monica sat down at the table and Lauren joined her. She pulled off her knit cap and the static made her blond hair stand away from her head. She smoothed it down and reached into her pocket.

"I've just taken some pictures of Jeff hard at work maintaining the equipment—particularly the egg beater. People always seem to be fascinated by that." Lauren smiled and the dimple in her cheek popped out. "Besides, who doesn't like looking at pictures of a handsome young man in a plaid flannel shirt with the sleeves rolled up."

"Are these going on our Instagram account?" Monica asked. She couldn't believe how many new things she'd learned about in such a short time—Instagram, TikTok—what was next?

Lauren pulled out her phone and handed it to Monica. Monica scrolled through the pictures. She had to admit, her brother was attractive. And if that's what it took to bring business to the farm, who was she to argue.

Janice bustled past with a black plastic bag full of garbage. "I'm going to put this in the trash." She stopped abruptly when she caught a glimpse of one of the pictures on the screen of Lauren's cell phone. She pointed at it.

"What did you say that's called? Food porn?" She shuddered and wrinkled her nose.

Monica laughed. "No, not this. This is more like beefcake." She held the phone up so Janice could see and couldn't help but notice how Janice's eyes lingered momentarily on the photo.

"Hmmph," she said. "What you have to do these days to run a business. It's scandalous."

"It's important to go with the times," Monica said. "Whether you like it or not. Life is always moving and changing and you have to keep up or you'll be left behind."

Janice said "hmmph" again and, tightening her grip on the bag of garbage, headed for the trash can, where she dropped it in with a resounding thud.

After Lauren had left, Monica was thinking of the expression *food porn* as she mixed batter for some cranberry bread. She wondered who was the first person to coin that phrase. It was certainly apt. All those beautifully arranged photographs of cakes, casseroles and people's restaurant dinners and lunches. Another phrase floated into her mind and she was so startled that she nearly dropped the spatula she was holding. *Revenge porn.* It had been in the news a lot lately. Was that how Lacey's picture had ended up on the Internet? Had Rip posted it to get back at her for throwing him out?

If that was the case, Lacey might have a motive for murder after all.

• • •

Monica was grateful for the warmth of her cottage when she got home later that afternoon. She made herself a cup of herbal tea and carried it into the living room, where she sat on the couch and huddled under a throw, Hercule lying contentedly at her feet and Mittens curled up beside her.

She debated for a moment but then flicked on the television. She was just in time to catch the evening news on WZZZ. The first segment was a report on the ongoing investigation into Kayla Moore's death. The news anchor relayed the story in somber tones as pictures of the crime scene flashed across the screen one by one.

Monica dropped her head back against the sofa cushions and was nearly dozing when there was a furious knocking on her back door. A delivery perhaps? She didn't remember ordering anything but perhaps Greg had.

"Coming," she yelled as she scurried into the kitchen. She quickly glanced out the window and was surprised to see Gina's car parked in the driveway.

"It's freezing out there," Gina said when Monica opened the door. Her coat was unbuttoned and she was holding it closed with one hand. She bustled into the kitchen. "I'm not disturbing you, am I? I simply couldn't wait to show you this."

"Show me what?" Monica thought Gina looked as if she was about to burst.

Gina held out her hand. A ring with a sapphire surrounded by diamonds glittered on the ring finger of her left hand.

"Mickey popped the question this morning."

"Wonderful." Monica gave Gina a hug. "You must be thrilled."

Gina couldn't stop smiling. "He brought me breakfast in bed—his special banana pancakes—and when I lifted up the napkin, there was the ring. I couldn't believe my eyes."

"How romantic." Monica took Gina's hand and admired the ring again. "It's beautiful. I'm so happy for you."

It sounded as if Mickey was a far better catch than Monica's father had been.

Monica led Gina into the living room, where she perched on the edge of the sofa. Almost immediately she jumped up again.

"I'm so excited I can barely sit still. I never thought I'd find someone again and certainly not someone as wonderful as Mickey."

Monica reached for the remote and was about to switch off the television when Gina cried, "No, wait." She gestured toward the screen.

The two WZZZ anchors—Tanya and Gary—sat behind the desk. On the wall behind them was a graphic featuring a large question mark.

"And now for an update on the Richard Taylor murder case. We still don't know who the mystery woman is who was in Richard Taylor's car when he was brutally murdered, do we?" Gary turned to Tanya.

She shook her head and the blond curls tumbling to her shoulders barely jiggled.

"No, Gary, we don't. No one has been identified yet. The police are hoping she might have seen something that will lead them to the killer."

"And no one has come forward?"

"No," Tanya said. "The police are still investigating."

Gary looked at his colleague, an eyebrow raised. "I wonder if the killer knows who the woman is? Surely, they must have seen her when they shot Taylor. Supposedly they were sitting in the car together."

Tanya assumed a shocked expression. "Do you think she might be in danger then?"

Gina gasped and put a hand to her mouth.

"Yes, I do. The killer might think she can identify him or her." Gary leaned toward the camera with an earnest expression on his face. "WZZZ has organized a tip line for anyone who has information that might lead to the identification of this woman. All you have to do is telephone the number on the screen. All calls will be kept confidential."

Tanya shuffled some papers on her desk then smiled broadly at the camera, as if to indicate a change of topic. "And now for the weather."

Monica looked at her stepmother. Gina's face had gone deathly white and she was shaking.

"They're right." Gina's voice cracked and she clutched the edge of her sweater. "The killer had to have seen me. And they might come after me next," she said with a horrified expression.

• • •

"How was your day?" Greg said to Monica when he got home an hour later. Hercule greeted him as if he hadn't seen Greg in months instead of merely hours. Even before he unbuttoned his coat, Greg bent down to scratch Hercule's ears and ruffle his fur.

Monica shrugged. "The usual. Janice had another pregnancy myth to share with me."

Greg chuckled. "What was it this time? They really are quite entertaining."

"Not if you're the one who has to listen to them." Monica peeked into the oven, where a loaf of corn bread was baking. "She's convinced we're having a boy."

Greg got a bottle of white wine out of the refrigerator and poured himself a glass.

He gave a hoot of laughter. "And what does she base that on?"

"Some nonsense about girls stealing their mother's beauty while boys enhance it."

"You do look beautiful." Greg put his arm around Monica and gave her a peck on the cheek. "Janice was right about that at least." He picked up the lid and peered into the pot on the stove. "Chili?" he said, his eyebrows raised.

"Yes." Monica took a spoon from the spoon rest and gave the chili a stir. "How are things going at the bookstore? Is the work almost finished?"

Greg blew out a sigh. "Yes, thank heavens. It's been quite the process. There was a bit of a problem with the wiring in the café—the electrician explained it, but frankly it was Greek to me. And he and his associate got into a bit of a spat about something and the associate threatened to walk out. But fortunately, it was all sorted out in the end and we're still on schedule for our opening." He ran a hand through his hair. "I can't believe it's almost here."

He glanced at Monica and raised his eyebrows. "Is everything okay? You look worried."

Monica turned toward Greg, a knife poised in her hand. "I am worried. It's about Gina."

"Oh? What is it this time?" Greg's voice held a smile.

Monica put the knife down on the cutting board and placed her hands on her hips.

"She still hasn't gone to the police to tell them she was in Rip's car when he was murdered. And now WZZZ has set up a tip line for anyone who can provide information." Monica paused. "But that's not the worst of it. The reporter pointed out that Gina could be in danger."

"But she was unconscious," Greg said as he got a container of sour cream out of the refrigerator. "She doesn't know anything."

"The reporter pointed out that the killer might think Gina saw something that would help identify them. And if the reporter thought of that, then certainly the killer has, too. She could be in danger." Monica's voice caught in her throat.

She remembered how she'd initially been hostile toward her new stepmother. Gina had stolen her father away and broken up their family. But as Monica got to know her, she came to like her.

"You know," Greg said as he grabbed some bowls from the cupboard. "Why bother to drug Rip and Gina at all? Why not just shoot Rip and be done with it?"

Monica went back to chopping cilantro. Greg was right—why put the benzodiazepines in the coffee and then shoot him? It was sort of like wearing a belt and suspenders. Unless . . .

Monica whirled around to face Greg, the knife still in her hand.

Greg faked alarm. "Hey, be careful with that thing."

"Sorry." Monica put the knife on the counter. "Maybe they thought they'd put enough benzodiazepines in his coffee to kill him." She frowned. "And maybe because he shared what was in the thermos with Gina, the drugs only made them both sleepy."

"Or," said Greg, getting silverware from the drawer, "they miscalculated how much was needed to be fatal."

Monica grabbed a pot holder and pulled open the oven door. The blast of heat blew tendrils of hair around her face. She removed a pan of golden cornbread and placed it on a trivet on the table.

Greg leaned against the counter and folded his arms over his chest. "The person had to have had a gun, so why not shoot Rip in the first place?"

"That is curious," Monica said, her head stuck in the refrigerator. She pulled out a tub of butter and put it on the table. "Maybe they thought the murder would be harder to solve if he'd been drugged? It could be they thought the police would rule it an accident or a suicide." She picked up a spoon and stirred the pot of chili on the stove. "Rip was having substantial financial problems. People have committed suicide for less."

"You may have hit the nail on the head." Greg squeezed Monica's shoulder.

Monica dipped a clean spoon into the pot and tasted the contents. "Needs more salt," she said, reaching for the salt shaker.

"You know, guns aren't exactly hard to come by these days." Greg scowled. "It seems everyone has one."

"But maybe the killer had to learn to shoot a gun. Even though Rip was shot at fairly close range, if they weren't used to using guns, they still needed to know how to operate a firearm." Monica shrugged. "I wouldn't know one end of a gun from the other."

"Frankly, neither would I." Greg grabbed the bowls from the table and carried them over to the stove, where Monica ladled hot chili into them. "So the person had to have practiced at the very least."

"What better place to learn how to shoot than a gun range." Monica took a seat at the table. "I think there's one not far from here. Maybe I can find out if any of the suspects were seen practicing there."

Greg reached out a hand and put it over Monica's. "Be careful. If the killer finds out you've been snooping around, they might come after you next."

Chapter 21

After breakfast the next morning, Monica flipped open her laptop and powered it up. She brought up her favorite search engine and typed in *shooting ranges*. She thought she'd seen signs for one nearby.

It didn't take her more than a minute to find it. Kooistra's Shooting Range. It was near Lake Ottawa, not far out of town.

Monica bundled up in a jacket, scarf, gloves and a hat but she still flinched when she opened the back door and was hit with a blast of frigid air. It didn't deter Hercule in the least and he bounded ahead of her until he reached the end of his leash. Monica stamped her feet against the cold and waited while he did his business. He wanted to dawdle on the way back in but she convinced him that a treat was in the offing if he hurried up and he finally condescended to follow her inside.

Monica doled out dog treats to Hercule, cat treats to Mittens, said goodbye and pulled the door closed behind her.

The drive to the shooting range was pleasant with occasional shafts of sunlight piercing the clouds. Monica passed Lake Ottawa—a small lake that was now deserted but would be alive with boaters, swimmers and tubers in the summer. A small sign nailed to a fence post pointed the way to Kooistra's Shooting Range.

The range was down a dirt road frozen into ruts and Monica felt every jolt even though she'd slowed her speed to under twenty miles an hour. She had a moment of panic thinking about the effects the bouncing might have on the baby even though her doctor had assured her the baby was well-cushioned inside the womb.

She was relieved when a low wooden building came into view. It was surrounded by a wire fence with a rusted metal sign attached that read *Beware: Guns*. Stuck into the ground was another sign, this one announcing Kooistra's Shooting Range.

Monica pulled into the gravel parking lot, got out of the car and walked toward the small building. It was weathered-looking and a few shingles were missing from the roof. Monica opened the front door cautiously and stepped into the cramped room, which was furnished with some tired-looking armchairs, a potbelly stove belching heat and various guns mounted on the walls. There was a bucket in the middle of the room, no doubt strategically positioned to catch the drips from the rotting roof.

A man stood behind a chipped and stained Formica counter. He had long hair going gray, a large handlebar mustache and was wearing a plaid shirt tucked into jeans. He had weary blue eyes and smelled of smoke.

He smiled at Monica and leaned his elbows on the counter.

"What can I do for you, young lady?"

Monica took a deep breath. She'd planned what to say on her way over in the car but suddenly the words deserted her.

"I wanted to learn how to shoot," she said finally. "And my cousin recommended your place."

The man looked her up and down. "Do you have your own gun? Because we don't rent to single people. We don't want any suicides." He smiled, showing tobacco-stained teeth.

"Uh, no. I mean, I didn't bring it with me. I was in the vicinity and thought I'd check this place out. My cousin, Lacey Van Der Zee, said she comes here for target practice and she told me it was quite reasonable."

"Nice lady, your cousin. Used to be married to that football player. What a shame that was." He cracked the knuckles of his right hand and the sound reverberated around the room like a gunshot. "She's just learning, of course, but she's improving."

"How long has she been coming here?"

"About a month or so, I'd say." He sneezed, pulled a red bandana from the pocket of his jeans, blew his nose and reached for a clipboard with a stack of papers attached. He pushed it toward Monica and pointed at it with a stubby finger.

"This here is our application for membership to the range. You'll need to fill this out if you want to join."

Now that she had the information she wanted, Monica wasn't quite sure how to extricate herself from the situation. Should she fill out the form with a phony name?

Fortunately for her, the man pulled a crumpled pack of cigarettes from his shirt pocket.

"You don't mind if I step out for a minute to have a smoke? You can leave the application right here when you're done." He rapped the counter with his knuckles.

Monica smiled and plucked a pen from the container on the counter.

As soon as his back was turned, she put down the clipboard, replaced the pen, picked up her purse and all but ran toward the door. She didn't breathe easily until she was in her car and on her way back down the dirt road toward Lake Ottawa.

Monica gritted her teeth as she bounced back down the rutted dirt road. She was surprised when she noticed a car coming toward her. Were they headed to the shooting range? As far as she could tell, there wasn't much of anything else in the vicinity. She felt her stomach drop to her feet as the car got closer. It was a Lamborghini. There weren't a lot of people in Cranberry Cove who drove a Lamborghini. As a matter of fact, she could think of only one—Lacey Van Der Zee.

Monica put a hand up to shield her face as the two automobiles passed each other on the narrow road. Had Lacey seen her? Panic overwhelmed her and she nearly steered the car into a ditch.

Would the fellow at the shooting range tell Lacey her "cousin" had been in asking questions? And had then taken off without even bothering to fill out the membership application form? If Lacey was indeed the killer, then Monica had put herself in a very precarious position.

She looked in her rearview mirror. What if Lacey turned around and came after her? Throughout the entire ride home, she kept an eye out for a flashy Lamborghini suddenly appearing behind her. The thought gave her goose bumps and she nearly collapsed with relief when she pulled into the driveway of her cottage.

• • •

"Where is everyone?" Monica said when she arrived, somewhat breathless, at the farm kitchen.

"Your mother is running an errand." Kit jerked his head toward the door. "And Janice has gone to deliver some product to the farm store."

"You've been busy this morning," Monica said as she slipped her apron on and joined Kit at the counter.

"No more than usual," Kit said.

Monica felt a slight sting. Was Kit saying she wasn't needed? That she wasn't holding up her end? She sighed and vowed to spend more time baking and less time investigating.

"Sean and I went out to dinner last night," Kit said as he tipped flour into the mixer. "We were walking down that alley next to the Pepper Pot, the one that leads to the parking lot, and we thought we heard someone coming up behind us." He gave an exaggerated shiver. "I suddenly thought of that killer—the one who shot that fellow in his car—what if it was him?"

"Or her," Monica said without thinking.

"Oh?" Kit's voice went up an octave. "Do you know something?" He folded his hands together as if in prayer. "Do tell."

"I'm only saying it could be a her. Rip Taylor left behind some angry women. His ex-wife, for instance."

"What about that woman who was killed and her body dumped in a ditch. Could there be two killers on the loose in Cranberry Cove?"

Monica found that thought quite alarming. She rolled the idea around in her mind. If she was right and Lacey had killed Rip, why would she kill Kayla as well? Because Kayla was the one who took Rip away from her? Lacey seemed to have put that behind her, but perhaps it was all an elaborate act.

Maybe she was wrong and Lacey wasn't the culprit. Maybe it was Tyler or Kayla herself and there really was another killer in Cranberry Cove. And then there was Jax Johnson. She'd almost forgotten him. But what reason would he have for killing Rip? Could someone really carry a grudge for that many years?

She shook her head. She was getting nowhere. It was time to focus on work.

• • •

Monica spent the rest of the afternoon on her feet, kneading dough, pulling sheets of cookies from the oven and mixing batter. By the time she got home, she ached from her head to her toes. She threw her jacket over one of the kitchen chairs, went into the living room and flopped down on the sofa.

She felt something wet on her cheek and turned her head to see Hercule's black button nose. She reached out a hand and scratched his ears before dropping her arm back on the sofa next to her.

She thought of soaking in a nice warm bath to ease the aches and pains. Maybe she'd phone Greg and ask him to get some take-out from the diner. Their hot turkey and gravy with mashed potatoes and green beans was actually quite good.

The telephone rang and she groaned. What now? It had better not be a robocall, she thought as she sat up and retrieved her cell phone from the pocket of her jeans.

"Hello?"

"It's me, Gina," Gina said in a breathless voice.

Monica frowned. "Gina? Is something wrong? You sound . . . strange."

There was a pause. "No, nothing serious. But my car broke down. I called Hal's towing and now I'm on the side of the road waiting for them. I was hoping you could come pick me up? I would call Mickey but this is his busiest time of the day. I tried Nancy but she isn't answering."

Monica closed her eyes and slowly counted to ten.

"Sure, I'll come get you," she said with more enthusiasm than she felt. "Where are you?"

Gina gave her directions and Monica promised to be there as soon as she could.

Of all the things, Monica thought as she put on her jacket and got into her car. Poor Gina though. Stuck on the side of the road in these freezing temperatures.

The address—actually it was just the intersection of two streets— was outside of town. Large trees grew on either side of the road with sparsely scattered houses set way back, down long driveways. What was Gina doing all the way out here? Monica wondered.

The sun was going down and Monica flicked on her lights. So far, she hadn't passed any other cars and the silence was eerie. Surely Gina would be around the next bend.

Monica breathed a sigh of relief when she finally saw Gina's car on the shoulder a short distance ahead. She put on her blinker and pulled off to the side of the road ahead of Gina's car. She switched on her flashers. While there was virtually no traffic, the shoulder wasn't very deep and she wasn't taking any chances.

She was surprised the tow truck hadn't arrived yet to haul Gina's car to the garage. She would have to wait till it came, she supposed. She looked out the rearview mirror expecting to see Gina walking toward her car but Gina appeared to still be sitting behind the wheel of her own vehicle.

Monica waited a few more minutes, tapping her fingers on the steering wheel and fiddling with the radio, unable to settle on any particular station. Finally, she decided to call Hal's Towing and find out how much longer it would be before they got there. It was nearly dark now and Greg would be home soon. She hadn't thought to leave a note, assuming she'd be back before him, and she hated to think of his worrying.

She sighed as she pulled her cell phone from her purse and punched in the number of the towing company.

"Hal's," a voice answered tersely.

Monica was surprised to hear Hal's gruff voice. She'd been expecting to get the answering service. Shouldn't he be on the road already? Gina had called him before Monica had even left the house.

She asked him how much longer he'd be. There was a pause.

"Who did you say this was?"

"I'm calling for Gina Albertson. She called for a tow about half an hour ago." Monica gave him the address.

Hal cleared his throat, a vast rumble that made Monica think of a volcano erupting. She heard him flipping through some papers.

"I'm sorry, miss, but your friend didn't call here. She must have called some other towing company, otherwise I'd be there by now. I haven't had a call for at least an hour. Not since I went to tow old Mrs. Singleton's Buick. That's the second time in two weeks she's called me. I told her she needed to take the car in for a tune-up but she's a stubborn old gal."

Monica heard him take a drag on his cigarette and waited while he blew out the smoke.

"But Gina must have called you. There isn't any other towing company in town."

"You sound like a nice lady, and I don't want to argue with you, but I'm afraid she didn't call here. Like I said, the phone hasn't even rung for the last couple of hours."

Monica was forced to admit defeat. She thanked Hal and hung up.

Who on earth did Gina call if not Hal's Towing? She thought back to their conversation. She was positive Gina had said Hal's Towing. She wouldn't lie about something like that. It made no sense.

Suddenly a chill crept up Monica's spine and her breath caught in her throat. Unless . . .

She glanced in her rearview mirror again. Gina still hadn't moved. She appeared to be clutching the steering wheel, and even though Monica couldn't make out her expression, there was something in her posture that told Monica she was frightened.

What did she have to be frightened of? Unless this was a trap with Gina as the bait and Monica had walked right into it.

She didn't know what to do. She toyed with her cell phone, picking it up and putting it down multiple times. Once she began dialing, but before entering all three digits, she abruptly ended the call. She'd feel awfully stupid if she called the police and everything turned out to be perfectly innocent.

Another five minutes went by. Still no sign of a tow truck and Monica wasn't surprised. But Gina hadn't gotten out of her car yet and had barely moved from her previous position.

Monica tapped her fingers on the steering wheel. What should she do? Call the police after all? And what would she say? Not only that, but would they believe her? Fortunately, Cranberry Cove was normally a fairly sleepy town, so the police would probably come out of curiosity if nothing else.

She picked up her cell phone and held her breath as she punched in the numbers nine-one-one.

The dispatcher's calm voice was very soothing and she reassured Monica that a patrol car would be on its way immediately. Monica was relieved the woman had taken her seriously but that didn't solve the problem of what was going on with Gina.

Knowing the police were on their way gave Monica a dose of courage. She opened her door, got out and began to walk toward Gina's Mercedes. It wasn't until she had nearly reached the car that she noticed someone sitting behind Gina.

And she had the muzzle of a gun up against the back of Gina's head.

Monica's limbs turned leaden and she froze in place, watching in horror as Lacey Van Der Zee slowly repositioned the gun, taking direct aim at Monica instead.

Chapter 22

Seconds ticked by but to Monica they felt like hours. It was funny how staring down the barrel of a gun could stretch time until it felt like an eternity. She contemplated making a run for it, but after glancing around, realized it would be futile. The ground next to the road was a tangle of vines and tree roots and she'd be bound to trip and fall before she got very far.

The door to Gina's car opened and Lacey got out, keeping the gun aimed steadily at Monica.

"I've heard that you're something of a snoop," she said, her lip curling disdainfully. "You must think you're like that woman on that television show where she solves murders before the police can even get their feet off their desks. Of course, nothing ever happens to her because they have to keep her around for the next episode. I'm afraid that's not going to be the case with you." She sneered. "It looks like your luck has run out."

This time Monica feared Lacey was right. She didn't see any way to escape.

"What you didn't know is that the man you talked to at the shooting range happens to be *my* cousin. He thought there was something suspicious about you. He gave me a call, and as luck would have it, I was already on my way to Kooistra's. I recognized you when my car passed yours."

So, Lacey had recognized her after all, Monica thought. So much for hiding behind her hand.

"Did you kill Rip because he posted that revenge porn? I saw one of the pictures taped up on the wall at Mike's Garage."

Monica noticed Lacey flush and it looked as if her finger had tightened on the trigger. Monica was tempted to close her eyes.

"I've never been so embarrassed," she said with what sounded suspiciously like a sob. "I didn't want to pose for those pictures. You've got to believe me. Rip kept insisting. He couldn't see what difference it made since I was used to wearing those skimpy outfits when I was a cheerleader for the Lions." She wiped away a tear with her free hand. "But I was proud to wear those outfits. We all were. It was like we were part of the team." She gave a loud sniff. "Rip teased me and said I wasn't any fun and that maybe he'd go out and find someone who wasn't such a prude."

"So, you did what he wanted so he wouldn't leave you?"

Lacey nodded.

While Lacey was talking, Monica had been looking around, but she could see no way of escaping. Gina was still in the car, seemingly frozen in place, her hands gripping the steering wheel just as tightly as they had been earlier.

"I begged Rip not to post any of those pictures and he said sure, he'd delete them if I gave him the money he was asking for." The gun quivered in Lacey's hand. "I had the money—more than enough—but I refused to give in to blackmail because that's what it was."

"So, he posted that picture on the Internet?" Monica said.

Lacey nodded. "He threatened to post more . . . worse ones." She gulped. "I had no choice but to give him the money he wanted."

"Did that stop him?"

"No." Lacey sobbed. "He wanted more and more. It would have never stopped. In the end the only solution was to . . . get rid of him."

Lacey shifted the gun to her other hand.

"I saw his car parked outside that house across the street and it was empty. The house was for sale so I assumed Rip was showing it to someone. Fortunately, he hadn't locked his car. I knew he always had a thermos of coffee with him—that had been his routine when we were married. I put some of those pills the doctor gave me, the tranquilizers, in his coffee. I thought it would kill him but I guess I hadn't used enough of them. Later, when I went to check, I could see he was still breathing."

"What did you do then?" If she could keep Lacey talking, Monica thought, it would give the police time to get there.

"I had recently taken up target shooting. My cousin talked me into it. He said it would be a good idea for me to learn how to handle a gun in case there was ever a break-in." She sniffed and rubbed a hand under her nose. "I'd only been to the range a couple of times but I knew how to load the gun, and I figured since I was able to get so close to Rip, aiming the gun wouldn't be a problem. I wasn't likely to miss."

There was a noise in the distance and Lacey spun around but no one was there.

"I hadn't counted on someone else being in the car with Rip. I suspect that's why the benzos didn't work. He didn't drink enough of that coffee."

"Why not kill her, too? You'd killed once already."

Lacey looked offended. "I'm not a monster."

"But why kidnap Gina?" Monica motioned toward Gina's car. "She didn't see anything. She didn't even go to the police."

"I realized I'd been foolish. What if she had only been pretending to be unconscious? I couldn't take any chances."

Monica frowned. "And Kayla? I can understand you might have resented her for stealing Rip away from you, but murder?"

Lacey gave a peal of laughter that sent goose bumps down Monica's spine.

"Kayla? You think I murdered Kayla because of that?" She shook her head several times, as if in disbelief. "She did me a favor taking him off my hands. No, I had to kill her because she took up where Rip left off. She knew about those pictures and she was threatening to post all of them online if I didn't pay up. I wasn't about to let that happen. I didn't kill Rip for nothing, after all."

Monica was running out of questions and she could sense Lacey was getting impatient.

"I think it's high time we got on with things," Lacey said, all trace of her previous vulnerability stripped from her voice. Her face even looked different—cold and determined.

Monica listened for any telltale sounds that the police were on the way but there were none. No engine sounds in the distance or rumble of tires on the road. Had the dispatcher understood the address Monica had given her?

She wet her lips and took a deep breath. She suspected pleading with Lacey was futile, but if it would buy them time, it was worth it.

"You don't have to do this," Monica said. The words sounded like the clichéd dialogue of every victim in every bad gangster movie. "Gina and I won't say anything. From the sound of things, Rip wasn't a very nice person, and neither was Kayla. They won't be missed."

"You're right. Rip wasn't very nice and neither was Kayla, but I'm afraid that doesn't change anything. There's no way I can trust the two of you to keep your mouths shut. I'm sorry it has to end this way, but unfortunately, I don't have any choice."

Lacey raised the gun a bit higher and braced her right arm with her left hand.

Monica tried to swallow but her mouth had gone completely dry and her tongue felt two sizes too big.

"The police are on their way," she blurted out suddenly.

"Then we'll have to make this quick." Lacey tightened her finger on the trigger.

Just then the engine of Gina's Mercedes sprang to life with a soft purr.

"What the . . ." Lacey said. She spun around.

Gina's face behind the wheel was a mask of determination, her eyes narrowed and her mouth set in a hard line. She stepped on the gas and the car shot forward.

Monica didn't hesitate. She immediately jumped out of the way. Lacey wasn't as quick and the bumper of Gina's car caught her mid-thigh and pushed her backward until she was sandwiched between the Mercedes and Monica's car. The gun flew out of her hand and landed by the side of the road.

"Back up," Lacey screamed, waving frantically at Gina. "I'm trapped. Back up."

Gina tilted her head to the side and slowly smiled.

Just then they heard sirens in the distance and two patrol cars, kicking up loose gravel as they rounded the corner, came into view. They skidded to a stop behind Gina's car and almost immediately their doors flew open and the two police officers jumped out.

Lacey wiggled frantically but was unable to free herself, and within moments the officers had her in handcuffs. Gina slowly backed her car up and Lacey was dragged away, protesting loudly.

Monica sagged against the bumper of her car, waiting for her heart rate to return to normal.

Gina jumped out of the driver's seat and ran over to her.

"Are you okay? You're not hurt, are you?"

The words refused to come out, but Monica managed to shake her head. Finally, she caught her breath.

"I'm okay. At least I think so." She gently rested her hands on her stomach.

"Oh my gosh, the baby," Gina exclaimed. "We need to get you to the hospital."

Monica held up a hand. "I don't think that's necessary. I'll call Dr.

Wilson in the morning and make an appointment."

"Are you sure?"

Monica suddenly went very still. She barely dared to breathe.

"What's wrong?" Gina asked, her eyes wide with panic. "Is something wrong?"

Monica looked up and a slow smile spread across her face.

"I just felt the baby move," she said, with awe in her voice.

Chapter 23

Monica had butterflies in her stomach as she waited for Greg to open the doors of Book 'Em for the ribbon cutting and inauguration of the new bookstore café — Monica's Café. Greg had already popped a bottle of champagne and filled glasses for Kit, Gina and Mickey, and Jeff and Lauren had brought along some sparkling punch for Monica.

They were about to raise a toast to Book 'Em's new venture when someone banged on the front door.

"It's Nancy," Monica said, rushing to let her mother in.

"Sorry I'm late," Nancy said as she slipped out of her coat and hung it on the coat rack. "My telephone rang just as I was about to leave."

"Here you go," Greg said, handing her a flute of champagne. He raised his own glass. "Here's to the success of Monica's Café."

"Hear, hear," everyone chanted as they held their glasses aloft.

Nancy put a hand on Monica's arm. "How was your doctor's appointment this morning?" she asked in low tones.

"Everything is fine." Monica couldn't help smiling. "We heard the heartbeat for the first time."

Nancy clasped her hands to her chest. "Thank heaven for that. When you told me what happened yesterday, I was terrified that something might go wrong."

Monica shook her head. "The doctor assured me that everything is perfectly normal and there was no harm done."

"That's good news," Gina, who had been listening, said. She gave Monica a hug.

"How are you feeling?" Monica studied Gina's face. Color had come back into it, thank goodness, and she seemed none the worse for wear. "You must have been terrified having Lacey kidnap you like that."

"When I think about how things might have turned out . . ." Nancy pretended to swoon.

Gina patted Nancy's shoulder. "What's that saying? All's well that ends well?"

"It's almost time," Greg announced, and everyone turned their attention in his direction. He rubbed his hands together then reached into his pocket and pulled out a ring of keys.

"Time to open up."

He unlocked the front door to Book 'Em with a flourish and everyone clapped. No sooner had he stepped away than the door opened and the VanVelsen sisters walked in. They pulled off their gloves and hung their matching tweed coats on the coat rack.

"Quite chilly out there, isn't it?" Hennie said to Monica.

Gerda nodded and smiled at Monica. "How are you feeling, dear?"

"Very well, thank you." Monica supposed she would have to get used to people asking her how she felt for the remainder of the nine months.

Moments later the door opened again and more people poured into the store. Tempest swept in in a swirl of purple velvet with Bart right behind her, wearing a fresh shirt with his hair still slightly wet and slicked back from his forehead.

He made a beeline for Monica. "Good news," he said with a smile. "Gus is out of rehab. The doctor said he made an amazingly quick recovery. The old geezer is tough as nails. He should be back in his usual position at the diner within a week or so."

"That is good news. I'm so happy to hear that."

"I know he plans to say a special thank-you to you for all you did to raise money for his hospital stay. He was extremely grateful."

Monica felt herself blush. "It was nothing." She was relieved when Greg clapped his hands and everyone fell silent.

"Shall we go upstairs for the ribbon cutting?"

A cheer rose from the crowd as they followed him up the spiral staircase to the second floor, where a thick red ribbon was stretched across the opening to Monica's Café.

At the back of the café, a table was set up with an urn for coffee, hot water for tea and various bite-sized pastries. A waiter in black pants and a pleated white shirt was waiting in the corner with a tray of hors d'oeuvres.

With a theatrical gesture, Greg handed Monica a pair of gold scissors that had been procured especially for the event.

"No, you should be the one . . ." Monica tried to hand the scissors back to Greg.

"It's your café." Greg gestured at the name on the wall. "You're the one who should do the honors."

Monica could tell it was useless to argue. She felt her face turn pink as she took the scissors, approached the ribbon and briefly closed her eyes. She said a quick prayer, opened her eyes and sliced through the ribbon, which fell to the floor on either side.

Monica's Café was officially open for business.

Recipe

Cranberry Walnut Muffins

4 tablespoons unsalted butter
2 cups flour, sifted
1 tablespoon baking powder
½ teaspoon salt
¼ teaspoon ground cinnamon
⅛ teaspoon nutmeg
1 large egg
¾ cup sugar
½ cup milk (whole or low-fat)
½ plain Greek yogurt (fat-free is fine)
1 teaspoon pure vanilla extract
½ teaspoon orange extract (optional)
1½ cups fresh or frozen cranberries
½ cup chopped walnuts

Preheat oven to 400 degrees. Grease muffin tin and set aside.

Melt butter in the microwave and set aside to cool.

Combine flour, baking powder, salt, cinnamon and nutmeg in a mixing bowl and whisk until mixed.

In another bowl, beat the egg until frothy. Add the sugar, milk, yogurt, vanilla extract, and orange extract, if using.

Slowly add the cooled butter to the egg mixture and whisk until combined.

Add liquid ingredients to dry ingredients and mix. Do not overmix! Gently stir in cranberries and walnuts.

Spoon batter into greased muffin tin and bake for approximately 20 minutes or until toothpick inserted in muffin comes out clean.

About the Author

Peg grew up in a New Jersey suburb about twenty-five miles outside of New York City. After college, she moved to the City, where she managed an art gallery owned by the son of the artist Henri Matisse.

After her husband died, Peg remarried and her new husband took a job in Grand Rapids, Michigan, where they now live (on exile from New Jersey, as she likes to joke). Somehow Peg managed to segue from the art world to marketing and is now the manager of marketing communications for a company that provides services to seniors.

She is the author of the Cranberry Cove Mysteries, the Lucille Mysteries, the Farmer's Daughter Mysteries, the Gourmet De-Lite Mysteries, and also, writing as Meg London, the Sweet Nothings Vintage Lingerie series, and as Margaret Loudon, the Open Book series.

Peg has two daughters, a stepdaughter and stepson, and two beautiful granddaughters. You can read more at pegcochran.com and meglondon.com.